The History *of* Sound

Also by Ben Shattuck

Six Walks: In the Footsteps of Henry David Thoreau

The History *of* Sound

Stories

Ben Shattuck

Viking

VIKING
An imprint of Penguin Random House LLC
penguinrandomhouse.com

The following stories were published previously in different form: "The History of Sound" in *The Common* (anthologized in *The Pushcart Prize XLIV: Best of the Small Presses 2020*); "Edwin Chase of Nantucket" in *The Harvard Review* (anthologized in *PEN America Best Debut Short Stories 2017*); and "The Silver Clip" (as "Scrimshaw") in *The Harvard Review*.

LIBRARY OF CONGRESS CATALOGING-IN-PUBLICATION DATA
Names: Shattuck, Ben, 1984– author.
Title: The history of sound: stories / Ben Shattuck.
Other titles: History of sound (Compilation)
Description: [New York] : Viking, 2024.
Identifiers: LCCN 2023032804 (print) | LCCN 2023032805 (ebook) | ISBN 9780593490389 (hardcover) | ISBN 9780593490396 (ebook)
Subjects: LCGFT: Short stories.
Classification: LCC PS3619.H3569 H57 2024 (print) | LCC PS3619.H3569 (ebook) | DDC 813/.6—dc23/eng/20231024
LC record available at https://lccn.loc.gov/2023032804
LC ebook record available at https://lccn.loc.gov/2023032805

Printed in the United States of America
1st Printing

Designed by Alexis Farabaugh

to Jenny and Ida

HOOK-AND-CHAIN:

A song or poem form popularized in eighteenth-century New England, in which the first and last lines rhyme and contains rhyming couplets within.

As in: *A BB CC DD EE FF A.*

The second half of the couplet often completes the sentence or sentiment of the first.

Contents

The History of Sound ... *1*

Edwin Chase of Nantucket ... *27*

The Silver Clip ... *53*

Graft ... *71*

Tundra Swan ... *99*

August in the Forest ... *117*

The Journal of Thomas Thurber ... *157*

Radiolab: "Singularities" ... *187*

The Auk ... *205*

The Children of New Eden ... *221*

Introduction to *The Dietzens: Searching for Eternity in the North American Wilderness* ... *255*

Origin Stories ... *269*

Acknowledgments ... *307*

The History of Sound

I was seventeen when I met David, back in 1916. Now I don't very much care to count my age. It's April 1984 here in Cambridge. White puff balls that must be some sort of seedpod have been floating by the window above my writing desk for days now, collecting on the sidewalk like first snow.

My doctor suggested I write this story down, due to the recent sleeplessness that started when a package from a stranger arrived at my house: a box of twenty-five wax phonograph cylinders, sent from Brunswick, Maine. A letter taped to the box read, *I saw you on television. I admire your work. These are yours. I found them when cleaning out the house we bought.* Of the three books I've written on American folk music—with moderate success and thus the television interviews—I've never written about that summer with David. So, here we are.

I FIRST SAW HIM in the fall, after my first term at the New England Conservatory, when I was out with my friends in the pub. He was across the room, at the piano. I remember watching how his shirt stretched and slacked across his back.

"What do you think?" my friend Sam asked, tapping me on the arm.

I hadn't heard his question.

"What are you looking at?" he said, turning.

"I know that song," I said. It was "A Dead Winter's Night," a tune my father used to play on the fiddle back in Kentucky. A slow song to the tempo of "a sitting person's breath," as he'd say. An old English ballad from the Lake District, I've since researched, about a man and a woman lost in the woods, having run from their homes to elope. Thinking of it now reminds me of lying on the porch in the summer, moths flitting around the lantern, my father's foot hitting the floor—the scratch of his boot on the wood. Katydids in the trees, stitching the night together. My brother sitting nearby.

"Excuse me," I said to Sam.

I pushed through the crowd, to the piano. I watched David play. His eyes were closed, so at first he didn't notice me standing there. Cigarette held between his lips. Dark hair combed back. His head jolted when the chorus arrived. I watched his hands.

"Where did you learn that?" I asked when he ended.

"Oh," he said, looking up. "Some swamp in Kentucky." He ashed his cigarette on the floor. A deep voice. Words spoken too fast. He played a C chord with one hand and picked up his drink from the floor with the other.

"I'm from Kentucky," I told him. His hand paused on the keys. He looked up again.

"Yes, well. Sorry." He held out his hand. "David."

"Lionel," I said.

"What department?"

Likely everyone in the pub that night was from the Conservatory.

"Voice," I said.

"Well, fa-la-la. I'm composition. This"—he played the melody once—"a hobby. In the summer. To get fresh air. Song collecting."

From across the room, my friends motioned that they were leaving. I waved them on.

"Ever been to Harrow?" I said. "That's where I grew up."

"Harrow. Two summers ago. Sky-blue gazebo in the center of town."

He seemed unsurprised by the coincidence, so I, likewise, didn't react. There weren't many Southerners at the Conservatory then, and absolutely nobody from Harrow, a town of two thousand between the rivers Cold and Solemn. (I'd come to Boston because the school's music teacher noticed my voice. She wrote to a friend in Lexington, who'd attended the Conservatory, who then visited Harrow and consequently organized my scholarship.) But here was David, having passed through my town on one of his collecting trips. Perhaps we'd even seen each other. I was once homesick, I remember.

"There was a reel I remember learning there," he said. "'Maids of Killary,' I think?"

"I know it. Do you know 'Seed of the Plough'?"

"Should I?" he said.

I told him that my mother used to sing it.

"Go on. Let's hear it."

"No," I said, shaking my head.

"What key?" he said, playing one chord to the next, down the piano. He edged forward on the bench. "What key?" he repeated, touching out an A.

His eyebrows lifted. I noticed then a dash on his upper lip, a scar, a smudge of pale red that I'd later learn was from his father.

"Don't think you could put a piano to it," I said.

"The floor is yours." He pushed away from the keys, slipped another cigarette from his pocket, picked a candle from the headboard, and cupped the flame to his face. Waited.

I was told I had perfect pitch when I named the note my mother coughed every morning. I could harmonize with a dog barking across the field. I was the tuner for my father's violin—standing at his elbow, singing out an A while he pinched and tightened the pegs. Early on I thought that everyone could see sound. A shape and color—a wobbly circle, blackberry purple, for D. I only adjusted the shape I saw, and then locked into the correct decibels. Tastes started to accompany the notes when I was thirteen. My father would play a bad B minor and waxy bitterness filled my mouth. On the other hand, a perfect C and I tasted sugary cherries. D, milk.

I sang for David then.

I've always felt as if what came from my throat and lips was not mine, like I was stealing rather than producing something. This body was mine—the constriction of my diaphragm, the pressure in my throat, the lips and the softening of my tongue that shaped the sound—but what left me, ringing through the crown of my head so my skull felt more bell than corporeal, flooding my ears' timpani, vibrating through my nose, wasn't my own. More like the sound of wind over a bottle. Or, better, an echo of my own voice, coming from my mouth. A repetition. I can't sing like that anymore—and I miss it. Now I have this weak warble, this drone that nobody tells me isn't any good.

As I ended the song, the color yellow faded to the taste of wet wood.

"Where in hell did you learn that?" David asked.

I shrugged.

"I wouldn't be puttering around school if I had a voice like that," he said.

When he stood to get another beer, I saw he was inches taller than anybody in the room.

We stayed together until dawn. Me singing to his piano.

I might have been able to hum a D at both octaves, but I'd never met anyone with a memory like his. I'd later learn he had maybe a thousand songs in his head, and could hear a melody only once to repeat it, note for note. That night, tilting his head, plugging an ear with a finger, humming a note or two to tease out the song, he only fumbled a line when he was absolutely drunk.

"Let me buy you another beer," I said, not moving from the piano's side, the gray morning light filling the dusty windows of the pub.

"Yes," he said. "You've kept me up all night. You owe me."

"Anything you want," I said, staring.

"No. I'm tired. It's morning. I'm going to bed. I live across the street. Walk me back."

His apartment was bare—only a bed, a piano, and a chair. Dirty plates and glasses were scattered on the floor, along with pages and pages of music. No desk. I asked him for a glass of water, because the room was spinning. He brought a water glass from the kitchen, said he only had this one clean one, took a long sip, and then spit an arc of water at me. I opened my mouth to catch the stream. He did this until the glass was empty and I was wet but had managed a few sips. He placed the glass on the floor, and then walked to me, took off my glasses, folded them and put them on the windowsill. He pulled my wet shirt up over my head and led me to his bed.

I woke when the sun was high and David was gone, with a headache and the room still moving. I'd been drunk before, but not like this. I crawled from the sheets and saw a note on the floor: *See you in a week.* I gulped water from his sink, then filled the glass and walked into the living room. I sat in his one chair, drank until the glass was empty, then went back to bed, put myself under the covers. When I woke again, just before sunset, he was still gone, and so I gathered my clothes, folded his note, and put it in my pocket before leaving.

Every Tuesday night thereafter, David was at the piano and I was buying us drinks with my scholarship stipend. On nights that weren't Tuesday, I sometimes stood across the street from his building, looking up, trying to see who it was walking around his apartment. I was only curious, I told myself. I really don't think I've ever been jealous, which was a problem with every relationship I've had since David. Like Clarissa, whom I dated in my forties, and who left me after she admitted she was sleeping with my friend. I'd already known about her affair, and when I told her so, saying I only wished she'd admitted it to me earlier and supposed we could work through it, she got upset, as if I'd been the one doing the cheating, that I didn't care about her anyway, so why should she stay? Most of the other men I've been with—Alex, William, Alistair, others—have lasted no more than a few months. Vincent was the longest. I met him in Rome, where I lived for over a year, in 1929 and 1930. An uncommonly gifted musician, originally from Milan, charming to every stranger we met, a gap between his two front teeth and a laugh that echoed all the way down the city's narrow streets, Vincent was a cellist who practiced in the same chapel where I sang. When, eventually, I said I needed to go home, back to Boston, for career reasons, he only said, "*Americano*," like it was the worst word he could think of.

I WON'T DWELL ON the particulars of David's departure only half a year after we met. It was 1917. America had entered the war. Classes were disbanded. He went to Europe. I didn't, because of my bad eyes. I wrote my Harrow address in his journal, told him to send me French chocolate.

I returned to Harrow, to the farm, to help my brother, who, not very long after I arrived, also went to Europe. Maybe that was the end of my time with David, I thought. A dozen Tuesday nights in Boston. I thought of him in the way you do when you're young: in the mornings, lying in bed listening to the songbirds, sheets tangled around my legs; when I stood in the kitchen watching the kettle, waiting for it to boil; when I was pruning, grafting, staking, and guying the fruit trees; after work, walking to the streambed and listening to the spring peepers; sitting on our porch, listening to a thunderstorm clear its throat on the horizon in three notes, the smell of dirt released under the storm's coming. As in, always. I sometimes woke with an impression of his face in my eyes, with my hand reaching across the bed for him.

My body remembering his, even if I tried not to. Gray-blue eyes with a pale copper ring around the iris. The scar on his lip. An Adam's apple stark as a broken bone. His hair smelled like tobacco, his neck like fermenting fruit. I didn't experience the guilt that some men in my time would have. I just loved David, and I didn't think much beyond that. My error was that I thought David was the first of many. That I'd had a taste of love. I was eager for my future. How could I have known that all the rest—Alex, Laura, William, Vincent, Clarissa, Sarah, and most recently George—were only rivulets after the first brief deluge?

Summer and autumn passed. Winter arrived on the farm. Snow once, but nothing like Boston. I spent months writing bad music, drinking too many cups of coffee, walking for hours. Wondering when life would resume, when the war would be over and I could go back north, back to classes, back to Boston, where, I was sure, David would return after his service.

I visited my grandfather sometimes, who lived on the outskirts of town in a house his father had built for him and his six siblings. My own father had died years earlier, in the orchard, and my mother had taken the change by going on walks that sometimes lasted into the night. So, without my brother around, the house was empty and quiet in a way I didn't like. My grandfather would sit in his chair beside the fire, summer or winter, wrapped in blankets. We drank coffee, talked about the war in Europe and if I'd heard from my brother, and then he'd ask me to sing. He never asked me about the Conservatory. He didn't like to talk about anywhere north of Kentucky. He'd been in the cavalry, watched his friends "de-limbed" in Antietam. He was not a bad man—just angry. Just missed his friends and missed his wife. I'm struck now, only writing this, by how many wars have swept through my family's lives. My brother never came back from the war.

DAVID'S NOTE ARRIVED at the farm in June 1919. The return address was Bowdoin College, up in Maine. He'd written on the back of a sheet of staff paper—on the front were two bars of arcing quarter notes. A paragraph, only:

> My dear silver-throated Confederate: I hope this note finds its way to you. How is life on the farm? As it stands: I just returned from a walking tour, you might say, in Northern Europe. God help me. But the day is getting brighter. I have a position up at Bowdoin, here in the evergreens. Last month a man visited the Department to show off a new phonograph prototype. The Chair thought it a Fine Idea if I was elected to record folk songs in this boreal wilderness for Dept.'s regionalist leanings. I can't drag this talking sewing machine by myself—how about a long walk in the woods this summer? The journey points north. A bed of pine needles under the stars? Birch beer? Don't dally, just come.

I turned the paper over and hummed what I could read of the two bars. A student's jolting melody, surely. All the notes I've gotten from David were directives: *See you in a week*, he wrote that first morning. And then: *Don't dally, just come.* He gave me instructions, and I followed.

That night, I lay in bed with the note on my face.

I told my mother I got a job up north and left a week later. The farm would go untended. The orchards would become overgrown, and if I stayed away long enough, the fruit would overripen, fall to the ground, and rot. I didn't care. I left as if I were running away, took the train from Louisville to New York, New York to Boston, Boston to Augusta.

I've never cared much about objects. I don't care when a dish breaks—and when my house here in Cambridge was robbed some years ago I can honestly say I didn't feel very bad, only confused and troubled by the cost. The walls of my house are bare, and I ask friends to never buy me Christmas or birthday gifts. It might be considered frugal or meaningful, but it was a problem when I was younger. I used to lose everything, leave my coat on the church pews, forget my schoolbooks, leave a hammer in the grass. I gave a lot of stuff away to other kids—toys, my father's violin rosin, coins. The worst was our family dog. I liked a boy at school and so one day walked our dog to his house, tied her to a tree on his lawn, and walked home not thinking too much of it. My father whipped me for that.

Yet I still have that note David sent, asking me to come north. Still have all the notes he left me on the floor of his apartment. Still have the cigarette he rolled and forgot on the piano one night, and the box of matches from the pub where we used to meet. I didn't keep the statuette Vincent gave me before I left Rome, or the watch Clarissa gave me soon after we started dating, or the landscape painting Sarah made, or the sea glass I collected on Cape Cod with Alex. But with David, I was a devoted magpie.

In the Augusta train station, I saw him before he saw me. I stood some distance away, watching. He was wearing a light blue shirt, a dark jacket. Hands in his pockets. He'd grown a mustache and looked thinner, sharper in the cheeks. When he stretched his arms above his head, I felt an actual jump in my chest, like a muscle I didn't know I had started up again. I waved, caught his attention, and he pointed at me like his hand was a pistol. Around him were the cases of recording equipment.

From August through September 1919, we must have walked a few hundred miles, collecting ballads and tunes from the rocky coast to the endless interior of colonnaded forests and back to the coast. Walked through foggy marshes, forests loud with singing frogs and moss that we sunk up to our knees in, along coastal roads where the wind nearly knocked us off our feet. We visited towns, of course, but also granite quarries and farms where we'd heard there were good singers. David was always the one to introduce us, while I stood back, smiled. We worked off recommendations—someone's cousin might know someone's aunt twenty miles north. Sometimes we stayed in the houses of those we recorded, but mostly we slept in a canvas tent that David lugged around. Or, when it was a clear night—as there were many that summer—we slept without the tent, in fields or under the pines. Our limbs tired from the day's walk, and sleep compacting us together.

My grandfather once said that happiness isn't a story. So, there isn't much to say about those first weeks. Though the heavy phonograph recorder straps dug into my shoulders, the blackflies left bloody welts all over my neck, and my boots blistered both my heels, I don't think I've ever been happier—in the plain, dull way that resists any further articulation. It comes in images: sun hatching out of clouds while we walked through a hayfield flattened by days of rain, droplets lighting up around us and birds shouting. Bathing under a wispy waterfall with David, and afterward having sex on the rocks. Running out of food, finding a blueberry barren like it was a gift, and eating for an afternoon until we were sick and happy and too full to keep going, so we napped there, until a woman woke us with her boot. Later that same evening, under lavender twilight, him asking me to stick out my tongue, and then him showing me his—both blue from the berries. I thought of the untended fruit trees back in Harrow, of the birds eating the fruit and the grasses rising up through the orchard, and didn't care.

It was my job to work the machinery: unwrap the wax cylinder from its paper covering, brush the surface clean, fit it on the rotator; position the horn right to the singer's face and ask him or her to sing down the tube; move the stylus to the wax; turn the crank slowly. David transcribed the lyrics and notes in a booklet, along with a short interview about the origins of the person and the song, after the recording was made. I liked the songs, but didn't love them, not like David loved them. I don't know exactly where the passion came from—he didn't grow up with the songs, not like me and my brother. But then again, I didn't know much at all about David's early life—whenever I'd ask, he'd shake his head, wave his hand like he was swatting away a blackfly, say it wasn't interesting. I only knew that he was born in Newport, that he lived for a few years as a boy in London for his father's work—the profession of which I didn't know. He did once mention an uncle in

England who played the fiddle and took him to Ireland for a weeklong trip. Perhaps that's where his collecting started. Now, in my eighties, I know that most things we love are seeded before we're ten. When I asked what he liked about the songs, the ballads especially, he said—I remember his words exactly—that they were "the most warm-blooded pieces of music" he knew. I see what he means, that the songs are filled with the voices of thousands who've sung and changed them, and that they are always stories of people's lives. Not like the baroque music I began to love at the Conservatory, sharp and abstract and ornate like coldly glittering pieces of jewelry. The folk songs had soft underbellies, could put a lump in your throat just by the melody. Emotion in song; nothing fancy. In the years immediately after our collecting trip ended, for reasons that will become apparent, I didn't want to sing the old songs. I turned to choir music, to arcing solos in cathedrals, which is why I took that position in Rome in 1929. It was only when my voice gave out in my fifties that I found the one thing I wanted to write about was American folk music, the traditions that trickled in from Europe and blossomed and twisted into something fresh and new. It was just by chance that my writing coincided with the folk revival in New York and Boston, and so my books sold well. It's not beyond my understanding that I was writing them as a sort of memoriam to David, without mentioning his name. And I honestly began to love the music again, the old Scotch-Irish songs from my home state and throughout Appalachia, in a way that had eluded me for so long.

Of all the recordings that summer of 1919, I felt like we were missing the best sounds. I wanted an aural journal of the days between our work sessions. The sound of a windstorm coming up a valley. The sound of the pines' broomed limbs brushing overhead. The *kapock-kip-koop* of eight children's wooden spoons hitting wooden plates down a table south of Augusta; the crackling lard around a side of meat burning in a skillet. I wanted a recording of David whispering "Holy Jesus" when we first came to a field glowing with fireflies in Dog Hill; of the scrape of a snapping turtle's claws across a table in Lincoln; the time in Cowper, when Nora Tettle and her three daughters, each so eager to have their songs recorded, singing at once entirely separate songs, each Tettle trying to outdo the others until David had to quiet them by knocking two cooking pans together. Love Williams in Southwick, seated in the middle of her kitchen, singing a modal tune while I tried to fix the phonograph, her six children and five stepchildren all sitting around her, quiet, until Love came to the second refrain, when the children couldn't restrain themselves and one by one joined their mother. Twelve singers, four harmonies.

I wanted all the chiseled ridges of sound that went missing. The vibrations that had been released into the world and never concentrated down the phonograph's tube and to the stylus, that had never been impressed to wax. I wanted a record of the sound from the years before. The first time David spoke his name to me in the pub. David inviting me to his apartment. Asking me one late night if he should join the war or not, and me saying yes because I thought that's what he wanted to hear. The history of sound, lost daily. I've started to think of Earth as a wax cylinder; the sun the needle, laid on the land and drawing out the day's music—the sound of people arguing, cooking, laughing, singing, moaning, crying, flirting. And behind that, a silent sweep of millions of sleeping people, washing across the Earth like static.

As the weeks passed, I noticed a darkness in David that I think he tried to keep hidden. His hands shook. He had trouble rolling his cigarettes. A few times I'd wake to see him standing some distance away from where we had made our bed. He was a black column under the moon, like a pillar of some ancient ruin. When we sang songs during our walks from town to town, he'd sometimes stop in the middle of a verse, repeating the last line, searching for the next one. I startled him once by coming up behind him too quietly. He sprung forward, as if electrocuted. I assumed it was the war, as it was for so many men.

One day, tired of his silence, I asked if he'd ever shot anyone. He raised his hand in the air, and didn't respond.

BY SEPTEMBER, a week before David needed to return to Bowdoin, we had only three cylinders left. We were on our way to Kingdom, a coastal village with a granite quarry. We were looking for the house of John Winslow, the cousin of a woman named Mary Conway, who, Mary said, had a bank of songs in his head. "And his wife, Rosemary, is one of the best cooks in a hundred miles. She'll set you up good."

Some kids at the waterfront directed us to the end of a long dirt road going inland. It was one of those too-cold, late-summer evenings, when a wind from a few months out was already blowing a chill over the land. The fog we'd seen all day on the water had folded in. Nestled in the woods was the house—or shack, really. A corrugated metal roof, patchwork of clapboard. Dozens of deer antlers nailed to the exterior. A dog chained to a stake in the muddy yard sprang awake and barked, ran toward us, and then was jolted back when the chain snapped tight. A flock of blackbirds lifted from the rain-darkened trees around the house, then dissolved farther into the woods. I got what you'd call a bad feeling.

David knocked. Nobody came to the door, so he walked around the house, called into the woods.

"Let's go," I said when he came back around. Now, thinking back on that house, I seem to remember that there weren't any windows.

The dog kept barking. Pulling at the chain. Jumping and choking itself. Huffing and snapping. A big dog. A bear dog, I think. Gray and brown with a white chest. Ears looked to be cut short.

"Shut up!" David yelled at the dog. "Let's wait until he gets back," he said, turning around and peering down the road. "I don't think I can walk another mile. I'm thirsty and we're out of water. We're here."

He shrugged off his pack, sat on the steps to the front door, patted his pocket for his tobacco, and then rolled a cigarette. He closed his eyes, rested the back of his head against the door.

I slipped my shoulders from the recorder's straps, laid it carefully on the ground, sat beside him.

Then, for the first time that summer, he asked me if I thought we'd see each other again, after the trip.

I said that I'd like to.

He asked if I worried about what we were doing.

I said I didn't, because I didn't.

He rolled his head against the door, as if to massage it. There was a slick of dirty sweat on his forehead. He then drew his legs up to his chest, leaned forward, put his chin on his knees, kept his eyes closed as if he were praying.

"I think I admire you," he said.

The dog kept barking. The chain snapped and clanged.

I was just about to ask him why, when he scrambled to his feet and strode toward the dog. As he approached, the dog lifted onto its back legs, the taut chain holding it upright. Like an axe head about to fall.

"What are you doing?" I said. "Careful."

David put out his hand, stepped closer. The dog was choking and wheezing as it pressed against its collar. David stood there looking at it, only a foot away, then flicked his cigarette at the dog's feet.

A man called from the forest's edge, "Hey!"

I jumped up. David spun around. The dog went quiet.

The man had a long beard, mostly white but streaked dark. Over his shoulder was a pole hung with dead rabbits. He held a gun in one hand.

"What in the hell are you doing?" he said, dropping the pole and holding up his gun.

"Hello!" David said cheerily, as if there wasn't a gun pointed at him. "I'm David White, and this is Lionel Worthing. We're friends of your cousin, Mary Conway?"

"Mary," he said. "And?" He put the gun at his side and picked up the staff with rabbits tied to it.

"You must be John," David said. "We're collecting songs, and Mary said you had a few?"

"Not interested," John said. He walked toward us in that slow, intentional way that some woodsmen have. Like he felt the length of a day more than the rest of us and didn't need to rush.

"It would only take a moment," David said. "Can I ask where you learned the songs?"

"Not interested," he said again, leaning the staff on the side of the house. The rabbits—there were three of them—must have just been killed. Blood dripped out of the mouth of one and tapped a bed of dry leaves.

"Mary said your family is from the west of Ireland?" David said.

John didn't answer. Pulled a knife from his belt, cut the rabbits from the pole, and laid them out on the porch, side by side.

"Which town?" David asked. "I've spent some time there, way back. That's where I first learned 'The Shepherd's Way.' Maybe you know it?"

"Now look," John said. One of his eyes, I saw then, was blood-red, I suppose from a broken vessel. His cheeks were sunken. His whole face twitched, clenched, and then loosened. "I'm not interested. I told you that once. I told you again. I'm not trying to be rude here. I see you have come a long way, if you're coming from Mary's. Come back later, maybe later. A week or two, and I can help you then."

David's gift of persuasion, I think, was only in that he couldn't stop going after something if he wanted it. If it wasn't for Mary's impassioned suggestion to record John, and for the fact that we wouldn't be anywhere near his house in a week, I think David would have stopped there. John seemed unlike the others, who at first always refused because they were shy or suspicious. Instead, he refused in a way that was final, unforgiving. His back was already turned to us, and with his knife he cut into one of the rabbits, then began pulling away the skin.

"Is your wife here?" David said. "Perhaps she'd like to sing? Rosemary?"

John turned to David, knife in hand, blood all over. Behind him, the rabbit's skin hung off its hind feet.

"Or water," I said. "We've run out of water. Could you spare some water?"

He sighed. Stepped back.

"I am a Christian," he said. He laid the knife on the porch, and then shuffled up the stairs. When he opened the door, sunlight spilled into the house and illuminated a woman's body, lying flat on a table in the center of the room. He didn't shut the door when he walked to the back of the house. The woman's dress spilled off the table, as if a tablecloth. The hem billowed in the wind coming through the doorway. On her chest was a bouquet of flowers. David and I didn't speak, as we both looked into the wake. When I heard John walking across the floor again, I turned and stared into the trees.

He came out with two glasses.

"For the thirsty musicians," he said.

"Thank you," I said. I avoided a thumbprint of blood on the rim of my cup.

He picked up his knife and continued skinning the rabbit, finally tearing the skin off the feet. It landed with a wet flop when he threw it on the stairs.

"And is this what you do," he said, "go and ask people to sing down a tube?"

"I do," David said. "Yes, I do. But not him." He pointed to me. "This one is a singer. He might have the best voice in New England."

"Is that so?" John said. He stabbed the knife into the porch so it stood upright. "Go ahead. Sing us a tune, then."

The water tasted metallic, bitter.

"I wouldn't know what to sing," I said. My head was still messy with the image of the woman on the table.

John touched the other rabbit. "I'm sure you'll think of one."

The first song that came to mind was "Lord Randall," one of David's favorites. He'd taught it to me one of the very rare mornings when we lay in bed in his apartment, when he didn't leave before I woke.

"O where have you been, Lord Randall, my son?" I sang. I closed my eyes, tasted burnt butter, and saw the color pale green. "Where have you been, my handsome young man?"

"Christ," I heard John say somewhere a hundred miles away.

"I've been at the greenwood," I sang. "Mother, make my bed soon. For I'm wearied with hunting, and fain would lie down. And what met you there, Lord Randall, my son? And what met you there, my handsome young man? O, I met with my true love. Mother, make my bed soon. For I'm wearied with hunting, and fain would lie down."

The ballad is long and repetitive, the mother questioning her son to figure out why he is so sick and tired. He tells her that his lover made him fried eels for dinner, and that when the dogs ate his scraps, they died. The mother tells him that he's been poisoned. He agrees, and asks her again to make his bed so he can lie down and die, too. He tells her that he's leaving her the family cows, leaving his sister his gold and silver, and leaving his brother his house and property. The mother asks, "What did you leave to your true love, Lord Randall, my son? What did you leave to your true love, my handsome young man?" He replies, "I leave her rope on yon apple tree, for to hang on. Mother, make my bed soon. For it was her who poisoned me, and I fain would lie down."

When I finished and opened my eyes, John and David were both looking at the ground. The sky appeared violet.

"I'm sorry about your loss," David said to John.

"Thank you for saying," John said.

David looked at me. "Good choice in song," he said. "Poisoned in love." He hooked his arm through the strap of his pack. "I didn't think you'd remember that one all the way through." He hefted the pack, shifted it into place on his shoulders. "Strange he calls her his true love right to the end. His killer, that is." He turned and walked away, down the road, past the silent dog, without waiting for me. Without saying goodbye or thanking John, as he usually did with our hosts.

If John was disturbed by David's sudden departure, he didn't show it.

"A beautiful song there, lad," he said. "I know it, too. You changed the end, though."

"Did I?" I'd only sung what David had taught me.

"The end. It's usually, 'I leave her fire and hell.' Not an apple tree and rope. I think I like your version more. Gentler, like."

"Thanks for your time," I said, going over to the phonograph and lifting it onto my back.

His whole body shifted, as if whatever he was going to say had gotten bent and clogged in his throat. "Good luck, son."

Another punch of cold wind rushed over the trees, as if summer was already gone.

At the Augusta train station, I told David I could stay in Maine longer, help him catalog the recordings. I could find a house near campus, just for the fall semester, if he needed help. But I should have been more direct. For once, I should have been the one to give him directions. If not staying in Maine, I could have told him to come with me to Boston. Maybe things would have turned out better. Instead, he shook his head for reasons I understood only later, and said that we'd collect songs again the following summer. He told me we'd write.

The fall months were busy, back in Kentucky. In that time, David hadn't answered any of my letters, so in January I wrote to the Bowdoin music department. I explained I was a research assistant of David's, a fellow graduate of the Conservatory, and that I'd been the one to join him on the song-collecting journey the summer previous. *Could you*, I asked, *send me his address, as I may have the wrong one, and there are some papers I'd like to share?* Or some lie like that.

The letter I got back, weeks later, was kind, I think. The department chair wrote that he was very sorry to be the one to deliver the news that David had passed away in the fall of 1919. He went on to say that he was also sorry to report that he didn't know what cylinders I was referring to—that David's job had been teaching music composition, not history, and the department had not sponsored a trip for song collecting. *I'm sorry I cannot be more helpful*, he wrote. *If I find the cylinders you're referring to, I'll be sure to forward them your way.*

I folded the letter and walked outside, toward the orchards, and then realized that I didn't want to go to the orchards, so I walked to the blue gazebo, but that wasn't the place, either. I ended up at my grandfather's house, miles out of town. We had tea. He showed me a new trick his dog had learned—balancing a stick on his nose. I didn't tell him about the letter. He said I "looked a bit sideways," asked if I was drunk, and when I said no, he poured me a glass of whiskey and said, "Go on, then." I slept at his house that night and for some nights following.

In a follow-up correspondence with the department chair about where the cylinders might be, I discovered that David had had a fiancée, named Belle, and that he'd been engaged since the spring before our trip.

IT'S BEEN A FEW DAYS NOW, after starting this. Yesterday I called Hal, my friend at the Harvard Peabody Museum who I knew would have access to a phonograph. I told him about the surprise package that arrived at my door. He said I could come by anytime.

I walked the box of cylinders five blocks to the museum, met him at the door. He brought me past the gemstone collection, past skeletons and glass flowers, into the back offices.

"I haven't used one of these since I was a boy," he said, slipping the dust cloth off the phonograph.

He helped me fit the first cylinder onto the rotator. He hooked the tube to the stylus base, and then placed the needle on the cylinder. Put his hand on the crank, turned it. What came from the horn was a man's voice, from a seaside town just north of Portland, singing a ballad as trim and haunting as when I first heard it.

The cylinders were each labeled on the ends with the song title and singer's name and date of recording, which is why my eye was drawn to the last one in the box: OCTOBER 20, 1919—a month after I said goodbye to David at the train station.

"Let's see what's on this one," I said, pointing to that cylinder.

He unfolded the paper, fit the cylinder on the rotator. Started the crank.

"Hello, Lionel," David's scratchy voice said into the room.

My heart hurt like it had been kicked. Clenched into something that gave me the same hot pinpricks in my arms and legs that happened the moment before I crashed my car years ago.

The phonograph's metal horn slushed out silence. I sank into the nearest chair.

"Are you OK?" Hal asked.

I nodded. Smiled.

"Thank you for this summer," David said. "And for last year. I am sorry I am not the same as when we first met. There's something in me that I can't get rid of. Some rotten spot."

More slush of silence—more static. The sound of him thinking. The silence was a high G.

"I can't see around it," David said. "The horizon of it just keeps speeding out ahead of me."

More static. And then he started humming.

"What's that he's singing?" Hal said.

"'A Dead Winter's Night,'" I said.

I closed my eyes, leaned back in the chair.

"'One going west, the other east,'" David sang in his stony baritone. "'Two still figures at trees' roots.'"

I tasted salt and tobacco, saw the round shape of the color indigo thin into a rod of deep orange, then flash into a point of black that filled my mouth with the taste of stone.

I'm not sure what I expected to hear, what I wanted to hear, but what came to mind was that famous story about the phonograph—that it was Edison's only invention that worked immediately. He drew out the concept of a stylus jittering over a soft surface, had his engineer mock one up, and it just worked, right then, the first time. It was that—the plain physicality of it, those hair-thin antique canyons chiseled by David's voice—that I concentrated on, looking at the skin-colored cylinder on the rotator. Edison hadn't thought to use the phonograph for music. He imagined doing what David had done here: recording messages, that it could be put beside a person's deathbed so he or she might give final instructions. Or that you could record a baby's voice, then the voice of the same person twenty years later, then as an old person, so that in one artifact you'd have an entire life. That it would be a comfort to people left behind. But this wasn't a comfort. Only a reminder of the regret I thought I'd let go. I should have stayed on the train platform in Augusta, or forced him to come with me to Boston. It was only a reminder that I actually, amazingly, still loved David. That my feelings for George and Clarissa were mindful, thoughtful, compared to this bone-deep kind that David's voice had shaken loose. How to put it? This type of sadness. Not nostalgia. Not grief. Just the obvious and sudden fact that my life looked an inch shorter than it could have been. That the best year really had come when I was twenty. Walking over to the museum with the cylinders, I imagined I might be soothed by flipping through the audio scrapbook of that summer. That hearing Mary Conway's or the Tettles' voices would stitch a wound, in the same way that when I'd met up with Clarissa in Harvard Square years after we'd split, I was afterward attended only by happiness at what might be an enduring friendship. The same with George—who regularly sent me updates on his life in Savannah, and who assured me he only felt thankful for our time together. But this cylinder reminded me of what I'd missed—which is, I think, a life that I didn't know but of which David was a part. The real one. And how ridiculously short it had been. Only a few months. The memories of fireflies and swimming naked in the waterfall did nothing but make very fine and long incisions in the membrane of contentedness I'd built up over the years—a good home, a successful career, kind neighbors, a few great relationships. A wasted life. Maybe that's why people started using the phonograph for recording music—because why the hell would you want to listen to the voices of the loved and dead?

The song ended. The needle drifted off the cylinder.

"Do you want to listen to any others?" Hal said, detaching the cylinder and wrapping it in its paper. "Any specific one?" He fidgeted with the cylinders, turning them to read the labels.

Still, despite my shortness of breath, I wanted more. A dog gnawing at a bone, licking for marrow.

"Let's start from the beginning," I said. "The first one."

I looked out the window, to the street, where the fluffy white seedpods were still blowing down the sidewalk, looking for a place to grow.

Edwin Chase of Nantucket

When my father and I were younger, he taught me how to count the days in a month. Put your fists up like this, he said, side by side. January is the first knuckle, the peak. February, the valley. The peak has more days. The valley, less. January has thirty-one. February, twenty-eight. March, thirty-one. April, thirty. And so on, down to the pair of knuckles for late summer. I was ten or eleven when he showed me that, years after we moved to Nantucket. I lay in bed that night, searching for other timepieces. I touched twenty-four ribs—the daily hours. Eyes, nostrils, mouth, and ears that made the seven days of a week. There might be moon phases down my spine; days between the equinox and solstice somewhere in my feet. I could be made of three hundred and sixty-five bones.

May is a knuckle. I know that without counting because on the thirty-first, 1796, a man and a woman—carrying between them nothing but a satchel of clothes, bread, paintbrushes, paints, and notebooks—arrived unexpectedly to our farm on Coskata. I was twenty when they came.

It had been raining all morning. Puddles held in the sand. Winter had been long. April ended in a blizzard, and snow still lay in ditches and in the house's shadows. So much of my day then was shaped by the sky—the way a cloud gathered itself up and fell in rain or snow or sleet. Nantucket starts and ends with weather. Which way the wind was blowing and why. What clouds meant. How coming storms moved the sea.

This was over a year since my father died. The evening he disappeared, I found his coat in the grass beside the pond, which had recently frozen over. I brought the coat home, told my mother, Laurel, that he'd probably gone on one of his walks. That he didn't come home that night wasn't rare—Laurel and I often ate dinner alone, found my father the next morning asleep in the garden, or in the shed, or out on the beach, or in the dunes. Usually naked, saying sorry when he woke up, holding his hands over his penis and asking to help find his clothes. He'd only been too hot in the night, he'd say, just too hot.

When I walked across the pond the day after finding his coat, I saw him out near the center, face down, under the ice. His shirt had ridden up over his head, so that when I stood over him it seemed that wind was blowing across his back, or that he was undressing. One shoe was missing. A thinner and clearer skin of ice had refrozen across the hole he'd fallen through.

In the coldest part of winter, my father cut ice from this pond. The blocks he carted home sometimes held feathers, or hairs of green winter growth, or a brown and bent rush. The day I found him, the ice was thin enough to break with an axe. With Paul Pinkham's help, I looped a rope around his body, and with the rope hitched to our horse, Sadie, standing in the grass, we pulled him from the water. His hair was clumped with ice. Hands balled into fists. Feet pointed inward so that his toes touched. Mouth open. Ice in his beard and eyelashes. A white film of frost already on his skin. The bald patch on his head puckered. He looked surprised, the skin on his face looked tauter. So much was still there, but more missing: his deep voice; his quietness; his limp from the leg broken in the war. I waited with him at the edge of the pond while Paul rigged up something to carry him back.

WHEN I SAW WILL and Rivkah walking toward our house—though I didn't know their names then—Laurel and I were by the shed rubbing oil on Sadie. Her fleas had been bad that winter. I should have kept her stall cleaner. Before fleas it was thrush—the bottoms of her hooves smothered with white rot. All horses' maladies are poetry, my father said. Bog spavin. Seedy toe. Our old horse Julius had moon blindness. Both corneas dyed milk-blue. Laurel and I led him through the dunes and along the beach for exercise on our evening walks because he was scared into laziness by his cloudy eyes.

Sadie stepped back and turned her head when she saw them. That's the way it always is—an animal noticing first. Like gulls crowding in a field hours before a storm.

They were in the middle of the sand road that nobody used. We were miles out from Nantucket town, and the only building beyond our house was the lighthouse, a mile away at the end of the point. Nobody came to our house. The only prints on the path were made by me, Laurel, mice, and the birds—which were like the punctuation of our solitude, the commas and periods in the footsteps of animals that distanced us from others.

"Who's that?" I said to Laurel.

"What?" she said, looking up at me. She used the back of her wrist to brush her hair from her forehead. Oil dripped from her fingers.

She was thirty-seven then. That makes her seventeen when I was born. The bones in her face were severe in a way that might have been ugly. A straight nose, thin lips, narrow face, deep eye sockets. But it happened that everything was placed well, beautifully even, and she could easily have remarried if we weren't all those miles from town. Two suitors did ride to our farm. One was John Throat, the butcher. He came for Laurel cleaner than usual, with a bundle of meat tied to his horse. My mother was polite, fixed him tea, and then asked him to leave. The other suitor was my uncle Amos, my father's brother, who stayed for two nights in the upstairs storage room. On the third day, he told us at breakfast that he'd been mistaken in coming, apologized, and left. I haven't seen him since.

"Behind you," I said to her. "Down the road."

She turned.

"Oh," she said, stepping back. "Yes." She touched her hairline. "Or—no."

"What?"

"I thought it was—but no, there are two. So I suppose not."

"Suppose not what?"

"Nothing," she said. "It's not Paul?" She turned back to Sadie and poured another ladleful of oil. "And Maggie?"

Paul Pinkham, I should have said, was the keeper of the lighthouse, that mile north. He lived there with his mute wife, Sarah, and their daughter, Maggie—a few years older than I and to whom I was engaged. Paul had a long white beard that you could see from a far way off. And they wouldn't have been walking like that, the way these two were separated.

"No," I said. "And that's not Maggie behind him."

Laurel turned again. Put her hand up to her forehead to block the sun.

"I don't know, Edwin. I guess we just have to wait and see."

As we watched the two figures hobble forward, through the wet sand, there were the sounds of gulls screeching, of the wind passing over our house and the dune grass, and of the sea feeling the land, saying to it with each wave, *Here you are, here you are, here you are.*

OUR HOUSE WAS A SACRIFICE to the wind. The wind rattled the fireboards and casements at night. The wind threw sand on the windows and guided it through the siding, no matter how many times I resealed it. Sand came down the chimney. Pooled on the hearthstone. Snaked over the floorboards. Banked up on all sides of the house. Collected at the feet of the table. It came in on my clothes, in my hair, under my fingernails, and filled my bed. I dug it out of my eyes before I fell asleep. My shoes were shovels. I swept the house every day, and still. "At least we won't need to dig the graves," Laurel would say, "when we're buried here."

My father left for the war in 1780. He came home in 1783 with burn marks down his arm and neck under his shirt collar. He was more wordless than before. He disappeared for long walks, swept the house in the middle of the night, talked to himself. He pried up floorboards by the chimney and front door and put hexes under them—one of his shoes by the chimney, an eelspear by the door—to stop whatever was tormenting him, he said. He often woke at night screaming, one time knocked himself out by running through the house and hitting a post. Sometimes he pulled me out of bed, always yelling about a fire in the house, and dragged me and Laurel outside. We'd stand in the dunes, under the stars, looking back at the dark house, until his mind resettled. We had to wait, though—when Laurel at first tried to go back to bed too early, he dragged her by the feet through the sand. Laurel squatted on the ground, knees drawn up to her chest, forehead resting on her arms. He'd stare at the dark, quiet house where, I suppose, he saw flames. And then, after a few still minutes, he'd turn to Laurel, ask what they were doing out there, to which Laurel would rise from the sand and walk back to the house without answering. She must have been very sad, thinking back, maybe scared. "Sorry," he'd say as she walked away. "Sorry, sorry," he'd repeat too quietly for her to hear.

He'd likely run himself into the pond to escape a fire he imagined. The burial was days later. Paul Pinkham, his assistant, William, and I lit a fire in the sheep pasture to thaw the ground. It was night by the time the fire died down enough to dig into the embers. Every few inches of mud they cleared would let the embers spill onto icy ground beneath and thaw another inch. We cleared the fire and mud, gathering branches from dead trees to refill the fire. Shoveled away burning soil that was wide and long enough for a person.

Especially at night, after dinner, I thought of how my life might change, what sadness or unexpected joy might settle in. Every summer I'd be digging up marsh mud to better the soil in the hotbeds for vegetables. I'd cut marsh hay and pile it on staddles. Sheer the sheep. Cut peat. Collect eggs. Mend fencing. My life then was comfortable, I think. I would have enough tea for a few cups a day. I would marry Maggie Pinkham. I would help Paul paint the lighthouse every few years. My mother might get sicker, though maybe not. My father would continue to not come back from the pond. Sadie would get fleas again. The sheep would lamb. The seals would continue to stare at us from the waves. This might last another forty years. The only unpredictable parts of a life are what comes with war and bad health. That is my experience.

I SAW THAT WILL, almost at the fence, held his boots. On his shoulder it looked like he was carrying a small, dark sack. A cat. A gray cat with its tail crossing his neck.

"Should I get the gun?" I asked Laurel.

She was breathing hard. She smiled to herself. Coughed. "I know who it is."

She untied her apron, wiped her hands, and draped it over her shoulder. She tucked her hair behind her ears. That was a habit of hers—always touching her hair, brushing her fingers across her forehead.

She pinched her cheeks to bring blood to them, something I only saw her do right before we walked to Meeting, before the men and women of town watched us take our seats.

She turned away, scraped at her teeth with her fingernails, and spat on the ground.

The cat's tail batted Will's chest. He opened the gate, passed through, dropped his boots, shrugged off his satchel. Waved. Laurel waved back.

"Jesus," he said, walking forward. "My legs feel as if they've been beaten."

He lifted the cat from his shoulder and put it on the sand. "I was going to quit three miles back." He waved behind himself, toward Rivkah. "But she was too thirsty."

He smiled, tilted his head. "Hello, Laurel."

I stepped around Sadie.

"Look what I found," he said, pointing to the cat rubbing itself on Laurel's leg. "For you. A late housewarming gift."

"You're here," Laurel said.

"I am," he said. He threw his arms up. "A few years late, I know."

"Why?" she said. "For what?"

"We are going south. A ship leaving from Nantucket. I would be forever guilty if I didn't see you on our way out."

He held open his arms. She stepped forward and hugged him.

"This is Edwin?" he said, looking at me when they stepped apart.

Sadie shifted, and I avoided her hooves.

"Yes," Laurel said. "Edwin, this is Will."

He squinted. Blond hair. A thin beard. Blue eyes. He smiled, and long, crescent dimples appeared.

"I haven't seen you since you were this big," he said. He sank his palm to his knee.

"Two years old," Laurel said.

"Is that so?" he said. "You look like your mother. More than your father."

"Who are you?" I asked.

Will looked at Laurel, and when she didn't say anything, he said, "A friend of your mother's."

Laurel touched her hairline. "Yes," she said. "Will and I grew up together."

"Neighbors," Will said, and drew in a breath. "Then she met your father and he moved her out to this island and so she left us all. Nearly twenty years ago?"

He smiled and touched her shoulder.

"How long can you stay?" Laurel said. "Now that you've finally come?"

"Tomorrow," Will said, quickly. "The ship leaves tomorrow. In the morning."

"Well," Laurel said.

The gate clapped shut. We all turned.

"Here she is," Will said.

Rivkah—tall as Will, unsmiling—was dressed in black. Her steps were heavy and short.

"Who?" Laurel said.

"Rivkah Seixas," Will said. "My wife. From Newport."

"Your wife," Laurel said.

Rivkah put her hands on her hips, took deep breaths. Long hair covered her face and shoulders.

"Good afternoon," she said, nearly bitterly.

"Why didn't you get a carriage from town?" Laurel said to Will.

"Why did Silas build a house so far away? And where is he, by the way?"

I hadn't heard my father's name spoken aloud since Paul Pinkham would come around the house asking for him. With Laurel, it was "your father." To hear his name was like seeing him suddenly.

"He died," Laurel said.

"Oh, no," Will said.

"Last year."

"I didn't know. I'm sorry. I didn't know."

She waved her hand. "Why would you? We all meet our Maker. How did you two meet?" She pointed to Rivkah then Will, Will then Rivkah.

"I . . ." He paused. "I painted her father's portrait," he said.

A silence fell over the four of us. Rivkah looked down, touched a pine cone with the tip of her boot. I was never good at understanding what exactly made people uncomfortable.

"I'm glad you came," Laurel finally said.

"Good," Will said. "I'm glad we came."

"You must be thirsty and hungry," Laurel said. "Edwin—milk?"

I nodded and went inside, happy for the excuse to leave.

When the English occupied the island, they stole from the houses and farm fields in the name of war, so Laurel asked me one day to put our dishes and paper money in a box and bury it in the marsh. My father was already away at war. Perhaps it was because of those years, fearful whenever a soldier came to our house—which happened sometimes—and watching the soldier watch my mother make a meal, that I wanted to tell Will to leave.

You never let a stranger into your house, is how I felt, after seeing what the soldiers had done to some of the farms as they retreated. I looked through the window above the sink at my mother laughing at something Will had said, and I felt like gathering up our Bible, my father's books, our glassware and silverware and the brooch Laurel wore only once a year, and burying it all.

Rivkah walked away from Laurel and Will, and sat on a stump, unlaced her boots and pushed them off, followed by her stockings.

I filled two glasses from a jug of our cow's milk, walked outside.

"Here," I said to Rivkah.

She took the glass, nodded, then put it in the sand. She touched her feet. Her thumbs made circles over blisters on the tops of her toes. Her hands were not like Maggie's or Laurel's—they were bony and thin, with longer fingernails. Embarrassed, I turned away. Yellow puffs of wood dust were falling from the edge of the barn roof—one of the carpenter wasps. They were everywhere that spring. Boring dozens of holes in the barn and house, and I didn't know how to get rid of them. Laurel had suggested smoking them out. I'd nearly burned the barn down when I held flaming grass under the roofline.

"Thanks," Will said when I handed him his glass, and he gulped down the milk that our cow had made from dead grass.

"Darling," Laurel said. "Why don't you get us a duck? I've seen teals landing in the marsh all week."

"Duck," Will said, handing the glass back to me. "That would be something. I haven't had one in some time." His hand wandered over Sadie's ears.

I nodded, went inside for the gun.

My job was simple then: introduce a ram, triple the heartbeats every year, then reduce. That might be the story of the living. Pull a fish from the sea. Take milk from a cow. Cut peat from the ground. Shoot a duck from the sky. Take a little bit of everything from everywhere. At the end of the year I'd pray I'd added more than all we'd taken to stay alive. In the winter, if a late flock of geese landed on the pond, I shot as many as I could and kept them hanging to dry on the laundry lines between the shed and the house.

Rivkah still hadn't moved from her seat on the stump, but was now staring at Will and Laurel.

I stepped between the two fresh sets of footprints, going the other way.

MALLARDS SLID ACROSS the black-watered marsh. An egret's wings gulped over the grass. Laurel's teals were rafted by the far edge, just below the small windmill of the saltworks, the drying vats of which I'd covered in the past week because of the storms. Buffleheads landed near the sandbar. More circling overhead.

I sat in the grass, waiting for one to paddle close enough so that I wouldn't waste a shot. Toward Wauwinet, two hay staddles stood like wardens over the marsh.

Weather painted the horizon. There was the smell of rain like wet stone, and of the marsh. Bits of quahogs and seaweed spread over the sandbar, which would soon sink under the incoming tide. I imagined the day when the tide didn't stop, when it washed through the spartina, lifted and toppled the cut hay; when it crept through the bayberry, pushed wavelets onto the dunes, touched our floor, mixed our fire's ashes, rose through the chimney, and over our house. One hurricane, I saw a barn float out into the ocean, hay spilling from its loft.

I put my gun under my knees and tented my body with my jacket as the cold rain began to fall.

There had been unexpected arrivals in the past. After the war, packs of dogs roamed the island looking for food. That was one bounty—for dogs' heads. Then there was the man who lived in the dunes for days until my father walked him back to town. There was Maggie's former suitor, who I'd seen walking past our house, near running past our house, to, I found out later, try to talk with her after she discovered he had another family on the mainland. There was the shipwreck carrying horses down at Great Point. The captain, gun in hand, sat in the sand beside two dead horses with broken legs. Paul had put a blanket over him. At least I could figure out the scene when I came upon it. The storm, the man, the gun, the broken legs, the dead horses. Cause, effect, and the blanket to finish it. This scene, Will and Rivkah and how my mother was breathing so hard and fidgeting when she talked with him, I couldn't see, entirely.

I looked up, and there was a black duck, right overhead. When I shot, it folded from the sky and slapped the water. I waited for the wind to push the duck to the edge of the marsh. I picked it up, slit its neck to bleed it, and started home. A dead animal's heat always makes me uneasy.

I watched shorebirds draw between waves. Soon it'd be summer, then winter. And then a year would have passed. In the marsh, a swan struggled to lift into flight, leaving a long white track. I cut a handful of rushes.

THE RAIN HAD PASSED, and the orange bits of cloud over the house looked like pieces of the sun. Sparks washed out the chimney. When I passed through the gate, I saw Rivkah in my bedroom window, upstairs, bent beside a candle on the sill. When she saw me, she lifted the candle and sank back into the dark room. I went around to the peat shed and tucked a few bricks under my arm.

Laurel and Will were sitting by the fire, so close to each other that their knees touched. When the door knocked the wall and Laurel saw me standing there with the peat bricks, she sat upright.

My father had carved a clock into the floorboards just inside the door—an arc of numerals. During the day, the doorframe's shadow kept time on the floor. At night, the numbers were caught useless in the wood.

"Close the door," she said. "The cold air is coming in."

"The hunter," Will said, reaching down for a bottle of fermented cider on the floor, refilling his and Laurel's glasses. There were two empty bottles on the floor beside his chair, and a basket of wild hazelnuts that I had been saving for baking was on the table beside them.

"Did you get one?" Laurel asked.

She rose, and touched the fire with a poker. Sunlight leaving the wood, my father used to say of fire. I held up the duck, shut the door, and hung my coat on a peg beside Will's satchel.

"Why are you using the wood?" I said to Laurel, nodding at the fire. In the summer, we only used peat. Wood was for the winter. I didn't mind so much that they'd drunk the cider.

"We're celebrating," she said.

"Bit of a damp chill in the air tonight, isn't there?" Will said. "You'd think the sky was wrung dry by now."

"Is Rivkah in my room?" I asked.

"Yes," Will said. "She is tired." He reached into the basket, cracked a nut with his teeth, and spat the shell into his hand. He tossed the shell into the fire.

"You can stay in my room tonight," Laurel said. "It's just for one night. Or you can make a bed by the fire if you want."

I filled the kettle and put it to heat on the chimney crane. I laid the duck in a pot, twisted its neck so the whole thing fit, and then poured in the water. When the duck floated, I pushed it down with a spoon.

"I was saving those nuts," I said to Laurel.

"I hear you're skilled with cooking," Will said. He reached around his seat and into his coat pocket. "I brought these from town." He held out a few peppercorns. "For you."

"Thank you," I said to him, and then put the peppercorns in my pocket.

I hung the duck on the chimney crane, and singed off the rest of the feathers. A skin of fire stretched over the body.

"What a painting that would make," Will said.

I nodded. Untied the duck and rested it on the hearthstone.

My presence had locked some silence over their conversation. Laurel produced stitching. Will went to his satchel for his journal, and with a nub of charcoal from the fireplace began drawing. The only other sound was the occasional creaking of floorboards upstairs.

Cooking is a funeral. Most of the recipes I know I learned from Laurel, before she stopped cooking. The butter I rubbed on the duck that night was its rite. I wrapped cubes of potato in bacon, stuffed cornmeal into the bird's cavity. In the kitchen, rosemary, thyme, garlic, hyssop, yellow docks, mint, drying on the ceiling like an inverted, withered garden. On the counter, pickled vegetables and onions. I crushed a peppercorn and sprinkled it on the breast. I piled the pot with embers and waited.

"Why is it that you do all the cooking here?" Will said, laying his drawing on his lap.

Because my father had started lining up his fingernail clippings on the mantel. Because he'd sometimes walk outside without shoes. Because he'd leave me and Laurel alone for hours in the afternoon and evening. Curious where he went, I followed him, sometimes. Mostly he'd just find a spot out of the wind, sit down, and do nothing, miss dinner. One night, Laurel said to me when I returned from the saltworks, "I don't care what you eat, but I'm not cooking for you or your father anymore." She put her mother's recipe book on the table. She might have a pickled beet for dinner. Or a boiled egg. So, I started cooking. In my father's long disappearances, I improved my recipes. Under the storms battering the house, cooking was the one thing I could control. Everything changes for the better with heat and time: onions go sweet with butter; potatoes soften. Of the raking, mucking, harrowing, it was the hours inside, out of the wind, in the kitchen, where I felt the weight lift away. Under our feet, in the cellar, with blocks of ice from the pond, I kept cheese, a bushel of quinces, apples, dried cherries, pears, a side of dried venison. Turnips and potatoes. And, depending on the season, I put berries into pies: gooseberries, strawberries, meal plums, cranberries, beach plums. When Laurel retreated to the bedroom early, I improved my dessert recipes. I made custards, cranberry tarts, ginger and treacle cakes, pound cakes, bread pudding, and hazelnut cake. I'd leave my father a plate on the table for when he returned.

"Because I like the warmth by the fire," I said to Will. "Something to do at night."

"I've never heard of a man your age spending so much time cooking."

"Is that an insult?"

Will laughed. "You are very serious, aren't you?"

"He's always been like this, even as a little boy," Laurel said. "An ornery old man. Always."

"I'd rather you not talk about me like that."

My mother put her finger up to her lips, looked at Will, shushed him, and then shook with laughter. She was drunk. Will smiled and looked down at his paper.

"Laurel," he said, gently admonishing her. He picked up his charcoal and made swift strokes across the paper.

On the mantel, I saw a small painting of a songbird standing on a table, with a blue ribbon tied to its leg.

"What's that?" I said, pointing.

"Oh," Will said, looking up. "A present for Laurel. One of my paintings."

"You did that?" I said, too honestly.

Will looked up from his lap. "I did. Do you like it?"

I approached the painting. The feathers and the beak and the feet seemed to be full, had depth. The ribbon looked real, as if it were spooling out from the small canvas. I touched the painting, right on the ribbon.

"A still life," Will said.

"Isn't it something?" Laurel said.

I had never seen anything so wonderful. It felt something like remembering, the way the painting looked familiar, but new. I wanted to ask him a hundred questions about it.

"The duck will be done soon," I said instead. "Should I tell your wife to come downstairs?"

"No," Will said. "Let her sleep."

I knew she wasn't sleeping.

"I'll leave a plate for her."

If cooking is the funeral, eating is its burial, grace, eulogy. I served the duck on three plates. Laurel and I always ate in our chairs by the fire.

We sat in silence, eating slowly. Will shifted in his chair, grunted.

"I should tell you," he said. "I should tell you about her."

"Tell me if you want," Laurel said. "Some things are best left alone."

He smiled. "Perhaps," he said. "We are going to Barbados. She has family there."

"I never thought you would marry."

"I didn't, either."

My father said that every story is a confession if you listen closely enough. Will had done nothing but confess, in some way or another, since he arrived—but somehow I still didn't know why he'd come.

Even without Will there, Laurel would have stayed up to watch the fire go out, until the logs broke to ash. Sometimes I found her still in her seat by the fire in the morning.

She had brought out a bottle of apple brandy after dinner. That winter, just as my father had done every year, I rolled a keg of cider outside to freeze out layers of ice, night by night, until all that was left was the alcohol that coldness couldn't pull any ice from. The alcohol was so strong that you could smell it from the cellar when we stored it down there in the spring.

They were talking only to each other, about people from their years in Falmouth. About how many children those people had, who had died, who had inherited property, who had left Cape Cod for New York or Boston. I spent the whole time staring at the painting of the bird, wondering how Will had made the ribbon look like that. How you make something that isn't real look so real.

"Good night," I finally said. "I don't mind sharing the bed. I'd rather have a bed than sleep on the floor."

"That's fine," Laurel said. "As I said."

I packed my pipe and walked into Laurel's room.

How familiar, a house. I knew every mark on the floor, the color of each stone of the chimney that I'd stared at for years. But I didn't know this bed. It would be the first and only time I ever slept there.

I took off my shoes, but kept on the rest of my clothes. I sat up in bed for a while, smoking, watching the ceiling and listening to the flooring creak as Rivkah paced. I heard the poker touching the firedogs as Laurel snuffed the fire. Banking it up, covering it with its own ash to insulate a heart of embers ready to light the next morning. Closing up the night. How long had that fire been going? If we tended it correctly, weeks—the last ember of the night to light the peat in the morning. In the winter, it could be a month before we used the tinderbox. Somewhere, spread in the field, were the ashes of hundreds of fires. Maybe sucked up by a root, added to a vegetable, cooked again.

They stood outside the bedroom door, telling each other "Good night," back and forth. "Good night, Laurel." "Good night, Will." "Good night, Laurel."

I concentrated on the bowl of my pipe. I inhaled, and held in the smoke.

"You're still up?" she said, closing the door behind her.

She undid her braid. All these daily rituals I never saw. Her standing there, pulling her hair out of its braid, getting ready for bed. Her hair was longer than I expected, far past her shoulders. It made her look younger.

She stood there for a moment, swaying.

"Are you drunk?" I asked.

"Close your eyes," she said.

I did, and heard the laces snap through cloth, the sound of her skirt and jacket fall to the ground, her boots kicked across the room, and then the ruffle of her body fitting into her nightgown. I felt the bed shift as she put herself down, as far away from me as possible.

"Have you always done that?" she said, pointing at my pipe. "Puffing away up there?"

"Some nights."

"I'm surprised you didn't suffocate yourself."

I closed my eyes, and let the back of my head rest on the wall. The sand in my hair crunched as I turned it from side to side, massaging my scalp on the knots in the wood.

"Who is he?"

At first, she didn't say anything from under the covers.

"I knew him before I knew your father."

"But I'm curious as to your relationship with him."

She was quiet.

I doused the tobacco with my thumb, and pressed my head against the pillow.

"It should be obvious that he and I were once very close," she said. "We were meant to be engaged. What you are seeing is an example of regret, Edwin. Of two people who might have married, but didn't for circumstances out of our control."

In her pause, I heard sand swept up by the wind hissing on the window.

"And now he will leave with his new wife, who he doesn't seem to like very much, and you and I will go back to our lives. And I'm not sure what the lesson is in that, but here we are. At least you might understand now."

"I'm glad to know," I said.

I thought she had soon after fallen asleep because her breathing had become labored and thick. But when her hand went up to her face, I realized she had been crying.

"Are you curious about the circumstances that drove us apart?" she said into the dark room.

I wasn't interested in hearing what I already knew, what I had heard in parts from my parents' arguments: how Laurel said she had been taken away from her home, brought out to live here, an island she hated and which she told me and my father both was ugly and depressing.

"No."

"Good night, then," she said, and rolled away from me.

Around the house, the dunes shifted one sand grain at a time in the ceaseless wind.

RAIN CRACKLING ON the roof. I was wide awake, as usual. Pure awake. The wind punched the windows. Rain gurgled through the shingles. Waterfalls pounded the ground in a constant whine. A wet wind had found our roof and was gnawing at it.

Laurel snored beside me.

I hadn't been sleeping more than a few hours, anyway, for the past few years. I might make tea and walk down the beach. In the summer, when the moon was full enough, I weeded the gardens. On my hands and knees under the stars, picking grasses. It made me feel good—to wake in the morning to a pile of uprooted weeds by a patch of cucumbers, for instance. It was like I had gained a short, dark day nested in the night. I sometimes fell asleep in the garden, in the barn, or against the side of the house.

I left the bed, shut the door quietly behind me. The fire glowed from under the ash. I lit a candle, and lifted Will's satchel from the peg by the door, put it on the dinner table. I laid out the contents: a shirt, string, razor blade, paintbrushes. Under that, small glass jars filled with molasses-like brown liquid. Under the bottles was a notebook. Not the one he'd been using earlier that night.

It had a soft leather cover with a worn, peeling spine. Overstuffed with papers. I sat, and opened it on my lap.

Stretching across two pages was a drawing of a breaking wave. The next page, a juniper branch full of berries. A cloud passing over the landscape. A shadowy copse of trees. A woman, naked, floating in the water, her hair fanning out around her. Rivkah, I imagined. Her face and figure were repeated throughout the book. Then one of a man hanging from the gallows. And finally, near the end, before the book's gasp of blank pages continuing to the back cover, a stack of loose papers. Letters.

They were in Laurel's cramped, jittery handwriting. The first one I read was dated ten years earlier. She wrote that she wanted to see him, that she missed him. She signed it *L.* The next one was dated only a month later, asking him to come visit her, that Silas wouldn't be angry this time if he came. She wrote about how bored she was. That she wasn't happy. Some letters were only a few lines, some were pages long. Some included poetic descriptions, but all were filled with general sadness. She ended every single letter with the exact same phrase: *Please come.* Only one was more graphic, saying that she had dreamed about his neck. I thought of my father's burned neck.

There must have been fifty or more letters. Fewer as years passed. Compared to the dozen in 1786, there were only two letters from 1788. In the earlier ones, she described memories of them together. The later ones were more direct. *I can't remember your eye color,* she wrote in July 1789. *I used to be able to close my eyes, and see your face so clearly.* In a letter from June 1790, she described a day I remembered well, when my father, she, and I walked out to Great

Point Lighthouse. Along the way, we found a crate of oranges that had washed ashore. We sat in the sand, eating as many oranges as we could because, my father said, they would soon rot. In her letter to Will, she described the smell of the oranges, how they had made her so happy, how the oranges might have made a nice painting for him. She didn't describe me or my father—had nearly made it sound as if she were alone on the beach. She also didn't mention what I later saw through the open door of her bedroom: that she had saved a few peels and rubbed them in her hair and down her forearms. The last letter was from September 1790—the only letter she sent that year. *Dear Will,* she wrote. *Yesterday I walked to the north side of the island. I saw a dark line—small, a dash—on the horizon. Cape Cod. Where you are, I think. Or, maybe you have moved. I haven't heard from you in some time. Why don't you write? Have I done something? Tell me.*

Once I finished reading, I stacked the letters neatly in the back of the notebook and retied the twine.

Had she received letters from him? And if so, how hadn't my father or I noticed? Or had she written to him, for years, without response?

I listened to the rain on our roof. I replaced the notebook in the satchel, then hung the satchel on the peg by the door.

THE NEXT MORNING, when the sky was gray with the light of a cloudy day, I heard Will and Rivkah shuffling upstairs. I looked over to Laurel, who was asleep on her back, her mouth hung open and the air halting through her nose and throat. I nearly woke her, but looking closely, I saw her eyes quivering under her eyelids. I was told by my father that you could kill someone if you woke them when their eyes were doing that.

I listened to Will and Rivkah walk downstairs and, I imagined, rummage through the cabinets for food. I listened to glasses filling with water from the jug, to Will whisper something, to their glasses placed on the counter. I heard Rivkah laugh quietly, and rising quickly, I moved to the edge of the door. I saw Will touch Rivkah on the back, and kiss her on her ear. She reached her hand up and grazed his cheek.

When they left, I walked out to the kitchen. Will hadn't left a note, hadn't left anything. Had snuck away early in the morning to make it to his boat with his wife, off to the Caribbean.

I lifted the water jug that they'd emptied and carried it to our well. I opened the coop door and let out our hens, collected their eggs. I would make an omelet with, if I could find them, mushrooms that might have bloomed in recent damp days. In the sand that had been smoothed and soaked by the night's storm were Will's and Rivkah's footprints—side by side and broken through the top, wet layer to the dry, white sand below.

Laurel was still asleep when I went back inside. I would wait until she woke to cook.

I stoked the embers in the fireplace, then rearranged the chairs—pushed them apart and placed them where they had been before Will arrived. The gray cat, which I hadn't seen since Will dropped it at Laurel's feet the day before, appeared on the stairs, stretched on the bottom step, and then rested flat on the hearthstone. Sitting in my chair, lighting my pipe again, I saw on the mantel that Will left the painting he had brought. I'm not sure why, but I assumed he would have taken it. I picked it up and turned it over. On the back, written in ink, was the title and signature: *The Captured Bird, William M. Snowe, 1795.*

I put the painting face down on the table, got the inkpot, quill, and a blank page torn from one of my father's poetry books. I studied the handwriting on the back of the painting, the way all the letters were linked and slanted. The way the *w*'s in his name were wide and angular. The *o* of *Snowe* was pinched narrow and its *e* overdrawn, as if a loop of thread.

Thank you, Laurel, I wrote on the paper. *Love, Will*

Though I didn't know exactly what it would mean for her, and I didn't fully understand their story, I folded the paper in half and left it with the painting on my mother's chair, which was already warm from the heat of the fire I had built for us that morning.

The Silver Clip

In 2008, I was living in my grandmother's house on Nantucket—an old Colonial with beams dyed so dark brown they were black, the cupboards filled with dishware too valuable to use. Gran's dementia had taken a bad turn that year. She couldn't live alone on the island anymore, so my dad had moved her into a nursing home on the mainland. The taxes and upkeep of the house were too high, my parents said, so they were going to sell it. I had just graduated from art school and, with no plan, asked if I could stay at the house until they put it on the market that summer. My dad said sure, if I did some work on the walls and windows and floors. "Good luck," he said. He'd grown up on Nantucket, and said he'd never spend another winter there again.

I arrived to the island on the car ferry on a warm September afternoon. The house did not sit on a bluff overlooking the Atlantic as one might imagine a Nantucket house. It did not have columns or a widow's walk or a picket fence or a secret garden rimmed with heirloom rosebushes. It was small and stout, deep in a nest of cobblestone streets downtown, near an old cemetery, packed in a line of houses that were evacuated in the fall. If I opened my bedroom window, I could reach out and touch the weatherworn shingles of the neighbor's house.

I moved Gran's furniture to the edges of the living room, put down a drop cloth, and set up my painting easel. I arranged my paints, lined up my brushes. I stood in the kitchen, drinking coffee, looking through the antique windowpanes smudging the view outside. Bubbles, small as fizz, were caught in the old glass. I listened to the silence of the house. A cat crossed the neighbor's lawn.

There were immediate problems—with the pipes, the heating, the flooded basement. Worst was the cold. I didn't understand how Gran had lived there in the winter. No matter how far I turned the dial on the thermostat, frigid dampness passed right inside. I once watched a tumbleweed of dust and hair make its way across the living room floor, blown by a draft coming from the rotting French doors, which, my dad wrote in an email, had to be reframed and rehung. Most nights, by October, I sat beside the fireplace, drinking coffee, listening to the autumn storms in the trees. With a flat metal instrument, I stuffed a tide of embers back into the shallow hearth, and loaded on more wood.

Soon the days felt the same. I woke in the late morning, put on a hoodie and long underwear under my pants, made a big pot of coffee, painted. After a couple hours, I made toast, and then worked on the house—I removed the doors, scraped and repainted the windows, replaced the cabinets, sanded the beams, and did whatever else my dad's emails instructed me to do. Sometimes after dinner, bored of reading, I would walk the streets of downtown, past the few houses where people still lived on Orange or New or Main streets. Gran and I used to walk together in the summer nights, getting lost in the streets and finding our way back. You saw people's lives framed in their illuminated windows: a man reading a book by a fire; a woman upstairs combing her hair; two people making dinner together and their daughter doing homework at the table; a man in front of his computer; a woman up late, making a sandwich.

On one particularly rotten December afternoon, I was on my knees in the fireplace preparing to clean out the chimney that, my dad said, was a powder keg waiting to blow. I dismantled the flue vent so I could push up a broom. It took nearly an hour to thread out the bolts that were rusted and covered with a century of ash and creosote. I detached the vent and started to bring it down when I felt something hard and cold roll from the vent and touch my hand. A small, white, ceramic vase fell onto the bed of ash.

I picked it up, turned it in my hand. It was swelled in the middle and no bigger than a comb, shaped like a toy rocket without the fins. It was hollow, too, and made a musical *plink* when I flicked it. On one end was a quarter-size hole fitted with a cork.

I brought it down to the kitchen and washed away the mold and dust with a sponge. I unplugged the cork and filled the cavity, shook it, and then emptied the water. I rubbed the ceramic with a dish towel, and saw hairline cracks in the glaze running along the length of it. Porcelain, I thought. It couldn't be a vase, because the tip was rounded and it wouldn't stand up. Maybe it was an old flask, or something medical, like a pillbox.

I put the ceramic on the windowsill, then laid my hands flat in the sink and let the warm water run into the bays of my fingers. Steam rose over my arms and face, fogged up the window. I felt bad that none of us had known how cold Gran must have been. I wondered if she missed this house, even with the cold and drafts, now that she was in the nursing home. She didn't have a car, and was allowed only short walks on the property, if, apparently, the staff thought it was warm enough. When I asked my dad if he'd been visiting her, he said not enough.

Antique flask, I searched on my computer that night. *Nantucket porcelain flask. Porcelain pillbox. Antique ceramic in chimney.* Each search turned up something bulkier and nothing so simple and seedlike as what was on my kitchen windowsill. It was nagging me, an object I couldn't name.

THE NEXT DAY, I was standing in the atrium of the Nantucket Whaling Museum, only a short walk from Gran's house, with the ceramic in a tote bag, hoping to find someone who could tell me what it was. A whale skeleton hung from the ceiling. It was early morning. A pale and wintry light passed through the bones overhead.

"Just one?" the woman at the front desk asked.

"I found an antique, I think, in my house." I lifted the tote bag. "I'm wondering if there is someone I could talk to about it?"

She picked up the phone, spoke quietly. Beside her desk was a misshapen, shell-like bone that was, the placard read, a sperm whale's ear.

"Someone will be down," she said after hanging up. "You can

walk around if you want." She gave me a sticker that read VISITOR.

Off the atrium was a gallery with an exhibit called *Arctic Exploration*. A gray, skin-lined kayak hung from the ceiling, and grainy, colorless photographs labeled INUIT HUNTERS were on the walls. A walrus tusk was mounted beside a narwhal tusk. I stopped in front of a painting the size of a door. Big swaths of pink icebergs crushed a ship at sunset. Ice cut with an ultramarine stripe floated nearby. A seal with the face of a catfish sat in the foreground. A ship in the far background, spewing black smoke, pushed through the ice toward a polar bear.

"Quite a painting, isn't it?" I heard from behind me.

The approaching woman was tall, in her seventies, I guessed, with thick, gray hair braided and clipped to the top of her head like a crown. She was wearing a black coat over a pale gray sweater, and had delicate, frameless glasses.

"I'm Mallory Dart," she said. "Exhibitions manager."

I introduced myself. Her earrings were two silver leaves. Aspen leaves, maybe.

"Can you believe it?" she said, pointing to the painting.

"What is it?" I asked.

"Alistair James Sanford, 1859. Trying to find a passage to Asia. There was a thought then that the North Pole was open ocean. That if you could break through the ring of ice around Greenland and Ellesmere Island, you'd make it to a hidden sea. He thought there might be islands and undiscovered civilizations up there. The follies of man. Imagine spending a life trying to find something that wasn't there?"

In the corner of the painting was a man standing on the ice, looking out to the horizon, all by himself.

"So," she said, "what's a young man like you doing way out here, with winter coming?"

I explained the situation of Gran's house.

"Ah," she said. "Wash ashore. Do you have a job?"

"I'm an artist. A painter."

"You're making a living off that?"

"Not really."

"I used to paint," she said. "And my husband, he was a great artist." She moved her glasses up her nose. "But, blah. You've brought something for us to see?"

"Maybe it's nothing," I said.

"This is my favorite part of the job," she said. "When someone says that."

I reached into the tote bag and found the artifact between my book and wallet. Holding it in front of Mallory, I regretted having not wrapped it in newspaper or bubble wrap, to show that I cared for old things.

She took it gently in her hands.

"Oh," she said, smiling. "You don't know what this is?"

"I thought maybe a flask?"

"No," she said. She sighed. "Where did you find it?"

"In the chimney," I said. "In the bedroom."

"That makes sense. Well, there's no polite way to say this. It's a, well, a phallus."

"A what?"

"A dildo. From the Pacific, likely. Whalers would buy these off the Chinese coast, after Atlantic whaling died. Either as a joke, a trinket, or to give to their wives. Mid-to-late-nineteenth century."

She twisted out the cork.

"In here," she said, pointing to the cavity, "was for hot water. It actually isn't that rare to find these, sorry to say. We have about a dozen in storage. It's impossible to date them. I tried to put them on display one year for our *Women in Whaling* exhibit, but the board put the kibosh on that. People get uncomfortable. But I think it's just wonderful. That's life. Life went on here."

She smiled, corked the dildo, and handed it back to me.

"Men went away for years whaling," she said. "Widowed their wives, for all intents and purposes. These are called 'he's-at-homes.' Like, *He is at home.* For clear reasons. To promote fidelity. But I think it's the women who had the last laugh here." She clasped her hands in front of her.

"Anything else?" she asked.

"No." I put the dildo in my tote bag.

"You should make sure to look around where you found it. Often there are other artifacts stuffed together. Stashed away. Not to be too sensational but sometimes there are laudanum vials."

"What's that?"

"Old opium."

"Oh," I said. "I'll look."

She tipped her head to the side. "Hear that?" She pointed to her ear, then out the window. "Catbird." She smiled, and so I smiled back at her. "Singing. So out of season."

We listened together, to the light notes—airy and deep.

"Thanks for coming," she said. "I have a call now. But feel free to look around the museum."

Just before she left, she turned and said, "I'll look into the deeds of the house if you want, see who owned it before your grandmother. Find out whose artifact this was."

I told her only if she had time.

"Very good," she said. She then hurried up the stairs. "Good luck with painting!" she sang out, without looking behind her, as she disappeared over the top step.

Outside, the clouds were charcoal, and fluorescent whitecaps flashed over the harbor. The wind snapped the flagpole's ropes in front of the museum.

I SAW MALLORY AGAIN a few days later, when I was walking on a beach far out of town, in Coskata. I rarely saw anyone else out there, besides, once or twice a week, the same man and his two dogs.

"It's you!" she said, when she approached. She was dressed in rain boots, a black woolen sweater, beret, and a navy scarf wrapped up to her nose.

"Mallory," I said. "Thanks for the other day."

She hooked her scarf with her finger and brought it down below her chin. She was wearing bright red lipstick.

"Have you made any other discoveries?" she asked. "Ripping apart your house?"

"I haven't. I was painting. Trying to paint."

"Did you have a productive day? Inspired?"

"Not really. Which is why I'm out here. I didn't see your car in the lot."

"I didn't drive. I live right up there."

She pointed to a house behind and above the dunes, one that I walked past every time I went to Coskata. The house had a view of the ocean, with a beautiful wraparound porch painted blue, a modest turret, and Scandinavian flourishes of woodwork in the gables.

"You live there?" I said. "I think that's my favorite house on the island."

"Well, thank you. Yes, somehow it's survived all these hurricanes. Do you want to see it? I can take you for a tour."

"Oh, you don't have to do that."

"I'd love the company. I haven't had the chance to talk to an artist in years. This island is overrun with bankers."

I wondered if she'd seen me any of the other times I'd walked that beach.

"Come in for tea," she said. "I insist."

THE HOUSE SMELLED of rosemary or some other herb, mixed with the mildewed scent of a basement. I kicked sand off my boots, hung my jacket. Down the front hallway were plain geometric paintings of ships and—she later told me—her husband, Tim's, ancestors: stiff-necked, top-hatted, and wide-eyed.

"They baked hardtack for the sailors," she said of the portraits. "Biscuits. Made a fortune. A monopoly on crackers, if you'd believe it."

The floorboards creaked under our footsteps as we walked from the front hall to the living room.

"Tim's family went totally nuts, as families of the wealthy eventually do. His aunt had a pair of dogs that she brushed and made yarn from their fur and then a coat for herself. It's all rot here—dusty books and threadbare old rugs and a cracked tennis court. That wasn't me. I wouldn't want you to think this is me. I just married into it."

"Where are you from?"

"Not here," she said. "Michigan."

She pointed out where Tim's father had added to the house, and then where Tim had added a breezeway and a library. "It used to just be a little shack for a sheep farmer," she said. "Before it became this sprawling thing."

We walked into the dining room, where I stopped to look at a beautiful, small painting in a Dutch-black frame.

"Do you know William Snowe's work?" she asked.

I shook my head.

The painting was of a standing bird, a robin, with a cerulean ribbon tied around its leg.

"Quite famous in his time. He died very young. In the Barbados. He made a name for himself painting merchants in 1700s Newport. Tim found this one not unlike how you found your artifact—tucked away, in the back of the woodbox by the fireplace. Who knows how these things end up where they do? I just love it, love it, love it."

I looked closer, to the flash of white in the bird's black eye.

"Does that ever happen to you?" Mallory said. "That you see a painting that seems made for you? Anyway, it started me on his trail, and we just mounted an exhibit of Snowe's work at the museum."

The brushwork was loose, not like the tight, small strokes of the painters in his time. I wondered if she was mistaken in the date. It looked too modern, too much like an Impressionist's touch.

"There's a trick to it," she said. "You can see it if you look closely at the blue ribbon."

I stepped closer.

"My granddaughter was the one to notice it."

I stared at the ribbon. It was curled in such a way that it simply folded over the bird's foot.

"It's not tied."

"Very good!" she said. "The bird is free to go. So why is it called *The Captured Bird*? The bird only thinks it's captured? I love riddles."

She continued the tour. A shadowbox of butterflies was hanging in the library, and on the side tables were bell jars filled with small, taxidermied birds. On the walls of the library were photographs of the same two girls.

"My daughters," she said. "They don't visit anymore." She pointed to a wall of letters framed behind glass. "And those," she said, "are my hobby. Or an obsession, whatever you'd like to call it. Collecting old letters. Love letters, I suppose."

I walked up to the wall.

I felt very bad after you had gone, I read, from a letter dated 1859. *I did not know what to do with myself. I went upstairs and cried till my head ached and felt most sick. It is dark and cloudy out to-night and I expect you feel rather lonesome. I have such a sense of loneliness come over once in a while that I don't know what to do. You were all the World to me and now you are gone.—Martha.*

"They are all very sad," she said. "Letters went only as fast as the wind could push a ship. My daughters thought I was nuts to buy them. But I find them refreshing."

My dear husband, another read, *it is impossible to write what I feel. I sit to the window and watch for you as I us'd to, but you do not come.* Signed, *Ann Burgess, a kiss for you.* The "kiss" was circled in a heavy line of ink, bled wide by a hand pressing too hard on the paper for too long.

"Stay for dinner," Mallory said suddenly. "I'm cooking a chicken. I would love the company. A whole chicken. I don't know what I was thinking. I'll never finish it."

I had nothing to do. I was hungry. I hadn't shared dinner with anybody in months.

"Thanks," I said. "Sure."

"Oh, look," Mallory said, looking behind me. "The first snow of the year."

Snowflakes tacked themselves to the window. The sky was pressed in all around the house. Somehow, night had already come.

AFTER DINNER, after emptying a bottle of wine, we walked to the porch and watched the snow falling.

"So," she said, "what did you try to paint today?"

I'd set up a vase with flowers, spent the afternoon trying to paint sincerely, honestly, but it had just ended up looking like a bad replica of older, better paintings.

"A still life. But it didn't turn out well."

"Want to try again?" she said. "Tim's studio hasn't been used for years. I'd love for someone to use it. Bring some life back in the house. Come see it."

Before I could answer, she was walking inside. She picked up a box of matches in the front hall, lit a lantern. "Saves on electric bills," she said, carrying the lantern and her wineglass up the dark stairwell. "This way."

I walked behind her, then down a long hallway, following a circle of orange light the lantern cast on the floors. She opened the door to the studio. She put the lantern on a table, found the light switch. The smell of turpentine filled the room.

The studio looked as if Tim had just left. Paint rags were heaped in a pile beside an easel holding an unfinished, three-quarters-profile portrait. The head and upper body were sketched out, and he'd put down a warm layer of underpainting in parts of the face.

"That's me," she said, pointing to the portrait.

"Oh, yes. I see it."

"I just didn't see the reason to clear away all his things after Tim passed. I like coming in here. I have afternoon tea here. I like smelling the paints. Looking at the mess he made. It makes him feel more present. I don't understand why everybody doesn't leave a little messy room of the dead. It's been a great balm. I sometimes refill the turpentine jars to conjure the smell of him working."

Drawings and oil sketches and photographs covered the walls. I looked closely at one of the photographs—black and white, of a pretty woman sitting in a wicker chair in a garden, leaning back, one arm above her head and the other holding her hair up in a loose bun.

"Me in my younger days," she said. "In Paris."

I wondered if she'd been a model or an actress when she was younger, if she was a face I should have recognized, as might happen on this island.

"Tim and I went there every summer, before the girls arrived."

I walked around the studio, looking at his sketches, seeing that he had been, in fact, a skilled portraitist.

"I have an idea," she said, putting down her wineglass.

She walked to the center of the room, and sat in the chair set up in front of the easel.

"I think all the paints should still be fine to use, right?"

She removed her glasses, folded them and held them in her lap, then arranged herself in the same position of the unfinished portrait—with her body turned and her face angled toward me. Her neck tightened and ridged.

"You can start, if you want," she said.

I understood with some terror what was happening.

"Oh," I said. "No. I can't really paint portraits."

"Of course you can," she said. "I saw some on your website."

I said thank you, but no.

She still sat there, erect, head turned to the formal angle.

"I'll pay you," she said. She turned, breaking her pose. Her face softened, she smiled. "Please," she said.

The old windows shook in their frames from a punching, oceanic gust.

I touched the brushes kept in the jar. Long-stemmed, wooden, arranged in rounds and flats and according to size. They clinked against the jar's rim as I felt with my thumb how sharp the brush edges were. Tim had taken good care of everything.

"There's the turpentine," she said, pointing to the bottom of the table. She turned her head away, back to the three-quarters profile.

I picked up a tube of Titanium White paint, uncapped it, saw that if I were going to use it, I'd need to cut off a dry top layer. On the glass palette was a palette knife, waiting.

Her chair creaked. Tim had been right to paint her portrait. The way she held herself—her shoulders back, almost like a dancer, about to lunge forward—looked powerful, looked like something that I wanted to put down on canvas, something I wanted to remember.

Even though I didn't want to paint, I still stared at her. At her nose, where there'd be cadmium red on her nostril. At her earlobe, which I noticed was attached. Her pearl earring looked nearly orange in the light, highlighted by a bluish shadow that ran down the side of her neck. I couldn't name her eye color from where I stood, with the bad light. Something pale. Her hair—braided and looped up just as it was when we met at the whaling museum—would take hours to paint, each one of those braids twisting into one another. A silver hair clip shining at the top of her braids was, I noticed, already sketched out on the canvas in front of me. Its shape was both round and bowed, like an unremarkable phase of the moon.

I took a step back from the painting. Maybe the clip was a coincidence, I thought. Maybe the painting was, as she'd claimed, an idea she had just then, when we walked into the studio, and she had, by chance, been wearing the same clip as was in the portrait. I thought back to the first time I met her, in front of the shipwreck painting. I couldn't remember what was holding up her hair then.

"Have you begun?" she said, without turning her head.

I saw that she had a freckle on her temple. Also, there was a nearly turquoise shade under her eyebrow. The only part of her body that moved was her fingers, turning her folded eyeglasses over and over.

I looked again at the sketched-out silver clip, and then at the real one, beyond the canvas. If she had worn it for this moment—as in, if it hadn't been by chance that she was dressed for the portrait—when had she put it on? I imagined her standing at her window, staring out to the sea, seeing me down the beach, and then going to her bedroom, finding the clip in her bureau. Gathering her hair. Clasping it.

Deciding whether I should make a painting, whether I should spend weeks on a single work, I sometimes asked myself if I could title the painting before I began. If I could, there was some focus, some meaning in what I was looking at.

"Do you have what you need?" she asked, still not breaking pose.

The title of the painting came to me.

"Yes," I said. "Just turn to me, an inch more to the left."

I painted for an hour or more. Enough that I made my way through her cheekbones and eye socket, along the side of her nose and into my favorite part of any portrait, any face: that puffy, elevated skin sloping from the nose's ridge to the cheekbone.

The wind knocked at the windows; some door or shutter downstairs was opening and slamming shut. She was a perfect model. She didn't slump or shift or move, really, at all. We kept our positions—me behind the canvas, her on the chair.

Then, abruptly, she said she was tired. "I need to go to bed," she added.

I wasn't close to finishing. I had been softening up a small mound of umber with linseed oil, ready to move down her neck.

"Now?" I asked.

She stood from the chair, stretched, unfolded her glasses and put them back on.

"Tim never wanted me to see the painting," she said. "Before it was finished. I'll assume that's the same for you. You can come over in the next few days to continue, if you want."

I began washing the brushes in turpentine. I thanked her for dinner.

"Oh," she said, pointing to the brushes. "I can do that."

She seemed eager to have me out of the house. We said good night. I walked outside, somewhat confused by the sudden dismissal. The snowdrifts had reached nearly to my car window. By the time I had dug out my car, all the lights of the house were off, except for those I could see in the windows of Tim's studio.

I DIDN'T LAST ANOTHER month on Nantucket. I went back home, to the mainland, for Christmas, and then moved to Boston. I hadn't finished half of the projects I said I would do. My dad hired a contractor to come out later to finish the work.

I didn't see Mallory after I left her house that night. I didn't go back to the whaling museum, and though she said I could come back whenever I wanted to finish the portrait, she never sent me an invitation. I stopped walking on that beach because I didn't want to run into her. I was embarrassed, without really knowing why. She did, though, send me two things before I left.

First, she mailed to Gran's house ten photocopied pages of old town deeds. She had underlined the address on each page, beside a family name and a purchase date and price, from the early

1800s onward. I saw that my grandfather had bought it from a family named the Wilsons in 1958. The Wilsons had bought it from a woman named Susan Harcourt in 1874, who was given the house by her mother, Annie Barnes; given to Annie by her husband, Thomas, given to Thomas by his father, Calvin; given to Calvin by his father, Zachary; and given to Zachary by his father, John, grandson of one of the original purchasers of Nantucket in the year 1659. Mallory had underlined Susan Harcourt's name, and put a star next to it, I suppose to indicate her as the owner of the dildo.

Then, a week before I left Nantucket, I found a package on my doorstep: a small, wooden box wrapped with twine. There was a note inside. *Hope you find a good home for this. Consider it payment for the portrait.* Beneath bubble wrap and layers of wax paper was William Snowe's painting of the bird. I still have it, of course. Whenever someone comes to my studio in Boston, it's always that painting—old, tricky, rare—they pause to look at, then suggest I should do more like that one, that that is my best work.

Graft

In the Harvard Peabody Museum, on a warm and stormy afternoon in May 1893, Hope stood at a display case near the very center of the gallery. She was staring at a boy on the other side of the display case, who was looking at the flowers in front of him. There was a water lily, beside a poppy, beside a cornflower—a common-enough plant made rare by the fact, against close observation, that, like the dozens of other flowers in this exhibit, it was made of glass.

She folded and unfolded the pamphlet she'd gotten at the entrance. *The Blaschka Models of Glass Plants* it read on the front, and inside detailed how the flowers had been crafted over the small flame of a paraffin lamp, how long it took Leopold and Rudolph Blaschka—father-and-son jewelers from Bohemia—to build each petal and stem and root and thorn out of nothing but melted stone over wire, touched up with a little paint.

The boy was identical to Sam—her former husband, whom she hadn't seen in over a decade. The same black eyebrows over pale blue eyes, the same round face. The same protruding ears. It was the same face, beyond what she could describe in the terms of a nose or complexion or shape of a forehead. It just was Sam, as a child.

The boy touched the display case with both hands, as visitors were told not to do. The buttons of his coat tapped the case as he leaned forward, bringing his face right over the glass, looking closer at the poppy and then the cornflower.

Hope folded and unfolded the pamphlet again.

He was probably just another blue-eyed, dark-haired boy in Cambridge—at most, maybe a distant relative of Sam's. There was also the remote and frightening possibility, but reasonable because of this near perfect resemblance, that this boy was, in fact, Sam's son from his other marriage. The opening of the glass flower exhibit had attracted people from across the state, she read in the paper. Maybe Sam had come with his other family, on the train, all the way from Pittsfield. Maybe he was somewhere in the museum right now.

And, finally, there was this third possibility, the one that had shocked Hope into stillness at the side of the display case: that she was standing across from Eli, her son, whom she hadn't seen since he was baby, twelve years earlier, when she'd left him with her brother and sister-in-law on Cape Cod.

She looked over her shoulder, turned—afraid to see Sam in the room, even more afraid to see Davis and Annabelle. But she saw only her husband, Harold, still reading the exhibition description on the far wall, and an elderly couple, arm in arm, standing in front of the orchids.

Maybe the boy's parents were in the next room. Hope would see them, see that they were not Sam and his wife, or Davis and Annabelle, and that would settle the matter.

She heard Harold's footsteps behind her.

"Can you believe these?" he said, touching her elbow. "How is it possible these are made of glass?"

She nodded. "I know."

The boy looked up at Harold, then at her. The resemblance to Sam struck deeper now that he faced her. She smiled, said nothing. When Eli was a baby, there was something about him that looked like her father. Nothing like Sam.

The boy withdrew his hands from the glass, turned away from the display case, and moved to the next room, toward the Hall of Birds.

Maybe it was best to leave the museum now, Hope thought. The boy's hands had left thin, oily streaks on the glass. Under the streaks was the water lily. The roots were coated in fine, gray hairs. The father or son glassmaker had crafted the roots with as much attention as he had the blossoming white flower and its cupped, yellow organs, which were together beautiful enough to be a piece of jewelry, as they were, snapped from the stem.

Harold touched her shoulder.

"Ready to go?" he said.

Years earlier, Harold had been her art teacher at Wellesley. He had proposed to her the day after she graduated. They now lived in a modest house Harold had bought with his savings. She had a studio and a garden. They spent summers in Gloucester. He was a good man. That's what everybody who met him said.

He was an agreeable, sweet man, if not particularly handsome or conversational. The past years had been pleasant. No disruptions or excitements in their union, which she took as good fortune.

She had not told Harold about Eli, or about Sam, or her years in western Massachusetts where she'd met Sam, or even that she had a brother. As far as Harold knew, both her parents were deceased, and she never wanted to go back to her family home, in Barnstable, again. That was all true, if incomplete. She never imagined the time would come when it would be necessary to say anything more than that. If she had told him about her past, she was sure he would have rescinded his proposal. By keeping the truth from him, she was protecting Harold from his own bad judgment. He was happy with her.

"Let's keep looking," Hope said, watching the boy turn the corner, out of view.

It couldn't be Eli, she thought. She would know—some instinct would tell her that he was her son.

"It's your day," Harold said.

As she walked out of the glass flower exhibit, she paused at a pea shoot fixed to the wall. A semitranslucent tendril. Pale buds. This one had been made by the father, Leopold Blaschka. All she could think, from one flower to the next, was what Harold had said: these couldn't be made of glass. Maybe that was the trick, that Leopold had discovered some material characteristic of plants, that stems and flowers were akin to glass, best described in glass, shared a property of glass. Like, as Harold first told her in class, how oil paint had been invented to look like skin.

She let a reasonable amount of time pass before she turned away from the peas and followed the boy into the Hall of Birds, where, when she saw his parents, she would know that it wasn't Eli and could leave.

Twelve years earlier, in 1881, when Hope was twenty, she stood by the stone wall at the edge of her family's orchard, watching snow fall on the apple trees. It was November on Cape Cod. Overhead, a black line of clouds was swiping away what remained of a clear sky. She smelled the smoke rising from the chimney of her childhood home, drifting to her. Wood that was burned to weightless ash, brought into her lungs, the deepest pocket of her body, touched, she imagined, where her soul might live. She wondered if Eli, months old by then and asleep, strapped to her chest with the bedsheet she'd taken the morning she fled Hatfield days earlier, could smell the smoke, if his infant's mind knew what it was, maybe felt safer by the smell that meant warmth and rest.

The windows of the house glowed with firelight. Davis passed from the kitchen to the fireplace. He walked slowly. Carrying something. A pot. Dinner. And then Annabelle followed with two plates, one in each hand.

With the back of her hand, Hope wiped her nose, shifted from foot to foot, rocking Eli. She liked the weight of his small body against her, her silent then screaming companion on the journey that started over a hundred miles and five days back. She envied him, the way he was held close to her, swaddled, tended—not knowing he was suddenly fatherless as she was husbandless.

The dry snow creaked in the steps she took toward the house and then away, back to the stone wall, where she sat and waited for her breathing to calm, for a phrase of explanation for why she was home after four years gone. It was getting cold. The earth was turning away from the sun. Night would clap overhead. Eli would wake. She would have to knock on the door, give some explanation to Davis and Annabelle why she was carrying a baby, alone, near nightfall, in the middle of winter, without warning, without invitation, without a husband, without money, without, without, without.

She wouldn't have come home if there was any other place to go. Embarrassed to have returned; embarrassed for the reasons she ran away. The last time she was here, she was sixteen. That year, acne had spread from her cheekbones to the corners of her mouth. Girls had given her a nickname. Boys called her something worse. One winter morning, after waking from a dream in which she was trying to peel away a cloth tightening around her face, she went to the barn, broke the ice in the trough, and numbed her face with a piece of it. Then, with lye and the sharp side of a quartz stone she found in the grass, she rubbed her skin down, scraped at the boils and whiteheads on her cheeks and on her forehead. There was blood, then unimaginable pain when she came inside and her skin warmed. Her mother screamed when she saw her; Davis ran outside, looking for the person he thought must have done it to her. Then days of fever. She couldn't sleep. They wrapped her face in hot cloth. Then cold cloth. Davis put animal fat on her face every night for a week, along with sage and pulverized sassafras poultice. Though she was in pain, she wasn't worried—she knew that the skin would heal over smoothly, as the scars on her legs had healed over, as any cut healed. Smooth, pock-less skin. That did not happen. Her scarred, pitted face was left. Stretches of unnaturally pink skin. "Your father would be so ashamed," her mother said one morning, many weeks after she'd gone to the barn. "You have good bones. And eyebrows. You should have left well enough alone."

The only time Hope looked at her reflection was at night, in her bedroom window, when the lamps turned glass into a mirror that held a dim reflection. She sometimes stood naked in her room, and with a candle looked at all the unblemished skin across her body. She'd touch her stomach, her thighs, bend and touch her ankles, the tops of her feet, her toes. Bringing the candle close to her torso, she'd run her palm along her hip bone, up along her ribs, wondering how people would think of her differently if they saw only this, if they saw this skin instead of the only part that was uncovered to the world. She touched her neck, her collarbones, reached around to brush her hand over her lower back. Even the skin of her knees was soft, smooth.

She had decided to leave Barnstable before too many years passed, before she was humiliated further. If she wasn't going to marry—as her classmates had told her—she would live a more interesting life outside town. She wouldn't do chores for her mother, in her mother's house, until she was old herself. She told Davis she was going. As if he'd expected to hear it, he gave her five dollars and a knife, and said that he'd take care of explaining it to their mother. He likely didn't try to convince her out of it because he, also, wanted to leave. He'd once told her that he wanted to go to college, to study plant biology. But who would keep the orchard going? He seemed proud of Hope when she told him she was leaving, which was the only reason she went through with it.

She traveled to Lowell for work at the mills, which she hated, so she followed a tip about orchards needing apple pickers in the western part of the state. She settled at a large farm in Hatfield in the spring, helping with housework off-season. She didn't write to her family.

Heaven is filled with apple blossoms, she thought, looking at trees overstuffed with the petals. Apples comforted her. From growing up on the orchard, she knew to fertilize the stocks, what bugs to pick off, what ones to keep. She knew when to go around the neighborhood asking for people to save their cut hair and when to hang it in pouches on the trees to keep the deer away. She could taste the differences between a dozen varietals—the tartness, sweetness, citrus, woodiness. When she'd walked away from home earlier that year, she'd stopped by an apple tree at the edge of their property, cut away a sprig, and wrapped it in a wet cloth, hoping to save it for a graft, for wherever she lived next. It was as close to a crucifix as she wanted to carry. It died before she could find a new rootstock.

In her third year at the orchard in Hatfield, she met Sam.

ELI SHIFTED against her. The wind that had been stirring the trees died. She let the snow gather on her—on her dress, her shoulders, sleeves. She raised her hands, let it collect on her palms. She walked forward. Through the orchard. She could still name some of her favorite trees as she passed them. Ones that her father had named. Lucia. Edmund. High Crown. Thankful. Winter Tree. Each had grown from a shoot her father had grafted onto a root of another. It was magic to her as a child: how entire trees, and all their apples, were embedded in the bundles of the thin wands her father cut every winter and stored in the cellar.

Eli woke. She felt like there was a moth in her throat when she knocked on the door.

Davis stood in the doorway. He hugged her before he spoke to her. She looked over his shoulder at Annabelle, smiling widely, standing timidly by the fire, waiting her turn to hug her sister-in-law.

Oh, Annabelle's face. More beautiful than Hope remembered her from school.

Eli cried.

"Come in," Davis said, without asking why she was there.

HOPE NEVER WANTED to be a mother. She only wanted to be in love and loved, to wake in the morning and put her leg across a man's stomach and feel his strength and press her chest against his chest, to feel the warmth of the bed and not wanting to leave the bed because of it, to have a man's beard on her neck, to have him kiss wherever her scarred cheeks were not—on her shoulders, on her calves, thighs. She spent nights thinking about how it would feel to be kissed on the backs of her knees.

And she thought she had found him—the tall, deep-voiced man who had come to the Hatfield orchard two weeks before the end of harvest to oversee cidermaking. All the workers ate dinner together. Women on one side of the table, men on the other. She watched Sam the night he arrived, spooning stew. The way his lip rose to the spoon. Every dinner in the days following she tried to determine where he was going to sit so she could sit across from him. Then, one meal about a week into his visit, came an act of God: she had arrived to dinner late from the storage shed, and all the seats on the women's side of the table were filled. She poured her soup, walked to the table, and stood beside it, wondering if someone would move so she could have a seat, or, as was sometimes the case with those who were late, if she'd have to eat in the kitchen.

Sam looked up. "Just sit here," he said, and pushed down the men's side. "Oh, for heaven's sake," he said when he saw the other workers' faces. "Just sit."

Hope sat. They talked. Before the meal ended, he had put his hand under the table, on her knee. She could feel her heartbeat in her thigh. She touched her spoon to the soup and rested it there. Maybe, she thought only much later, if she had known more men, she would have seen his hand on her knee as a warning, and not, as she thought then, a prize that she was finally being awarded for her troubles.

When they had sex in the storage house when the harvest was done, she didn't hesitate to help him lift her skirt, to bring him toward her. The anticipation was so vast in her mind that she would have done it a hundred times before she paused to wonder what would happen if she became pregnant. Every day after that first one, they met in the storage house after dark. She usually got there before him, waited within the dark smell of apples, her hands cold, the sound of wood cracking in the night. Waiting to hear the metallic clink of the back door's bolt.

Sam seemed happy when she told him she was pregnant. They had a marriage ceremony—just her, Sam, and a priest—in Sam's friend's living room in Northampton when she was three months pregnant. Sam leased her a house. A small one, but with a good woodstove and not far from Hatfield town center. He bought her dishes. He gave her a ceramic, oval platter with a blue swan painted in the center. She arranged and rearranged the items in the cupboard he also bought her. These were the facts of her life. Things that were real: dishes, woodstove, blue swan on an oval platter.

She was happy that summer, for a few months, though she was uncomfortable—her legs swollen, her breathing shallow. It was one of the hottest summers anyone in Hatfield could remember. In the middle of the day, the nailheads on the shingling were too hot to touch. Muggy air swelled the doors. The birds had started singing in the middle of the night, perhaps because of the heat. Blankets stuck to her skin. Late one night, they were both awake and sitting up in bed, sweating, talking about how they'd never felt this kind of heat. Sam had gotten back that evening from one of his weeklong work trips, which he promised he would shorten when the baby came. They passed a cup of water between them, blowing air on each other's faces.

She asked him to tell her a story about his life. Any story, she said. He never talked about his childhood, or about his parents, and only once mentioned a brother who had left for the West. He mostly talked about apples, fermentation, and how much he liked being with her.

"About what?" Sam said.

"Anything. Or—no, something that you haven't told anyone else."

He was quiet, thinking.

"Have you heard of Iceland?" he said.

She said yes.

"My great-grandfather. He was from Iceland."

He told her that his great-grandfather came to Boston in the 1780s, after a volcano exploded and blacked out the sky over the island. People had to use lanterns all day, even at noon. His great-grandfather ate grass because ash had killed everything else. The sheep suffocated, coughed up black spit. Crops died, but even before their pantry ran out people were dying from suffocation. The first blue sky he saw was miles into the Atlantic Ocean, going west.

"And?" Hope said, when he stopped talking.

"And what?"

"That's the end? That doesn't tell me anything about you, about your life. I'm interested in your life, Sam."

"Why? It's boring."

"It's not boring to me."

They were silent, sipping water.

"I guess in some ways it is about me," he said.

"How?"

"I wouldn't be here if it wasn't for that volcano."

She later wondered if that was the only true thing she knew about him. That he had a great-grandfather who'd been driven halfway across the world by an eruption which eventually led him there, to bed with her.

"Well, I thank that volcano, then," she said.

It wasn't long after that conversation that the collapse came. A letter was left on Hope's doorstep when Sam was away, apparently visiting another orchard.

Sam is here, the letter read. *I thought you should know.* There was an address, two towns over.

Hope took a carriage. She knocked on the door and was greeted by Sam, two little children at his legs, and a woman sitting at a dining table behind him. He didn't say anything to Hope. Just nodded, then closed the door slowly, like he didn't know her. "Who was that?" Hope heard the woman say. "Nobody," he said from behind the door. She heard the door lock. She stood at the stoop, her limbs not working, the familiar feeling of punishment settling in her mind.

She returned to Hatfield. A week passed. Two weeks. He didn't come. She would wait for him. He would come. He would explain. A month passed. She wondered if maybe there was a misunderstanding, maybe that was his sister or a friend.

When she went into labor, her neighbor, Sarah, was the one to deliver Eli.

She was awake all day and night with Eli. Sarah checked on her sometimes, suggested they tell the priest about Sam, about what he'd done. No, Hope said. She didn't want to be humiliated even further. She wanted to never leave her home. Sarah brought her food.

She rehearsed what she would say to Sam. She would tell him that she never needed to be a parent. Never needed to have a child, like some women. This was not her desired life. He had ruined her, she'd say when he came back to explain.

Hope watched Eli's eyes as she rocked him. His open eyes were punctures in the night, disturbances, pain for her. He'd squirm in her arms, move his hands under her arms and pinch her. She squeezed Eli's hand in her armpit so he'd stop pinching while she nursed him. She put his little hand in her mouth, held it gently there. In moments, she noticed good things: the bottoms of Eli's feet were just as soft as his neck, because he'd never walked. She could smell his fragrant scalp from a foot away. She'd put her nose on Eli's head, breathe in and out to calm down.

Months passed of Sam not returning. She considered if she should bring Eli to that house, to show Sam what he'd done. But thinking of him shutting the door on her and Eli together, as he might do, was too painful. She gave up. She wrote down all the things she would say to him, folded it, and then burned it, along with the note she'd first gotten—she assumed he'd been recognized by a neighbor, or maybe by a visitor from his other town—of his other family's address.

She gathered up what she could take, the money she'd saved, picked up Eli, and left. She hated the woodstove, hated the dishes, the angle of the stairs, the floorboard in the hallway upstairs that creaked. When a man with a cart on the road out of Hatfield asked her where she'd like to go, she said Cape Cod, because it was the only place that remained in her mind, the only place in America that she remembered then, because every town and city and county and acre between Hatfield and Barnstable had disappeared when she'd seen Sam in the doorway, and in the sound of the door closing, the sound of an iron latch dropping into place to keep her out.

"I'll take you to the station," the man driving the cart said.

"Yes," she said, and got in.

She would have been kind to Sam, if he'd just told her that he had a family. She might not have continued to be with him, but she would have wished him well. She wasn't so naive to think that people didn't, at times, do selfish things. But why had he taken it so far? To marrying her? Wasn't that tiresome and burdensome, expensive? Had he given his other wife a collection of plates, another oval platter with a blue swan? God was punishing her for her vanity long ago, for abandoning her mother and brother, and, finally, for letting Sam keep his hand on her knee, under the table.

THEIR MOTHER PASSED AWAY the year Hope left, Davis said to her on that first night home. Hope nodded, felt far less than she thought she would. "We can visit her grave tomorrow," he said.

Hope put her finger beside Eli's mouth, brushed his face.

Davis said he and Annabelle had married the following year.

"God is not willing us parents," Annabelle said.

"Not yet," Davis said.

They sat by the fire after dinner. Annabelle had made stewed apples and cream for them. It was a scene that repeated every night the first week: sitting fireside, beside her brother and his sweet wife.

Hope told Davis about the orchard she had been working in. About the cider they produced and how it had been such good money, and maybe Davis should think about doing that. And, finally, in the briefest terms, about Sam.

WINTER PASSED. Crocuses filled the forest beyond the orchards. A yellow songbird smacked into the window above Hope's bed one morning. Spring had arrived.

Within months, Annabelle had started to get up at night when

Eli woke, to ask Hope if there was anything she could do to help. Annabelle heated up water, hung Eli's gowns and blankets by the fire, and touched the gowns to make sure they weren't too hot before fitting them on him. She bathed him, first putting her hand in the basin, swishing around the warm water, and bringing it to Eli's leg so he would feel the temperature.

Annabelle was a good mother. Better than Hope. Hope only wanted to sleep. She lay in bed for more than half the day, waking to feed Eli when Annabelle brought him in, and coming out only to get bread and apple jam, some tea that Davis would set for her as soon as he saw her emerge from the room. *How strange*, she thought when she fed Eli. *My baby and I are both swaddled here, in my old home.*

There was the time when they were all eating dinner, when Eli started crying and Annabelle rose from her chair and rushed to him, lifted him up, rocked him, patted him on his small back, and soothed his crying before she realized her mistake.

"Sorry," Annabelle said to Hope, who had also started to stand. "Sorry. You should take him. He wants you."

Annabelle drew Eli out of her embrace, held him out to Hope.

"No," Hope said, watching Eli grip Annabelle's dress. "That's fine. He is quiet with you. Take him."

How many times did this happen before Hope started staying in her bed, Eli crying, waiting for Annabelle to come in to comfort him?

"I WANT TO SHOW YOU SOMETHING," Davis said one early summer day, columns of thunderheads above.

Hope followed him through the orchard, to the final row of trees, where he stood, smiling, beside a strange tree. He touched the branches, where there were too many graft points—some cuts still wrapped in cloth and smeared in beeswax that leaked from the folds.

"Do you see?" he asked.

"What did you do?"

Her memory of her father teaching her and Davis how to graft might have been her first memory, or perhaps just the strongest of her childhood. He took them down to the root cellar, gathered the scions, then whittled their ends to wedges. He cut a cleft into a rootstock, fit in the scion. He covered the wedge with beeswax, and then wrapped it with cloth, as you would a wound. That spring, the sap would push from the root up through the scion, and so forcing two separate growths into one. It was an urgency rendered by the sun drawing out the leaves, by the leaves drawing up the sap; from the soil drawing down the roots. Trees pulling at both ends, up and down, their sap so vital that they would mend themselves to foreign bodies.

"Ten varieties," Davis said. He pointed to each of the graft marks on the one tree. "Crisp, Baldwin, Black Oxford, Cortland, Orange Pippin, Russet, Hyslop, Spitzenburg, Gravenstein, Pearmain."

"Will they live?" she asked. "I mean, it. Will it live?"

He brushed his hands over the young leaves.

"It appears it will."

Davis might be a genius, she thought. In the hand, in the eye, in patience. She imagined the tree come fall. Hung with so many different colors and sizes of apples.

It didn't surprise her that the Bible started with an apple tree. A young tree, maybe no thicker than two fingers, will make apples just as heavy as those a hundred years old. Even the young trees are required to give up fruit.

HOPE FOUND DAVIS WRITING at his desk one night. She stood in the doorway of his room, watching, listening to his quill scratch across paper and the occasional the clink of its metal nib dipped and tapped in the inkwell. Annabelle was in the kitchen, smacking a lump of dough with a rolling pin, readying it for baking the next morning. She'd refused Hope's offer to help, insisting that she rest by the fire. It was in moments like these, after dinner and when Eli was asleep, when Annabelle and Davis busied themselves with tasks before going to bed, that Hope felt most displaced, when she didn't quite know what to do with herself. During the day, Eli kept her attention, or when he was with Annabelle, she could distract herself with walking or chores. But these evening hours made her mind fray.

"What are you doing?" Hope said from the doorway.

Davis sat up quickly, turned.

"You startled me. Just some notes."

"On what?"

"Nothing, really. Just what's happening around the farm."

"Can I see?"

She walked across the room, sat on the edge of his bed.

"It's nothing," he said. "Yes, if you want."

He dropped his quill in the inkwell, blew on the wet line of words he'd just finished, then offered Hope his open journal.

"Nothing private?" she asked.

"Nothing you can't read."

His handwriting was clear and neatly spaced, but, also, nearly decorative—the crosses of his *t*'s spanned words, and some capital letters ended in tendrils.

"You have beautiful handwriting. I think this is the first time I've seen it."

"Annabelle says the same. Thank you."

She read a short paragraph on what trees were producing good apples, then flipped back a few pages to read about the weather, the rainfall, days of sun, days of wind and the direction of that wind, bugs, fungi, temperatures, observations of birds. On the inner cover was inscribed a list of blooms that came, in order, that spring. She read the list aloud: "Chickweed, groundsel, mayflower, crocus, smooth alder, speckled alder, beaked hazel, bloodroot, willow, henbit, coltsfoot, horsetail, cow parsnip, caraway, golden Alexanders, sweet cicely, evening primrose, buckthorn, blue-eyed grass, sidesaddle flower, sweet flag, bastard toadflax, garlic, liverwort. It reads like a poem."

"That would be a very bad poem."

"What's it all for?" she asked.

"I don't know, really. I do it every night. I suppose you could say it helps reveal our Maker? What the Lord has given us, day by day. It adds meaning, I think."

This was who her brother was: someone who kept notes on flowers, faithful to the world, sure of purpose. To her, observations did not render meaning. She knew better. Experience told her only actions made meaning. That scarring your own face, leaving home in a rush, sharing a bed with a man who was a devoted and creative liar—those were the items that created the plot of a life. Nothing happened when garlic bloomed.

"Liverwort," she read. "April eighteenth."

"You think it's silly."

"I think it's hopeful. I like that you're doing it."

SHE DIDN'T KNOW when it would happen. Maybe that summer. Maybe later, by winter. After the harvest. But it was coming: her second and final departure from home. She felt it all the time. The tightening in her stomach. She didn't like holding Eli as she used to, didn't like the way he looked at Annabelle when he was in her arms. She didn't like that his eyes had the same blue as Sam's, and, more, didn't like that she felt that way about her son. She felt shame. She was tired and lonely. Mostly lonely.

When she was sitting inside one day by the window, watching Annabelle play with Eli, who was on his back in the grass under one of the trees over-packed with white blossoms, she thought how simple the solution was. Easier for everyone, especially for Eli, if she just left. Annabelle was the rootstock, not her. This would be her gift to her brother and sister-in-law—her departure, Eli's new home. She felt relief at the thought, at the inevitability of her leaving, of its naturalness. She'd shed herself from her home, as a husk.

Beyond Eli and Annabelle, beyond the trees, beyond the salt marsh, out to sea, she saw the blue stitching of lightning, followed by the warm sound of distant thunder. One summer, when she was a girl, she and her father were sitting in a field he'd just mown. Piles of hay lay around them. Hope had just delivered half a loaf of bread and a jar of honey that her mother had sent for his lunch. The sky hung with yellow clouds. Her father said to her that it looked like lightning, and that they needed to go home soon. But it was so rare for Hope to be alone with her father—without Davis or her mother—that she said she wasn't afraid of lightning, and that it was fine if they just stayed there a little longer. Her father leaned back on his elbow, nodded at the clouds. "Do you know lightning turns sand to glass?" he said. "On the beach, one day when I was younger than you, a bolt struck ten yards from me. Before it hit, my skin felt how it does when you stand beside a fire on a cold day. My teeth hurt, too. I don't know why that would happen. Then I saw a bright light; lost my hearing, my eyesight for some minutes. When I woke up, on my back, the ground was charred, like a big fire had just been set upon it. In the middle of that ground was a circle of glass. Thick as my arm here. I ran home, told your grandfather, and he came back and dug it out. Looked like a branch, I remember, but glassy." He stood then, gave Hope the rest of the bread and honey she'd brought. Lifted his scythe and put it over his shoulder. "Turned to glass. That's what lightning does. It could turn you to glass. Now let's go." She missed her father. He'd died from an infected foot after an old nail in a rotten board near the barn went straight through his boot. His jaw locked up. She was eleven. Time hadn't eased the pain, as her mother had said it would.

Hope was about to warn Annabelle about the lightning, but Annabelle had already scooped Eli up and was carrying him against her chest. Hope saw her son's small hand pressed to her sister-in-law's shoulder.

She stood when Annabelle and Eli came inside. She said she was going for a walk.

"In this weather?" Annabelle said, looking out the window. "Are you sure?"

The living room was dimmed by the clouds.

"Still some time before rain," Hope said, gathering a shawl around herself.

Annabelle held Eli closer to her chest, and he reached his arms around her neck.

The air was still but fragrant, as if the landscape were sealed under glass. The smells of the orchard and farm were drawn out by the impending storm's low pressure. The scent of manure wafted from the barn. She smelled the pines, the grass, and, entering the orchard, the sweet apples. She passed the trees her grandfather had planted, those her father had grafted, and, finally, the saplings that she and Davis had together grafted. She arrived at Davis's tree—the limbs filling with the shapes and colors of the many varieties. Did the rootstock feel the burden of so many different grafts? She touched the beeswax on the cuts, the scars that her brother had been tending.

She wouldn't tell Annabelle and Davis she was leaving—they would refuse, or they would try to convince her out of it. She would just go, and then it would be done.

She walked away from the tree, found her way into the old barn, and, as if the universe had a narrative, as if she were at the mercy of its story, she saw that propping open the door was the half-moon-shaped quartz that, if it was not the one, looked very much like the one she had used years earlier, in the name of vanity, to change her destiny.

She picked up the stone, put it in her pocket, and walked back to the house.

In the Hall of Birds, Hope followed the boy. He walked past a goose with its neck outstretched and frozen in flight, mounted over a stone. He stopped at dozens of songbirds fixed to the wall. The longer Hope stared, the more she was sure it was Eli. He had a cowlick just like Sam's, but his expression, the way he furrowed his eyebrows while looking at the songbirds, was exactly something she did. She moved her lips, as if speaking. This was what her son looked like, she thought. This was how tall he was, how he held his hands. This was how he walked. Why was he alone? She should say something before he left. Before Annabelle or Davis came into the room.

"Look at those," Harold said to Hope, his voice booming. He motioned to the birds. "There is nothing an artist can make that is more beautiful than what nature has already created. That one looks like its dressing for a carnival." He walked away, stood beside the boy.

Hope didn't follow. She should leave now, she thought again. She walked to a wall of mounted owls. She stared into the black, glass eyes of a screech owl.

"Have you ever seen something so magnificent?" she heard Harold say.

"John!" a woman called from the other room, followed by the frantic footfall of a mother looking for her lost child.

Hope's chest clenched. She turned away from the owl to see a woman charging through the door. It was not Annabelle. The woman stopped in the threshold, said, "Thank the Lord!" She looked at Harold with dissatisfaction, then strode across the room, grabbed her son's arm.

"You can't just wander off!" she said. "We've been looking all over. Your sister and father have been waiting to leave." She straightened up and called through the door, "I found him!"

Hope froze in fear, still looking at the boy and his mother, as she listened to footsteps from far down the hallway. She then saw a man who was not Sam, followed by his young daughter. The girl said to her brother, "You shouldn't have done that."

The boy, still held on his arm by his mother's grip, looked to the ground.

"Time to go," the father said. "Come. Come. All is fine."

Hope turned back to the owl. She touched the glass. She felt dizzy. He was not Eli. And he was not Sam's other son. She closed her eyes and breathed. She listened to the mother scold the boy as they walked out of the room, back toward the glass flowers. As they made their way through the exhibit, Hope heard the boy ask his mother what her favorite flower was.

HOPE STOOD IN HAROLD'S study the next day, watering the plants, with a headache. She hadn't eaten since yesterday; she hadn't slept more than an hour the night before.

Plaster busts rested on pedestals beside fronds of tropical plants. Landscape paintings from Harold's former students filled the walls. Rain crackled on the tall windows by his desk. In the grass, just beyond the windows, she noticed bright blue juniper berries knocked out of the surrounding trees by the storm. As her eyes drifted over the lawn, she saw hundreds of berries, wherever she looked, coming in and out of focus. She thought of Harold standing beside the boy she thought was her son.

She had assumed she might visit Annabelle and Davis in some far future year, after she left Eli with them. She had only wanted to create a stable life before returning. She wanted her brother to be proud of her—that she hadn't made a mess of things like before. It took her four years to write them, after arriving in Boston. She'd suffered through too many humiliations to recall—as a sweeper, then as a washerwoman—but had finally found her luck by working as a maid in the house of a wealthy widow named Mrs. Wellstone, who was impressed by how much Hope knew about plants after she gave advice on a struggling hibiscus in the woman's greenhouse, and had arranged for Hope to attend the women's college. So, she started her letter to Annabelle and Davis by describing Mrs. Wellstone, and the classes Hope was taking at the college. She wrote about the botany lessons that she knew Davis would love. About the drawing classes that had become her favorite subject. She apologized for not having written sooner. But now that she was settled, she wondered when there might be a good time to visit.

It never crossed her mind, in all those years washing sweat and food and hair out of clothes, years of waiting until she was respectable enough to return home, that she might not be welcome. She was sure they'd be thankful to have Eli—so natural was Annabelle with him, so sad was Davis for not having his own children. She had done the right thing, making a clean break. They were happier, she was sure, without her. But still, she was Eli's mother.

Annabelle wrote back that she was sorry that Hope had not written sooner. She and Davis had been very worried about her, in the weeks after she suddenly left Barnstable. Nearly sick. *Not even a word from you*, Annabelle wrote. *Not even an address. Where had you gone?* They wondered if she was even alive. They expected news. Anything. Davis had lost weight, had even gone to Boston and asked around for her, and when that hadn't turned up anything, he'd gone all the way to the west of the state, visiting orchards she had told him about, looking for her. He had looked for Sam. *It has been a difficult few years*, she wrote. *I wish you had sent just a bit of news. Told us you were fine. I wish you had thought of us.*

She ended the letter with her response: It might confuse Eli if Hope visited. Unsure if Hope would ever be in touch, they had raised him as their own. It was probably better to keep things simple. Eli was now talking, Annabelle wrote. He had a certain understanding of the world that shouldn't be disturbed. They didn't tell him about Hope. Children had fragile minds. Aside from Davis's signature, he hadn't added anything to the letter.

HOPE UNLATCHED THE WINDOWS, pushed them open. She leaned forward, put her arm out, opened her palm skyward, and let the rain fall on it.

She quickly left the study to look for Harold. She found him in his upstairs studio, sitting on his stool and staring at an old painting of his.

Before she could speak, he said, "I've been thinking about those flowers. I can't stop thinking about them. Do you know"—at this, he held up a booklet he had purchased in the museum, on the way out—"that they not only look like the flowers but they are exactly, nearly mathematically accurate? Listen to this. Written last year by botanist Walter Deane."

Hope sat, still holding the watering can.

"'The eye is at first attracted by the great beauty of the flowers, as they lie on their white cards in glass cases, and, on a closer examination, are more and more surprised and delighted to find nature so accurately followed.' And it continues. Oh, here we go. Under a microscope. About the New England aster: 'Their models are the living plants, and every flower has its separate pattern, no two being alike.' And of the devil's-walking-stick, 'The work is almost magical. A complex inflorescence of multitudinous minute flowers almost beyond belief. I would estimate that there are two hundred and fifty to three hundred thousand individually crafted details *per specimen*'!"

Harold looked up at her, almost like a child.

"Every flower has the exact number of petals and alternating stamens and number of blossoms. They are, actually, perfect. Microscopically perfect! I mean, what in God's name would make this artist—because, love, he is an artist—put himself through this? Why spend those hours on precision far beyond what some botany student will ever need to understand pollination? To make detail smaller than an eye can see? It says here he made the thorns on a backside of a leaf, thinner than sewing needles, that lay against display fabric, which the viewer will never see. It is madness. It is genius. It is the most inspiring thing I have ever encountered, and the most mysterious."

He looked satisfied with his speech, with the conclusion of it, as if he might have been preparing it before she entered the room.

"Thinner than a sewing needle," he said, once more.

"Harold," Hope said, shifting in her seat, putting the watering can at her feet. "I have something to tell you."

He removed his glasses, smiled, closed the museum booklet.

"Yes, I've been blathering," he said. "What is it, love?"

She didn't know how to tell him what had happened yesterday. It wouldn't make sense. In a way, nothing had happened. But her past had come so close to her life that it might as well have arrived. She needed to tell Harold who she thought he'd been standing by, there in front of the songbirds.

She would start at the beginning. She would tell him what happened when she was sixteen, how she tried to change her life with a piece of quartz, and how her life had changed, but not as she thought it would.

Tundra Swan

Mark had been stealing from his employer, McAllister Farm & Nursery, throughout that fall. Only one or two trees per week, so Dave and the other managers wouldn't notice. He took the trees at night, and in the mornings, before the sales team arrived, he logged on to an office computer to delete a unit or two from the inventory. McAllister was a huge operation with three satellite locations spanning two towns on Cape Cod. Plants were misplaced or not picked up or improperly inventoried all the time—nobody would notice a few trees missing. He'd eventually rent a trailer and drive the trees south, to a farmers' market in Rhode Island or Connecticut, pay someone for their slot for the day. He'd done something like this with his brother when they were teenagers, in the eighties. They bought big bags of potatoes, beans, and onions from Stop & Shop, dumped them in old-looking wooden crates, splashed them with water, set up on a street in Woods Hole, and made a couple hundred dollars in a morning selling to weekenders and folks arriving for the Martha's Vineyard ferry.

By now, in late October, Mark had fifteen trees hidden away

in the woods at the edge of their property, down at the end of an old farm road nobody used anymore. It was early evening. Just after work. He walked from tree to tree with a hose attached to a tank loaded on his pickup. It was an odd group—these rarities for suburban homes; their root bulbs still wrapped in burlap, clumped together in a loose circle. He figured he could get somewhere near ten thousand dollars for what he was looking at: a Golden Spanish fir, Crimson Queen maple, Himalayan birch, Green Mountain boxwood, American hornbeam, Catalpa, katsura, Hinoki false cypress, Autumn Gold maidenhair, dogwood, Golden Curls willow, Jonamac, Siberian birch. They weren't very big—six or seven feet, at most—because he'd had to lift them into his truck by himself. The odd thing about these nursery-raised ones, which had been carted up from the south that spring, was that they were all mixed up season-wise. Most were still leafing out, while the overhead maples and oaks were already shedding for winter. He pointed the hose at the hornbeam and touched the soft, green serrated leaves. He heard the creaking whine of autumn's distant geese. He moved to the next tree.

When he finished giving them all a good drenching, he drove back up the old farm road, along a row of windblown wild cherries strangled by nets of bittersweet. A flock of starlings warped over a field. A migrating Cooper's hawk eased up and over a stone wall and then shot in front of his truck, gliding into a shock of tupelos. The sun was almost down, casting the earth's belted shadow on the eastern horizon. It was such a pretty night, and since Julia, his wife, and Ian—his twenty-year-old son who was now living with them—weren't home yet, he took the shore road back, around the bottom of the fields.

He drove up and over a sandy rise, and down in the salt marsh saw three tundra swans huddled together—bright against the dark water and browning spartina grass. He watched them follow and circle one another, capsizing now and then to graze underwater. A flock of black ducks lifted from the far side of the marsh. Maybe he'd take Ian out hunting tomorrow. It was one of the few activities they still did together.

He drove away from the salt marsh, over a cattle grate, back along the fallow farm fields, toward the house. It was an old Cape built by one of Julia's ancestors before the Civil War, the kind shouldering a burdensome roof that leaked every spring. It still had the wide floorboards and a huge old chimney with a beehive oven opening to all four downstairs rooms. The house was on the highest part of this low land, surrounded by walls where, at one time, dairy cows had been kept. Julia's grandfather said that before the fields had been cleared for grazing, there had been an apple orchard. A successful one. Sometime in the mid-1800s. There were still a few grizzly old apple trees scattered here—one particularly famous one that everyone in Barnstable knew about, one that appeared every year in the fall months of the town calendar. It grew at the edge of the property, where their driveway met the road. It was bent, knobby, wind-huddled, and thick in the base like the other old remainders. But unlike the others, it fruited out ten apple varieties. Bloodred Baldwins baubling over Golden Russets, Black Oxfords hanging limb to limb with Pippins. The town had designated the tree as a historic monument, and put a little white fence around it with a plaque describing each heirloom apple variety.

Julia had inherited it all—the house, the land, the strange apple tree, and the development and conservation restrictions that her grandfather had arranged with Massachusetts Audubon, which made the open fields unsellable and, so, nearly worthless.

Mark parked his truck in the grass near the back door. Julia's car was still gone. Her student-teacher conferences and curriculum review meetings that week had been keeping her out late. He kicked off his boots in the mudroom, hung up his coat, made himself a cup of tea, and started on rice and grilled chicken. Julia texted. She was going to Chili's with a few other teachers. He shouldn't wait up.

He stirred the chicken in the pan. He looked out the kitchen window to the beach plum bushes. He and Julia had met at McAllister, over those beach plums, twenty-five years earlier. She'd been walking up and down the rows, looking confused. He asked if he could help. She said she was moving into her grandfather's house and wanted to spruce up the front yard. "These ones are native," he said to her. "And they'll give you fruit every year." He helped her plant them at the house later that day and, in a way, never left. Every year they picked the plums together, boiled them down for jelly, packed the mash into cheesecloth bundles that hung from the kitchen rafters to drip into pots. The kitchen smelled sweet for days while they mixed in pounds of sugar. Whenever Mark opened a jar in the winter, the smell forced his mind to late summer, warm wind, and tree swallows lining the telephone pole wires. Picking the beach plums always felt like an anniversary. Somehow, he and Julia had missed it this year, and neither said anything until the fruit had already dropped to the ground and was rotting.

The rice boiled. He ate dinner alone at the counter. Maybe he had time to go to the nursery before Julia got home.

He unloaded the water tank from his truck and set down a tarp. This would be his last time. He would take the most expensive tree. The Attaryi Fullmoon Japanese maple, whose burgundy leaves went golden-tipped in cold weather and sold at McAllister for two thousand, one hundred fifty dollars, before tax.

"THERE ARE FIFTEEN TOWNS on Cape Cod," Ian's ER doctor told Mark and Julia that past spring, "and all fifteen have problems. We have a twenty-five-percent-higher opiate prescription than the state average. In this town alone, we had a hundred and twenty overdoses. In one year. That's not even considering the alcohol."

"Jesus," Julia said.

"It's happening all over America," the doctor said.

Julia and Mark had met at the ER early that morning. Ian had been admitted after a jogger found him in his car at dawn, down on the beach road. He'd hit a telephone pole. The fact that he'd passed out before his car hit the pole had probably saved his life, the doctor said. He'd broken his arm and two ribs, shattered his clavicle, sprained his ankle, gotten a bad concussion, and done something to his neck.

"He's in danger," the doctor said. "Probably more than we know. You have to stop this. Think of it as an infection. He needs care. Residential treatment is the best path forward. Keep him home, at your house, until he heals up. After that, to rehab. Right away."

Julia called the school, said she was taking a sick day. Mark took her hand. They were still paying off the bills from Ian's last stay at River Valley Recovery Center, a year earlier, which the insurance had only covered partly and left them with a twenty-eight-thousand-dollar bill. Julia's parents had plenty of money, but Mark and Julia learned long ago not to ask them. The subject of Ian's addiction and what they should do about it created an argument so bad that Julia and her dad hadn't talked for years.

"I'll ask Dave for another loan," Mark said to Julia. Dave McAllister—Mark's boss—had helped them last time. His daughter was going through something like this, which had gotten Dave and Mark into a discussion about the health-care system and prompted Dave to offer help.

At first, it was nice to have Ian back home. Back in his old room. There was a short time when he seemed to have been struck calm by the accident. He had a cast on his arm, a neck brace, and walked with a crutch. He moved slowly around the house. He ate dinner with Mark and Julia. They watched a few seasons of *Downton Abbey* together. Ian had stopped drinking—or he didn't drink in front of them. Ian's doctor had told Mark and Julia to keep the pain medication hidden away, and to give Ian a pill once or twice a day, depending. Because Ian couldn't drive, Mark took him around town to keep away cabin fever, sometimes all the way up to Provincetown. They'd park in an empty beach lot, watch the seagulls lift and drop over the dunes. Years later, Mark would think about these drives as some of his happiest days. Maybe because it was so unexpected, this sweet spot in the middle of that cold, rainy spring. Things seemed so good that Mark and Julia put off the conversation of River Valley. Ian seemed to be on a path to recovery, just by being back in the house. Some stability and home-cooked meals, Julia said. Not living with his friends. That's all he needed.

It didn't last long. By late summer, when Ian's cast came off, someone was picking him up at the end of the driveway almost every night. Now, Mark and Julia experienced something they hadn't felt since Ian had moved out when he was eighteen: waiting for him to come home, waiting all night for the sound of car tires coming up the driveway, with the fear growing as the night drew on. And then, one dawn in September, Mark found Ian asleep in the front yard, vomit on his shirt, with Julia's car on the front lawn and the door still open.

So, now it was clear. He had to go back to River Valley. First they'd get the money, then he'd go. That winter.

Dave said he was really sorry about Mark's situation, but he wasn't a bank, and Mark still owed him for the last loan. "I hope they sue those fuckers to the moon," Dave said of the pharmaceutical companies, then asked Mark if he could come in early the next day for a large delivery.

This was the first big lie Mark told to Julia—that Dave had said yes. He asked her to let him handle it, that she not talk about it with Dave. He wasn't sure if Dave would even press charges for what he was doing with the trees. But he honestly didn't think about it much. He thought of what the doctor had said: think of it as an infection that needed to be stopped.

Hours after sundown, Mark drove to McAllister with two tarps shuddering in the bed of his pickup. He parked at the deer fence in the back, where they kept the extra mulch. He turned off his truck. He opened the gate, walked past the boxwoods, the beeches and holly trees, passed through the minty smell of the firs. He grabbed a dolly from the shed and wheeled it toward the Japanese maples. The Attaryi Fullmoon was in the center of the row, given some space to show off its foliage. He edged the dolly under, pitched the tree back and forth until the root bulb was mostly on, and then tilted and pushed. It was one of the biggest trees he'd taken—heavy but not impossible. When he finally made it back to his truck, he detached the tailgate, aligned two stacks of two-by-fours to make a ramp to the bed. He heaved the dolly up the ramp, and rolled the tree off. He covered it with the tarps and tied it all down with rope. He returned the dolly, closed the gate, replaced the tailgate, and drove off. It was usually that easy.

On his way home, he drove past Chili's. Julia's car was still in the lot. There had been periods that fall when they might talk for less than ten minutes in a day. Julia got up before dawn to drive to school and grade assignments. She coached the girls' varsity soccer team, which practiced until dark now that the season was heating up. When she came home, they talked briefly about Ian, ate while watching a show, and then Julia would open her laptop to review assignments and write her lesson plans. She often said to Mark how exhausted she was with work, but he suspected she liked being away from home. Through the window of Chili's, he saw her laughing with two other teachers, Liz Lowell and Justin Cook. He'd stayed away from home, too, years back, when he and Ian would get into an argument nearly every evening. Home became the most uncomfortable place to be. Mark invented work that kept him late, volunteered for delivery jobs far away.

He woke the next morning to everything changed. Snow on the fields, the walls, the beach plums, and his bird feeders. He thought of the trees. The snow would probably melt away, but the cold snap was unsettling. He'd call about renting a trailer that morning and drive them south that weekend.

He poured lukewarm coffee from a pot Julia had brewed. She'd come to bed long after he'd delivered the tree to the woods, pushed him on the shoulder to wake him. She said she'd had too many margaritas, but that they were really good. He said that sounded fun. She asked if Ian was home. He said he didn't think so. He heard her sighing and shifting in bed for a while, awake. Years ago, he would have asked what was wrong, but he knew the answer and wanted to sleep, anyway.

He boiled water for oatmeal. Watched the snow fall. Wet flakes tacked against the window and dripped down the glass. He sipped coffee, then opened his laptop to search for farmers' markets. He found one in Mystic. He wrote down the address and time. He'd sell them at three-quarters value and hopefully be done by dinner.

The house was quiet. He wondered if Ian had gotten home. If so, he was probably sleeping—but with the snow, the roads would have been dangerous last night. Mark walked up the narrow stairwell, trying to be quiet on the creaking old steps. He put his ear to Ian's door, listening. He didn't hear anything. He should go downstairs, he thought, and text Julia, ask if she'd heard from Ian. But fear and impatience overwhelmed him. He knocked on the door.

"What?" Ian said.

Relief washed through him. "Sorry. I know it's early."

"What do you want?"

Mark didn't know what to say without annoying Ian. Anything but that he was just checking in. He looked out the hallway window, toward the salt marsh.

"You feel like hunting?" he said through the door. "Bad weather this morning. The ducks will be sheltering in the marsh." Nobody would notice if Mark came into work a little late. He could get there by nine.

"Sure."

"OK," Mark said happily. "I'll get the guns ready. Meet you downstairs."

In the mudroom, he found his waders, hat and gloves, binoculars, a couple decoys from the top cabinets, and his twelve-gauge and Ian's twenty-gauge from the bottom cabinet. He cleaned the guns at the dining table while he waited. The snow had already stopped.

Ian walked slowly down the stairs, heavy-footed, dressed in a hoodie and his camouflage hunting waders.

His son had a handsome face, that was undeniable. Julia's face. No matter how tired or angry he was. He kept his hair long and tucked behind his ears.

"Just let me get some coffee," Ian said.

He sat at the table, across from Mark. The smell of weed was so powerful that it made Mark feel suddenly nauseous. When Ian started smoking at fifteen or sixteen, he attempted to hide it. Now, he either didn't care or didn't notice how much he smelled.

The truck bumped along the field road, cutting tracks in the snow, toward the hunting blind at the edge of the salt marsh. Ian tipped his head against the window. He blew on the glass, put his finger on the foggy patch, and drew a crooked smiley face. When they arrived at the marsh, Mark reached into a box of shotgun cartridges, stuffed a bunch in his coat pocket.

"Ready?" he said.

Ian slipped out the passenger side.

After sweeping snow out of the duck blind, Mark stood in the water, in his waders, arranging decoys. He let them drift, re-tossed the anchor and string when they didn't sit right.

"How do they look now?" he called back to the blind.

Ian, mostly hidden behind the cedar cuttings that Mark had lashed to the blind that week, gave him a thumbs-up.

Mark climbed back into the blind. It was a small wooden shack with a bench just big enough for two. They loaded four yellow cartridges into their guns' chambers, which rang like four small broken bells as they set into place. Ian sat with his knees apart, gunstock between his feet, barrel on his thigh. A flock of cormorants came and went. Mark opened the coffee thermos. The only conversation he wanted to have was the one they'd had many times, the one that made Ian distant. He couldn't ask Ian how he felt, what he'd been up to the night before, if he'd had any luck finding work.

"Were you up when the snow started last night?" Mark asked.

"I don't think so."

"It's so early in the season for snow. It must be climate change."

"Yeah, I guess so."

Mark heard the rhythmic wheeze of tundra swans. He stood in the blind to see three of them pass high overhead—maybe the same three he'd seen the day before. They flew over the marsh, toward South Pond. Then, the one in front turned, and the other two followed, and now they were circling back.

"Look at that," Mark said, pointing to the swans. He lifted his binoculars. They were too large and bright for this day. Too beautiful for the gray sky and gray water, drab dunes, brown grasses.

"See them?" Mark said, following the swans with his binoculars. They flew low over the salt marsh, then the water, toward the blind. Their heads stayed level and low as their necks and bodies pulsed with the beats of their enormous wings, which were nearly touching the water and rendering those signature breathy whistles. It was odd that there were three. Tundra swans mated for life, sometimes pairing up for a year before breeding. Something must have happened to the fourth.

Mark knew all this—about the swans and their lives—because of Ian. He'd become a birder because of Ian. When Ian was in fifth grade, a man came to the local nature center with a falcon to talk about falconry. Ian instantly became obsessed with birds of prey, which was a surprise because he had never been interested much in anything. Mark and Julia were thrilled. Ian had been a hard child, in some ways. Uninterested in books or going for walks or being on the water. He liked to be inside, on his computer. This was different. Birds were interesting. Scientific, nearly academic. So, Mark and Julia went a little overboard. They bought Ian three types of field guides, a pair of expensive binoculars, a notebook for his Life List. They subscribed to *Audubon* magazine and gave him a "Raptors of the World" poster. Before work, Mark would take Ian out to the fields and forests, trying to identify songbirds and match the songs with the singer. And then, within a month, Ian lost interest. As quickly as it had come, it had gone. All that was left were the bird posters, the magazine subscription that went right into the recycling, the magnets on the fridge, the field guides, and one scientific book called *Handbook of Bird Biology*. It was in that book where Mark—who kept it on his bedside table—learned about bird migration. Songbirds migrated at night, he read, and used the stars to navigate. *Millions passing overhead in the dark*, the author wrote. *Appearing in spring as if from nowhere. Unseen by most.* Some birds migrated across oceans to return to the very same tiny islands or peninsulas where they'd been born, years after leaving it. And so, Mark became a birder by accident. And still, when he saw the season's first warbler, he'd think of those early mornings with Ian, listening for songbirds that had arrived from the night sky. That's what he was holding on to these days: birdsongs from one brief spring a decade earlier.

So, it was just a habit that Mark still pointed out birds to Ian—as with these swans, which Mark knew had flown over a thousand miles from their breeding grounds on the Canadian tundra to be here, on Cape Cod, to escape the frozen north and glean whatever greenery New England's winter had left underwater.

He asked Ian again if he saw them. The swans were trying so hard, Mark felt, had traveled so far to survive.

THE SOUND OF THE GUNSHOT and the swan's plunge into the water came at once. The ringing in Mark's ear came moments later. He dropped the binoculars. The smell of gunpowder then filled the blind.

"Fuck!" Mark said, touching his ear.

Ian was still seated, gun barrel resting on the edge of the blind. Mark looked back at the swan hammering at the water with one wing. It pushed its way to the edge of the marsh and lifted itself into the grass. The other two swans had risen high up and away, but were now circling back.

Ian looked stunned.

"What are you doing?" Mark said. "What?"

He pushed past Ian's legs and jumped from the blind. He jogged along the edge of the marsh, toward the swan. Blood streaked its white feathers and the snow. It was wheezing and turning around and around, as if looking for a place to hide. Its wing was limp and twisted up at a horrible angle. When Mark stepped close, the swan faced him squarely, its head quivering. It was making a strange, broken sound from its throat. Ian had shot it on the side, in the lungs. The swan dipped its head toward Mark, as if taking a long, sad bow.

"Come here," Mark said, reaching out, softening his voice. He needed to break the swan's neck so it wouldn't suffer longer. When his hand was close, the swan suddenly straightened, hissed. It drew its head back and whipped forward, snapping at Mark's hand, then charged and snapped again. Its twisted, bloody wing dragged behind as it moved.

Mark backed up, then jogged to the blind.

"Come with me," he said to Ian, as calmly as he could. "Bring your gun."

Ian, maybe intimidated, maybe shocked, obeyed. By the time they got back to the swan, it was huddled in the grass. It had given up trying to move. Or couldn't. It looked at them, its bill hanging open. No sound came out. Its neck swung from side to side. Blood dripped from the tip of its bill and onto the snow.

"Shoot it," Mark said. "Now."

Ian didn't move. He kept his gun barrel low, brushing the marsh grass.

"Ian," Mark said. "Shoot it now. In the chest."

"Shit," Ian said quietly and forcefully. Still, he didn't raise the gun.

Mark grabbed Ian's gun, lined up the sighting, and fired.

They stood there for some time, with the sounds of waves falling on the beach beyond the salt marsh, and the whistling wingbeats of the two other swans still circling overhead.

Ian shifted. "Shit," he said again, softer this time.

"That's a thousand-dollar fine if a warden saw you. What's wrong with you?"

"I didn't think I'd hit it," Ian said.

The snow started again. And maybe it was that, the change in weather, the clouds unloading themselves, that made Mark say exactly what he was feeling—which was the one thing he knew he shouldn't do, the one thing that made Ian go silent for days and always left Mark regretful.

"I don't care if you're stoned. Or if you want to sit in the blind pouting like a fucking child. You don't even have to talk to me. You don't have to try. But you can't do that. Whatever that is, you can't do that." Mark felt his face getting hot. He pointed at the dead swan. He felt a wave coming through him. "It's sick, Ian. What the hell is wrong with you?"

Ian walked away.

"OK!" Mark called after him. "I'll clean it up! Don't worry, Ian!"

Ian passed the truck, continued up through the field, toward the house. Mark picked up the swan by its neck and dragged it toward his truck.

Back at the house, he yelled Ian's name from the kitchen. He climbed the stairs two at a time, pushed the door open without knocking.

The room was cold. Ian had left the window halfway open. Snow drifted through, right onto the carpet. There was a mound of dirty clothes on the floor. A towel over the back of the couch. Ashtrays on the windowsill and coffee table. His sheets halfway off the bed. As a boy, Ian had been so neat. So particular. Like, he'd only eat his fruit if it was cut a certain way. He had a few favorite T-shirts that he folded himself and kept on a special shelf. He arranged his collections of sea glass and shells by color and size—and, before he understood it was trash, chips of lobster buoys and shards of colorful plastic mixed in line with devil's purses and bay scallops. What had happened?

Mark sat on the couch. He looked at his hands—dotted with dried swan blood. The snowflakes floated across the room, nearly to his feet. He had felt many things about Ian. Guilt, kindness, frustration, hope, disappointment, fear, anger. A lot of sympathy, just wishing his son a better life. But never this, never simply repulsion.

SPRING CAME ON A MARCH day five months later. A week of icy rain had ended, leaving in the fields and roads strips and dashes of water that reflected a blue sky. The landscape's hesitance had broken seemingly overnight. The trees were full, the fields regrown, and the salt marsh's spartina inched through last year's dead and folded grass.

Mark stood in the forest, at his trees, holding a shovel. Most had survived winter dormancy, even without his attention. It had been mild, anyway, barely any snow. He touched the trees. The dogwood was still alive. The hornbeam, too. The Himalayan birch. The willow with its drooping strings looked fine. Some were tipped over from the weather, a couple others were clearly dead.

The day of the swan was the last time Mark had seen Ian. After the second night he was gone, Mark and Julia drove to the hospital, the police station, to the public beaches and around town. On the way home, Mark told Julia that he and Ian had gotten into an argument down at the duck blind—that Ian had shot a tundra swan, and that he might have overreacted, might have lost control a bit and made Ian feel bad. Julia had been kind at first, saying he shouldn't beat himself up about every little thing Ian got upset about. The third night he was gone, Ian sent a text to Julia saying he was in Boston staying with a friend. Julia called him right away, but he didn't pick up—that day, or any day after. They eventually drove up to Boston, then around Cambridge, Somerville, looking at the sidewalks, until Mark said, "What are we doing?" On their way back to the Cape, out of nowhere, she asked him what he did with the swan, after Ian shot it. He buried it in the fields, deep down so a fox wouldn't get it. "It's such a waste," she said. "Ian will come back when he runs out of money," Mark responded. "Don't worry."

Mark texted Ian every day. But sometime in February, his texts stopped going through. He didn't know if Ian needed money, or had a place to sleep that night, or if he was even still in Massachusetts. His worry collected and complicated itself. He started having dreams of Ian as a little boy wandering around the house, asking for help.

He planted the trees mostly where they were. The Spanish fir beside the Hinoki false cypress beside the Catalpa beside the Crimson Queen maple and so on. It was the wrong season to plant, but they would all die if he kept them aboveground much longer. It took hours to dig the holes. It was hard, wet, clay-packed dirt. On his hands and knees, he lifted out stones, broke through root systems sent out by the taller trees. The last one he planted was the Attaryi Fullmoon, which he put in the middle of the circle. It was evening by the time he pitched in the last shovelful.

He dropped his shovel. His arms burned. His back hurt. He sat on the ground, took a few deep breaths, and stretched, then went all the way down, onto his back.

The peepers started up. A gust pushed through the forest. The first stars came. Soon, millions of songbirds would be migrating, flocks like storm clouds moving through the night, navigating home under the stars, passing overhead unseen.

Maybe the trees would live. Some, at least. The Golden Curls willow would probably die. The Attaryi Fullmoon Japanese maple might be alright if it got enough light. In a century, if the trees resisted hurricanes and moths and blight and the incoming sea, some might get as tall as the native ones, breaking up through the canopy. And maybe someone would walk down here, wonder what they were looking at, what this ring of rare trees within the forest meant. And by that time, all of Mark's and Julia's and Ian's problems would be so far in the past, so irrelevant, it would be as if they'd never even touched the earth.

August in the Forest

August first met Chloe in Concord. She was the doctor at the hospital—to where he'd driven himself, over an hour, sure that his appendix was bursting, stopping twice to throw up on the side of the road. She told him that his appendix was fine, that he likely had food poisoning and there was nothing to do but to let it pass. She prescribed anti-nausea pills. "You should go home," she said. He explained the long drive. She was sorry, but she couldn't give him a hospital bed for what he had. She told him to buy Gatorade. He slept in the car that night, in the parking lot, because his torso hurt too much to drive. It was a cold, bad night.

The next morning, he drove back to his cabin, a few miles outside of the hamlet of Wells Slope, in northern New Hampshire, with a population smaller than a football team and where he'd been living for the past three weeks. Wells Slope was a former slate mining settlement. Industry had moved on. Now there was a pizza shop, a laundromat, a bar, and a small museum dedicated to the history of slate mining. He'd moved there because of a misconceived statewide program that left the New Hampshire Arts & Cultures program with more money than they knew what to do with. Someone decided that sending dancers and composers and writers and artists on fellowships to small towns across the state—towns that didn't ask for them—was important. A woman offered to the program her summer cabin, which was grandfathered into the White Mountain National Forest. August's closest neighbor was miles away. There was a woodstove, a twin bed, and a kitchenette that evidenced there must have, at one time, been running water. The only power was derived from a solar panel the size of a laptop that was mounted on the roof.

It was October when he arrived. Overcast days by November made the cabin uninhabitably cold—so, he spent a lot of time at the slate mining museum, where there were desks pushed up against tall, arched windows, and a back room that was an informal and disorganized library. Big metal furnaces crackled through the day.

When the museum wasn't open, he walked along the road to keep warm. He only realized that the path behind his cabin was part of the Appalachian Trail when he stepped outside with his toothbrush one morning to see two guys with backpacks half as big as themselves trying to light a flame below a very small stove.

"Where'd you come from?" August asked.

"Georgia," they said. "Do you know where we could buy weed? Is there a town close?"

August said that the town was ten miles down the road, but they were unlikely to find what they were looking for.

August saw Chloe again some weeks after the hospital, while waiting in line at the bakery in downtown Concord—where he went every Sunday morning to add some shape to his week. He recognized her, but couldn't place from where. He introduced himself, and said he was sure they'd met before. He was excited he might know someone, maybe a friend of a friend, he thought, in a place where he hadn't had a conversation in weeks.

She tilted her head, smiled, and said she didn't think so.

He noticed the powder blue hospital scrubs beneath her unzipped jacket. Her pants were also powder blue. She wore clogs.

"Oh," August said, the memory coming back. "I know."

"Really? Tell me."

He asked if she was a doctor. She said yes. He said he knew her from the hospital. He looked at his feet, embarrassed remembering what he'd told her about his body.

"Sorry, I should have recognized you," he said. "I was pretty out of it. The food poisoning."

She looked at him. "Oh, right. Are you feeling better?"

"Much."

He squinted in concentration at the menu, handwritten on butcher paper hanging on the open door.

She smiled. "Good."

They waited in line, a few feet apart, in silence, for minutes. The bakery was recently famous and always crowded, started by a couple who left the city to set up somewhere rural. August had a lot of time to think about Chloe, standing at his back, and about how lonely he was most of the day, how tired he was of his own thoughts. Well, he might never see her again. He turned around, asked very quickly if she wanted to get together, maybe next weekend. For a walk. There were some beautiful trails near his cabin, he said. He'd only asked out one other person, ever, and that was the woman he dated for five years.

"You mean a walk, as in a date?" she said, flatly. "Everyone up here wants to go kayaking or hiking, and I never know if I'm actually on a date. Or are you asking because you want a hiking buddy?"

"No," August said. "I mean, yes, a date. Or, wait, are you not allowed?"

"Not allowed?"

"Because I'm your patient? Was your patient?"

"I don't think you're thinking of the right thing," she said. "You're over twenty-five, right?"

"Yes." He was twenty-nine.

"What do you do, again?"

"Poetry." He felt this was not going the way it should. "I write poetry," he said.

"For a job?"

August shrugged. "Kind of. It's a grant. A fellowship, kind of. I get a stipend. I might have a book coming out."

"Wow. OK. Sure, I'll go on a walking date with you."

"Thank you," he said, earnestly.

She laughed so loudly that the people all the way at the front of the line turned around to see.

"Sorry," she said, covering her mouth with her hand, shaking her head. "It's just, I've never been thanked for that before."

SHE TEXTED HIM THE MORNING she was supposed to drive out to his cabin for their walk, asked if he could come to Concord instead. Her apartment was an old and divided Victorian stacked with rooms twice as wide as a stairwell, creaking floors, and hallways that smelled woody and sharp, like black tea. She lived on the top two floors. In the month that they dated, he slept there a few times per week, but she never once visited his cabin.

She'd leave her apartment for the hospital early in the morning, when it was still dark. August would drink the remainder of the coffee in the percolator, wander around the apartment and read the news on his phone, delaying the return to Wells Slope. He left notes on her pillow. She never mentioned the notes, but they were always gone when he returned days later. Maybe she kept his notes in a special drawer or in a journal. Then he reached for a sock under the bed one morning and found all of them on the floor, covered in hair and dust balls.

She broke up with him at the Concord Farmers' Market, where she went on Saturdays to buy vegetables for a stew that she froze in containers and ate throughout the week. The decisiveness of the break—the confidence with which she did it, without pity or hesitation—made it easier on him. She appeared to assume he'd be fine, that whatever that month of him sleeping over could be called had meant little to them both. She said that she was too busy with her job to be dating, anyway. He shouldn't take it personally. It was hard to not take it personally, he said.

"I'll probably see you again soon," she said. "We always run into each other."

"I'm really glad I met you," he said.

She put a hand on his back. "That's a very, very nice thing to say, August." She patted his shoulder. "Just a very nice thing to say."

WHEN HE ARRIVED BACK at his cabin, he made a fire, and then called his best friend, Elizabeth. They talked once a week, sometimes more.

She and August had grown up in Vermont at the end of the same long road that led to two sheep farms their families owned. Some of August's earliest memories were of Elizabeth knocking on the front door, letting herself in, and yelling his name in the mudroom until he got out of bed and came downstairs. Neither had brothers or sisters. Looking back, their friendship shouldn't have lasted through middle school, but it did.

Elizabeth now lived in a nameless expanse of rainforest in northern Laos. Right out of college, seven years earlier, she'd taken a job for a mining company to engineer roads and water systems. All August knew about her job, really, was that she made almost a quarter-million dollars a year, which she told him when complaining about how hard and isolating her job was. She was doing it to buy her parents' farm, so they could retire.

"How was your night?" she asked, after picking up the phone and telling him she didn't have much time to talk.

It was morning where she was. She was breathing hard. A machine buzzed in the background.

August said Chloe had just broken up with him, and that his writing was going horribly, that he was always cold in the cabin, that he couldn't remember why he'd come to live here.

"I had a cobra in my kitchen today," she said. "Do you know how high a king cobra can lift its head?"

"Do you think I'm depressed?" he asked her. "Do you get depressed?"

"Five feet," Elizabeth said. "Up to my face. I have no idea if you're depressed. Sounds like you don't have enough daily surmountable problems."

"Daily what? Why do you talk like that now?"

When she didn't answer, August asked what happened to the cobra.

"One of the miners took care of it with a machete. I don't think he got what you'd call a clean hit. It must have thrashed around some—blood everywhere. All over the cabinets and floor."

"Oh God."

"Also, there was a centipede the size of my forearm in the shower a couple weeks ago. I sprayed it with window cleaner for like ten minutes, and it still didn't die."

"I don't understand where you live," August said. "Do you have walls? A door?"

"Anyway, about your depression? You should get a job. I don't have time to think about my feelings because I'm too busy. If I had time to think about how lonely I was I'd probably shoot myself. Plus, I haven't had sex in five months."

"I have a job. My fellowship. I'm sorry about the five months."

"Creative writing in a cabin isn't even remotely like a job."

"OK."

"But I'm glad you called. I was going to call you, anyway. Next week I'm flying into Boston. Speaking of five celibate months. To go see Emerson."

Emerson was Elizabeth's boyfriend. They'd been dating for over ten years, since freshman year of college. They'd broken up, gotten back together, broken up again and finally gotten back together just before graduating. He was from a big family—four older sisters—and the first of his family to go to college. He was noticeably smart and polite to a degree that felt nearly sarcastic. "He's been well raised," Elizabeth had said of him, when she was preparing August for Emerson's first visit to her house. He was also very handsome, which Elizabeth said had "kept her coming back to him," after she'd broken up with him twice. He'd taken a job in New York, in finance because, he said to August one day, though he didn't like the work, money made life a lot easier. Elizabeth took the engineering job and moved across the world. Elizabeth and Emerson had agreed they wouldn't get in the way of each other's professional paths.

"I thought I'd drive up to see Mom and Dad, and to see you at your cabin," Elizabeth said. "Before going to New York to see Emerson. He can't take off work. He can't come up."

"Oh, yeah," August said, looking around. There was chipped paint on the walls, and a single overhead fluorescent bulb emitting what would be called a headache of light on a plastic folding table that the artist-in-residence coordinator had moved in the day after August arrived.

"I don't think you'll like it here," August said. "Maybe I can drive down to see you."

"We haven't seen each other in a year. I want to see where you live," she said. "Just send me the address. I can only stay a night."

"There's nowhere to sleep here. Just my bed."

On his bed was an old sleeping bag that had lost much of its down, topped with every blanket he'd found in the cabin's closet.

"We'll figure it out," she said. "I'll call you when I get into Boston. OK, bye."

She hung up before he could say goodbye, or tell her to please not come to Wells Slope because there was nothing to do.

LATER THAT WEEK, when he was in the slate mining museum looking through the bookshelves in the back for anything to inspire a new poem, August found a stack of old *Wells Slope Herald* newspapers. He picked up the stack, and read through the headlines: World Wars, the Kennedys, lots about the logging and granite and slate industries, new tourism. At the bottom of the stack, he read a headline from 1929: THE FOG RIVER MYSTERY: NEW DISCOVERIES!

The article began by reminding readers what had happened: In 1908, at a logging site in Fog River, eleven bodies were found in a cabin, on the floor, with two others outside. The missing loggers' wives and parents had gone to the police when the loggers hadn't come home. The rescue party who found the bodies said they'd been there for some time. There were no signs of wounds or cuts or gunshots; no obvious causes of death, except for one of the bodies outside, whose skull was fractured and arm broken. There were other oddities: two horses were still alive in the stable, nearly starved. Socks were still hanging to dry from lines strung along the wall near the fireplace. Bowls were on the table, as if dinner had just ended. Stranger still, a couple hundred yards from the cabin were pants, shoes, a shirt, and an undershirt—as if one of them had undressed. And lodged halfway into a tree at the nearby logging site was a crosscut saw. The men didn't have time to even remove their saw during whatever had happened. It was treated as an unsolved mass homicide, though there were "stranger theories" the paper mentioned but didn't expand upon.

August put the paper down, looked out the window at the snow filtering through the dark and leafless trees stenciled against the pink winter sky. He wondered if the snow would keep coming, if there'd be ice on the roads, if Elizabeth would still come the next day. If it would be safe enough for her to drive. Maybe he should buy another sleeping bag for her—or maybe another mattress. Maybe he should text her, tell her not to come.

He turned the newspaper over. The next page revealed the new discovery: a journal from one of the loggers had been found at a junk shop in the town of Tully, a hundred miles from Fog River, which was a mystery in itself. The article went on: "The journal, acquired by the *Herald*, is written by lumberman Thomas Thurber, of Concord, who had no apparent connection to Tully. Mr. Thurber's widow, Mrs. Isabelle Thurber, who might have offered some light, has since passed." And with a final, commercial flare, the article ended with this: "Our editorial department will publish a selection of the entries in next week's paper. Don't miss it!"

August folded the newspaper closed, and looked through the stack of others. The next one he found was from 1931. He walked to the front desk.

"Hey, sorry," he said to Jan, the museum's only employee, who was watching a video on her laptop.

"Yeah?" she said, without looking up.

"Do you know where the rest of the old newspapers would be?" He held up the 1929 *Wells Slope Herald*. "The one the week after this one?"

"All we have is what's on the shelves."

"OK, I don't see any others. Do you have microfilm? Maybe it was recorded?"

"Microfilm?

"The little rolls?"

"Let me check." She opened a desk drawer by her stomach. She closed it. "Nope," she said. "No microfilm in here."

"It's just," he said, "there's this article about these loggers. Have you heard of this?" He showed her the newspaper. "In Fog River?"

Jan put on her glasses. Her lips moved as she read the headline. She took off her glasses.

"No."

"These loggers—they just died, in this weird way."

"I just read the headline," she said. "I bet it was a bear attack. It's always a bear." She looked back at her laptop. "I'm sure Stephen King's already on the case."

August returned to his seat by the window, and then searched online for the January 13, 1929, *Wells Slope Herald,* but found nothing. The paper had failed in the 1980s, long before anything was digitized. He searched for the story on the *Concord Times* website, the *Concord Herald*, the *Manchester Times,* Wikipedia. Nothing.

He watched the snow fall.

"Time to go," Jan said, shutting off the lights before he had finished packing his bag.

ELIZABETH TEXTED FROM BOSTON the next morning, saying that her flight was fine, and that it was freezing here. She was going to buy a coat in the airport, then go to the car rental place, then drive north. She'd hopefully see him midday.

August cleaned the cabin as much as he could, and then drove to Concord, to go grocery shopping and to the bakery to pick up some croissants and nice bread.

He was sitting at a table in the bakery, waiting for an egg sandwich. He closed his eyes and faced the sun through the window, which added a degree of warmth.

"August?"

He opened his eyes.

Chloe stood across the table. He hadn't seen her in a month.

"Chloe," he said. "What are you doing here?"

"I come here all the time. What are you doing here?"

He told her his friend was arriving that day, staying for the night, and that he was shopping.

She looked nervous. Her eyes were puffy and red, as if she'd been crying. He sat upright.

"Are you OK?" he asked.

She gripped her neck. She crossed her arms and nodded.

"Good to see you," she said. She moved past the table, out of the bakery, toward her car.

The barista placed the egg sandwich on the table. August looked out the window to see Chloe's car still in the parking lot. He watched her get out of her car, walk back into the bakery.

"What are you doing right now?" she asked.

"Eating," he said. "Then food shopping. Then back to the cabin to meet my friend."

"Oh, yes. You said that. Why is your friend coming?"

"We haven't seen each other in a while. She's back in the States for a bit, from Laos."

"I was thinking," Chloe said. "Can I come with you?"

"Where?"

"Back to your town. Or cabin or whatever. I need to leave for the day."

"Don't you have to work?" When they were together, she said the idea of spending her free weekend hours driving made her ill.

"I've been given the day off," she said. "I want to see your little cabin in the woods. How's the poetry going?"

"I didn't think you got days off."

"I don't," she said. "It's a mental health day. I just don't want to be in my house today, OK? Can I come, or not?"

There was something desperate in her voice, the way she was hovering over his table. "Sure," he said, hiding his hesitation. "Of course." He would text Elizabeth to explain.

She sat down at the table. "I can help you with your errands. Do you have a shopping list?"

She put her hands on the table, and started picking at her cuticle.

"Are you sure you're OK?"

She hesitated, then said, "Just, work. Sometimes you see bad things."

During their month together, when he'd asked about her life, she would answer briefly and then, in the same sentence, turn it around on him. All he knew was what he might find on her résumé. She was eight years older than him. She'd gone to medical school in Boston. Her father had moved from Denmark to Montreal, where she'd grown up, but her mother, from New Hampshire, had come back here after her parents divorced. She'd taken a job at a less-than-ideal hospital in Concord to be closer to her mother, even though she'd been offered a job at a prestigious research hospital in Atlanta. She spoke French and Danish. She had a lot of student debt.

"Do you want anything to eat?" August asked.

She shook her head, still picking at her fingers. "No."

They sat in silence as August tried to think of something to ask her.

"I had to call social services this morning," she said. "To remove a boy from his family. That's all I want to say about it."

She pointed out the window, at the dark clouds. She said that it seemed it would snow again this afternoon, looking at those clouds.

After breakfast, they walked the aisles of Market Basket. He pushed the cart while she walked beside it. Elizabeth called when they were on the road, halfway back to the cabin with the groceries and a new sleeping bag in the back. She said she was close.

IT WAS EARLY AFTERNOON in the cabin. The snow had not come; the sky had gone blue, and welcoming squares of sunlight cast through the windows stretched across the floor. Chloe, Elizabeth, and August sat around the woodstove, drinking tea. August put as many logs in the fire as he could.

Introductions had been made in the driveway. Elizabeth was tan and with bangs and a shorter haircut. At first, she seemed confused, maybe unhappy that Chloe was there, despite August's warning. But then she and Chloe fell into a conversation about how horrible the cabin was, about how they both felt sorry for August, and a small link had been forged.

"What are you writing?" Elizabeth asked August, sipping her tea.

"Nothing, really," he said. He had learned to not say too much to her about his writing. When he first told her that he wanted to be a writer, she responded that the world certainly didn't need more novelists. Engineers, hydrologists, physicists, biologists, community organizers, leaders—yes. He should do something useful, she told him.

"Come on," Elizabeth said. "Tell me what you're writing about. Couples slowly divorcing in the domestic sphere? A bit of adulterous intrigue?"

"If you're going to make fun of me," August said, "then, no."

"Come on," she said. "Sorry. Tell me. Really. I'm interested."

"Poetry," Chloe said, brightly. "Right? You told me you were writing poetry?"

"Oh God," Elizabeth said into her mug, with a look of sincere distaste. "August! That's. Well. That's what you're doing now? That is something. Has he read any to you?"

Chloe shook her head.

"And," August interrupted, "also nonfiction. An essay."

"An essay?" Elizabeth said. "Like school homework?"

"A mystery. I'm just starting it."

"A mystery?" Elizabeth said. "That sounds interesting. Not like you."

"Murders. I really haven't written much of it yet. I'm in the research stage." He had nothing more than a few disorganized notes, jotted down the night after his visit to the slate mining museum.

Chloe said, "A murder mystery? About what?" She kicked off her shoes, and pulled her feet up onto her chair.

"Lumberjacks," August said. "In the early 1900s. They were in a logging camp. Way up at the border. Between these two small lakes. A couple miles north of this town called Fog River. You can see it on satellite maps."

"This is how your story begins?" Elizabeth said. "A geography lesson?"

"The point I'm trying to make, Elizabeth, is that there was nobody around. Weeks after they were supposed to return to town, they were still gone. So, the logging company sent a rescue party. And what the rescue party saw was really kind of weird."

"What?" Chloe said. Her hands cupped her mug of tea, which was poised below her chin. She was honestly interested.

He told them what he'd read. The bodies lined up. That the loggers' things—their axes and bedding and soup bowls—were left there.

"Like from a disease?" Elizabeth asked.

"Another weird thing," August continued, "is that one of them was naked, outside. Like, he took off his clothes before whatever happened, happened."

"Hypothermia," Chloe said. "When people get hypothermia,

they act weird. Sometimes they think they're hot. They take off their clothes."

"And a tree nearby had one of those long saws stuck halfway through it," he said. "Why would they have stopped work all of a sudden? Maybe they saw something that scared them? Chased them away? But then, the bodies in the cabin."

The logs shifted in the woodstove, and the fire breathed brighter. They were all quiet for a moment. The metal of the woodstove crackled as new heat radiated out.

"OK," Elizabeth said. "That actually is weird. How much do we all believe in aliens here?"

"That kind of makes the most sense," August said.

"When's the essay going to be published?" Chloe said. "I want to read it."

"Not soon," August said. "There's a lot more research to do. I just have this one article right now. And I think I'd have to visit the logging camp before I started any writing. Get some sensory details. The lay of the land. See if there's anything still there."

"Is it far?" Chloe asked. "From here?"

"The camp?" August said. "About an hour north, I think."

"Should we go?" Chloe said.

"What?" August said.

"Let's go," Chloe said. "It'll be a good distraction. Adventure."

"Oh," August said. "No. We're having a nice time here."

"I would go," Elizabeth said. "Why not?"

"You just got here," August said. "From Boston. Aren't you tired?"

"She's not tired," Chloe said. "See? Let's go."

"No," August said. "Who knows if we can actually find it? I only think I know where the cabin is."

"You've tickled my interest," Elizabeth said, "with your writerly blah blah. And what else are we going to do here? I mean, honestly, August, this is depressing." She moved her head in a circle to indicate everything around her, and then took a sip of her tea. "Plus, I bet there's more snow up there. I haven't seen real snow in a year."

IT SEEMED AS if Chloe had immediately changed her mind about wanting to go, and showed it by sitting silently in the cramped back seat of August's truck, resting her head against the small window. She'd insisted that Elizabeth sit in front.

"Any more snakes in your kitchen?" August asked.

"New thing happened," Elizabeth said. A feral cat had gotten into her house and hid under her bed. She said she thought she could just leave it there, with the door open, and it would wander out. But she got impatient when it was time to go to bed, and so she reached under and tried to drag it out.

"The cat bit my hand," she said. "I had to get rabies shots."

"Isn't rabies really dangerous?" August said. "And why are there so many animals in your house?"

"The doctor said to me, 'You know Ebola? You have a thirty percent chance of surviving that. Rabies? Zero percent.'"

"Your doctor's right," Chloe said, speaking for the first time in many miles on the road. "What is it you do, again?"

"Mining, infrastructure in developing nations," Elizabeth said.

"Like colonialism," August said.

"Mostly power and roadways." She turned to August. "Sorry not all of us are quietly chiseling toward the beating heart of the human experience, August. One iamb at a time. And if that's what you think development is, you actually have to take an economics lesson."

"What happened with your rabies?" Chloe asked.

"I got the shots. And I caught the cat with a net—to bring it in to see if they could test it. Turns out that's not a thing. Maybe that's only something you do with ticks. Is it ticks? Or snakes? Anyway, the nurse looked at me like I was a wacko and took the cat away. Maybe to kill it? I feel bad about it now."

Chloe asked her if she really did bring a live cat into a hospital.

Elizabeth said yes. "For safety."

"So," Elizabeth said after a silence. "Can we talk about the elephant in the room? You two dated?"

"Elizabeth," August said. "Sorry, Chloe."

"What's wrong with that question?" Elizabeth said.

She turned in her seat, toward Chloe. August looked in the rearview mirror, trying to see Chloe's face.

"August is very secretive about his girlfriends with me," Elizabeth said. "He tells me everything, but not that. And now I find myself with an actual ex in the car as we're driving through the wilderness? Too tempting not to ask. I hope I'm not being rude."

"You are," August said. "That's right. You are being rude."

"No, you aren't," Chloe said. "I don't care. Why should I care? We dated for a month, and then I was too busy. And I think I'm looking for something more serious. I'm not sure I'd even call what we did dating. Hooking up?"

"And who asked who out?" Elizabeth asked.

"Please stop," August said.

"He did," Chloe said. "It was nice."

"Auggie!" Elizabeth said. "Swinging for the fences! No offense."

"She said yes, I'll remind you."

"Well," Elizabeth said. "Kind of. For a little while."

"And," Chloe said, "have you two ever? Dated or whatever?"

"Oh, no. No, no, no," Elizabeth said. "I have a boyfriend. And I saw August poop his pants in first grade when he couldn't find the bathroom at Ned Doherty's birthday party. So, I would say I've seen too much, you know?"

"This is actual hell," August said. "I'm going to drive into a tree."

He looked again in the rearview mirror.

"Elizabeth and I grew up together," he said. "Like brother and sister. It would be, like, incestuous."

"But you are very pretty, Elizabeth," Chloe said. "August, you must have had a crush on her. As a teenager, at least?"

"Yes," Elizabeth said, moving her shoulders. "Tell me, how could you resist this?"

August shook his head.

"I don't believe it," Chloe said. "You are a boy. I'm sure you did. She's so fun, too. You're fun, Elizabeth. And smart. And pretty. Like, objectively pretty."

"I am loving this road trip," Elizabeth said. She made a little bow. "Thank you."

"We have to talk about something else," August said.

"Not even a little fantasy?" Chloe said.

"I don't know what you want me to say. The answer is no."

"You aren't good at lying," Chloe said.

"OK," he said. "How am I supposed to respond to that?"

"I'm older than you," Chloe said. "I've seen more. I know. Boys are boys."

"What about Elizabeth?" August said. "Why wouldn't she be the one to have a crush on me?"

Elizabeth shifted in her seat.

"It doesn't work that way," Chloe said. "Her liking you. Not yet. Not until you're both older. Like, if she hasn't found someone by her mid-thirties, she might like you."

"I have found someone," Elizabeth said. "I have a boyfriend."

"Well, sure, but you know what I mean," Chloe said.

"Not really," Elizabeth said. "What do you mean?"

"Well," Chloe said. "If you and your boyfriend break up, you'll see in a few years that there's nobody good left to date. They all paired off in their twenties. What's left is bad. Very bad. Might look good, but is bad. Impossible to spend more than six months with. So, what you'll want is comfort. You'll see August differently in a couple years. I think you two would be a good couple."

Elizabeth didn't respond. August kept driving.

They passed a billboard between two trees in the middle of nowhere that read, KEEP NEW HAMPSHIRE GREEN! THIS IS GOD'S COUNTRY. WHY SET IT ON FIRE? AND MAKE IT LOOK LIKE HELL.

"What does that even mean?" Elizabeth said, tapping on the window with her fingernail. "Is someone trying to set the forest on fire?"

"Is that awkward to say?" Chloe said. "About you and August?"

"What?" Elizabeth said. "No."

August slumped in his seat. "I guess something about campfires," he said to Elizabeth.

Yes, he had had a crush on Elizabeth. For years and years. All through high school, just as Chloe had guessed. When they went to separate colleges, he thought about Elizabeth all the time. When he first returned home for Thanksgiving break, he walked across the sheep fields, over the two stone walls, to her house. He opened the door without knocking, as he'd always done, and saw Elizabeth reading in the deep pocket of a colorful chair in the kitchen. She had come back the night before, too. The kitchen smelled of bread her mom was making. It had been the longest time he'd gone without seeing her. Sunlight stepped from her head to her arm to the book pages to the kitchen floor. She looked up, smiled. "Hey, Auggie," she said. "I knew you'd be here first thing." He thought then, even if she was a stranger, he would still stare. She asked him how college was, and quickly told him that she had started dating Emerson, who lived across the hall from her. While they ate the freshly baked bread that afternoon, she told August how much she couldn't wait for him to meet Emerson. She talked about how smart he was, about how she'd never been so attracted to someone in her life, how she couldn't believe her luck that he lived on her hall. She loved college, she said. Sitting with her, something unfamiliar happened to August. He felt sad. Or *troubled* is maybe the word. Over the next few days, his mind reached something like a meltdown. He began to feel bitter toward her. Distant. During the rest of Thanksgiving break, Elizabeth kept asking about college, asking if he hated it. He replied that it was fine. "Then what's wrong?" she'd asked. He kept shaking his head. "Nothing," he repeated, smiling. He felt free, somewhat. He started dating somebody when he returned to college that winter, and he honestly let go of his crush on Elizabeth the longer he was with his girlfriend.

Years out of college, he read that the part of the brain activated for love and the part activated for grief were quite close, physically. Love can be a type of euphoric grief, the author wrote. There are stages: self-delusion, understanding, and—most important—the obsession, in a different way than grief, with another person.

FINALLY, THEY ARRIVED AT the point on August's GPS where he thought the old logging road started. There was about an hour of sunlight left, maybe less. They parked on the side of a dirt road that was bisected by another road blocked by fallen trees between which a few small pines had grown.

"We're here," August said. "The camp should be down there."

"Great!" Elizabeth said, opening the truck's door and letting in a gust of cold air.

"We're not going to get lost, are we?" he said to her, before she hopped out.

"This isn't 1800," Elizabeth said. "Getting lost in the woods isn't a thing that happens anymore. I'll bring my phone."

She lifted the handle to pop her seat forward, allowing Chloe to get out, then walked onto the old road, weaving around the new pines.

"Is this OK with you?" August asked Chloe, who was still sitting in the dark back seat.

"If we don't find anything," she said, "it's still nice to walk in the woods." She pushed herself up and out of the truck.

They walked in a line. The road was straight, almost never turning or bending. They passed through a boggy clearing spotted with pools of black water, and then up and down a knoll. They stopped when August noticed another, narrower road branching off from the one they were on.

"Straight? Or turn?" Elizabeth said. "It's really quiet out here."

"Let's try that way?" August said, pointing down the narrower road.

They came to an intersection of another logging road, this one extending in both directions, one way disappearing over a rock outcropping, the other around a sharp bend.

"Maybe we should turn back," August said, after going the direction Elizabeth had chosen. "It seems like—"

"There," Chloe interrupted. "Look."

Through the trees, August saw a stack of stones. It was a chimney—or part of a chimney. This was much easier than he had imagined.

"Bingo," Elizabeth said.

They walked to the clearing, stood around the stone stack. This must have been the inside of the logging cabin. The stones, August saw, were stained black.

"You're right," he said. "A chimney."

There was an arch of stones from the hearth up to the stone mantelshelf. August knelt, touched a piece of twisted, rusted metal protruding from the dirt.

"Look at this," Chloe said. She stood over a grinding wheel, half sunken into the ground.

They pointed out stones and pieces of metal to one another.

August touched the fireplace.

Chloe said, "I feel like we shouldn't be here. Like, I'm really getting a bad feeling. Don't you feel that?"

"I don't believe in the paranormal, if that's what you're saying," Elizabeth said. "But, yes, it is getting dark in the woods and clearly something bad happened here, so I get it."

Whatever else the loggers' search party had found long ago had been obliterated by a century of weather and decay, apparently fire. There was only forest, the chimney, the grinding wheel, the sound of distant crows, of sticks snapping under Chloe's feet as she walked away, through the trees.

August took out his notebook. *Unsettled here*, he wrote. *Much time passed. Something else? Ghosts?*

"What are you writing?" Elizabeth asked from the other side of the chimney. "Sensory details? 'The afternoon light filters through the pines and falls, perchance, atop the scene of this most enduring mystery'?"

"Exactly," he said.

She wandered away.

He wrote a small paragraph about seeing a chimney in the middle of the woods. *Relic*, he wrote. *Tombstone. A monolith.* He imagined the loggers sitting around this fireplace, their hair matted with sweat, their hands callused and marked with a few cuts. The acidic smell of wet socks, steaming warm, hanging from lines between the small bunks. The loggers' arms, heavy from the work. Sawdust in their clothes, in their beards, their hair, in the folds where their clothing touched their skin. The fire being the only light in the room; the lambent firelight on their faces illuminating their cheekbones and foreheads and eyes. Quiet and entranced, thanking the cook for the food. Or, within themselves, turning over the repeated thoughts or anxieties or hopes that shaped their characters: who they had disappointed or loved, how their fathers might have hurt them. Around them, the forest's silence. The handle of a ladle pinging on the edge of the soup kettle after one man filled his cup. The *thip-thip-thip* sounds of Thomas Thurber's pencil in his journal. A man coughing.

"Are we ready to go?" Elizabeth said. "Where is Chloe? My feet are freezing. You were right. This was a bad idea."

August looked up and didn't see Chloe.

"No way," Elizabeth said.

"What is it?" August asked.

"My phone is dead."

Elizabeth unzipped her coat and put her phone up her shirt, in her armpit.

"Maybe if I warm it up," she said. "Oh God, that's cold."

"I don't think you have to put it right on your skin," August said. "It's not hypothermia."

She yelled into the woods, "Chloe! Where are you!"

"You really know how to pick them," she said. "She's intense. In that humorless, maybe murder-you-in-your-sleep way? I mean, what was all that about you and me? I don't need life lessons from someone who's in the middle of a mental health crisis."

"That's not nice."

"Why? Didn't you say she had a breakdown?"

"I said she got a day off for mental health. That's not the same thing."

Elizabeth reached up her shirt, took out her phone.

"I wonder what happened. Imagine how bad it must have been

to push an ER doctor over the edge." She put the phone back in her armpit.

He heard crows. He looked up. A cloud caught by some atmospherically high wind was rushing along. The cloud was torquing and spinning off strands of saffron vapor under the low sun. He looked over to Elizabeth, who seemed troubled, her hands in her coat pockets, staring at the ground, touching a stick with her shoe.

"I wanted to ask you something," she said.

"Sure," August said.

"I think Emerson is going to propose."

"Propose?" he said. "Like marriage?"

"He said he had something important to talk about. Yes, marriage, obviously."

"That doesn't mean he's going to propose."

"No. But I know. The way he said it over the phone. Also, his mom wrote me a weird email about how excited she was that I was coming back to see him. How much she loves me and loves family."

"And?"

"What?"

"If he does?"

"I have to move my life forward, right?" Elizabeth said. "I don't think I'll meet someone like Emerson again. Chloe is right. All the good ones are taken in their twenties. I'd be stupid to give him up. I mean, just thinking about him in bed with someone else literally makes me sick."

August's hands felt cold then. He put them in his coat pockets.

"That doesn't exactly seem to be the right way to think about marriage," he said. "Does it?"

"Then what's the right way?" she said. "I want kids. I want a husband. I have to move forward. What I'm doing now is not building a life."

She reached under her shirt, took out her phone, and tried to turn it on again.

"No—still dead," she said. "And where is Chloe?"

"Do you want to be married to Emerson?" August asked. "Isn't that the question?"

"I want a home," Elizabeth said. "That's all I think about when I'm lying in bed at night. Like, I want to be ten years old again, on the weekend, on a winter day, wrapped in blankets in my bed and hearing Mom and Dad puttering around downstairs. The smell of pancakes. I can't go back in time. So I have to make it for myself, right? He's the best chance I have at that, I think."

August was trying to figure out a kind way to say that it seemed like Elizabeth was trying to force something that should come naturally, when Chloe appeared, a hundred feet away, and yelled, "I found it!"

She waved her hand frantically.

"Wow," Elizabeth said. "She's scary, right?"

"Come on!" Chloe yelled. She walked away, disappearing behind a tree.

"Well," August said to Elizabeth. "I think you should do whatever you think is right."

"I hate when people say that," Elizabeth said. "There are ten things that I think are both right and wrong about one situation, always. I'm sure people usually feel hesitant about marriage. Especially these days. Why are people even getting married, anyway?"

"I think it's something you should be excited about, is all I'm saying."

"I've been dating him for ten years—if I wasn't excited about him I wouldn't be dating him."

"I guess."

Elizabeth cleared her throat, then straightened up.

"How long was your last relationship?" she asked. "A month? Do you think you should be giving advice? I shouldn't have brought it up. I was hoping, as my oldest friend, you'd just say what great news and then help me conceptualize the whole thing."

"Conceptualize the whole thing?"

"Over here!" Chloe yelled again, from behind the trees. "Come! Now!"

"Oh my gosh, she's annoying," Elizabeth said. She turned away, toward Chloe.

August stepped forward to follow, and they walked in silence, one behind the other, to Chloe, who was standing in front of one of the biggest trees in that patch of forest.

"What is it?" August said.

Then he saw it.

"Look," Chloe said, pointing.

At about chest level, two rusty ends of a crosscut saw protruded from each side of the trunk. The wooden handles were gone, rotted away. The teeth of the saw were corroded to thin chips along the cutting edge. The tree had healed and regrown over the back edge of the saw. Bulging over the ends of the saw were rolls of bark, as the tree had widened and grown over the metal, absorbing it.

"That's insane," Elizabeth said. "I didn't know trees could do that."

August touched the saw. It was cold, and rough like sandpaper. Elizabeth touched the other side. They both moved their fingers along the metal. Elizabeth stepped forward, put her hand flat on the scarred bark, where the saw had first cut into the tree.

"I think we should go," Chloe said. "It really is getting dark. I just wanted to show you that. Do you want to take a picture or something?"

August shook his head.

Chloe left, starting back toward the chimney.

The last minutes of sunlight held in the clouds high above them. Crows moved through the canopy. The light drained from the forest.

August felt the tree, where the wood had healed over, when Elizabeth let her hand fall. He then told her what he thought.

SEVEN YEARS LATER and standing at the kitchen sink on a cold winter morning, August watched Elizabeth walk down their snowy driveway with their mail pressed against her chest. He heard her open the front door, stomp her feet in the mudroom. He'd later see the chips of snow that her boots had shed. She came in the kitchen, her cheeks flushed red with cold. She tossed her wool hat on their dining table. She spilled the mail on the kitchen counter and began sifting. She sniffled, her nose still running from the cold she'd had all week.

He saw the magazine before she did, at the bottom of the pile, under the stack of bills and the free weekly newspaper. He had asked the editor to notify him before she sent a copy, which she'd forgotten to do, apparently.

Elizabeth picked up the magazine. It was a small but famous publication, something they'd talked about before, something that could change a writer's life, something that August mentioned when Elizabeth became interested in his writing.

He saw his name on the cover, along with a few others.

"August!" she yelled. "What the hell!" She pointed to his name. "What?" Her smile was wide and sincere. "Why didn't you tell me?" She hit his shoulder with the magazine.

"I know," he said. "I know. It just didn't seem real until it was real."

He'd written the first draft so many years ago, in the days after Elizabeth left Wells Slope, when he was lonely and bored and cold in the cabin, when what she had said about Emerson, moving forward with life, wanting August's blessing as a tool to get her there, had fed a consuming anger that had cleared away all other writing projects. He'd set the story in the past, in the early 1900s. But, still, there was no way Elizabeth wouldn't recognize herself in the writing, wouldn't recognize her own words spoken by a character he'd named Eleanor.

"Sorry," he said. "I should have told you. But, yes. There it is. I didn't think it would ever really happen. I guess I was just being superstitious. But, well, wow, there it is."

She flipped to the front of the magazine, to the table of contents. He felt panicked.

The year he wrote the story, he'd sent it to a friend who knew the editor of the magazine. "It's a long shot," the friend said. "But who knows." The editor, amazingly, wrote August half a year later, apologizing for her delay in reading. She was intrigued, she said, and asked if he'd be willing to change a few plot points. He did, and she asked him to edit again. This went back and forth for years—through him moving from Wells Slope to Boston and, later, back to Vermont. He kept editing after he began renting the house down the road from his parents' house, and after Elizabeth quit her job in Laos, moved to New York. He edited after Elizabeth first accepted Emerson's proposal and then, after a few months, broke it off. He rewrote almost the whole draft, following the editor's notes, after Elizabeth moved from New York back to their hometown, where she'd come to her parents' house to recover from her breakup. He worked on it after she told August one day at lunch that she thought she was just going to stay in town for a while, maybe apply for a job in Manchester, and what did he think of that? He worked on it after they got drunk at Pete's Bar and kissed in the parking lot on the way back to their cars, and after the first night they spent together at his house, days later; through the months of taking turns making coffee for each other in the morning; through August telling Elizabeth that he loved her, and her saying it back. He kept writing and corresponding with the editor, long after his anger faded. He liked the deadlines, but was sure this problem—of his unflattering portrait of Elizabeth, now his fiancée, put into Eleanor's character—would take care of itself. There was no way it would actually be published. After every email, there was always a moment when he thought of writing the editor to please disregard the story, that he had other ones now, if she'd like to see them? But then he imagined, What if it did get published? It might be the chance to finally get an agent, to write a book. And so, anxiety, not excitement, settled in his stomach when the editor wrote a note of congratulations, to tell him she thought the story was ready and would be in the winter issue, and inviting him to come down to New York for the launch party at their Chelsea office before Christmas. He said he was sorry, he needed to look after the sheep and he couldn't make it down to New York, but asked her to please email him when she put his copy in the mail. She wrote back that "looking after my sheep" was the best excuse she'd heard for not coming to a launch party, and that she hoped he would keep the magazine in mind for future stories.

Elizabeth would never see it, he thought, if he could get to the mailbox before her. He hadn't planned anything beyond that.

"Isn't this, like, kind of a huge deal?" she said to him now, sitting at their dining table, flipping from the table of contents to his story. It was a big deal. This was his first publication.

He watched her eyes scan the pages.

"That's what they say," he said.

He filled a cup of water at the sink.

"Augustus!" she said, slapping her hand on the table. "What's wrong with you? Why don't you seem more excited? This is amazing! This is a huge deal. Are you shy?"

"I guess I am shy. Ha." He gulped the water.

"Shoot," she said, touching her phone and then standing from the table. "Actually, I'm late for work. But, can you read your story to me in bed tonight?"

She put the magazine on the counter, and then put on her heavy jacket. "I want to hear it in your voice," she said. "I can't believe you didn't tell me. So secretive."

"Sure," he said, smiling. "I'll read it to you."

"Can you make dinner tonight?" she said. "I'll be home at six-ish."

Just before she walked out the door, she turned around, crossed the kitchen, put her hands on either side of his face. "I'm proud of you," she said. "Even though that's cheesy, it's true. OK. Bye." She kissed him and left.

He stood in the quiet kitchen, sipping coffee, wondering if he should burn the magazine. When he imagined reading the story aloud in bed that night, he felt sick.

There was no way she wouldn't recognize herself, because one of the few sections of the story that the editor hadn't changed at all was the one he basically lifted verbatim from Elizabeth, when they were standing alone, after Chloe had left them by the cross-cut saw and half-cut tree at the old logging camp. And then he'd written what he almost said to her, what he was thinking at the time but what he was happy he didn't actually say.

The editor had highlighted that section in the first draft and commented, *This seems like the emotionally truest part of the story. Watching someone make a bad decision, a big thing like marriage for the wrong reasons, and the protagonist—who knows her well—not saying anything. Like, the motive is blurred, right? What's the feeling of both being asked to be supportive and being rejected? To be angry at someone you love? To know that if you tell them they're wrong, you might push them away more when all you want to do is be closer? Use his interiority to explore. More of that.* When he once deleted that section a few months after he'd written it, hoping the editor wouldn't notice, she pasted it back in, with a one-word note in the margin: *Keep.*

After Elizabeth left for work, he did the chores that he needed to do every day—spreading the hay for the sheep and feeding the dogs and the chickens. Then, because he didn't want to go inside, and the fresh, cold air felt good in his lungs, he spent the morning doing chores that were unnecessary daily and so had been neglected. He filled the bird feeders. He cleaned out the chicken coop, scraping away the droppings below the wood shavings, bringing a broom and dustpan in, laying down a whole new layer of shavings. He washed the green slime from the inside of the chickens' watering buckets. He brought wood from the woodshed to the woodbox, and then refilled the woodshed with logs from the pile behind the barn.

When he went back inside for lunch, he watered all the plants and then washed the windows.

Then he sat at the table, looking at the magazine. He picked it up and turned to his story. He read the first line: *Eleanor was born beside a slate quarry in 1888, had lived in New Hampshire's mountains all her life, and until now, at twenty years old, for reasons she couldn't explain yet, felt disappointment seeping into her life—like a fog moving through the valley, over the river, as it did on warm mornings every spring, and which had given the town its name.*

He flipped to the end, where Eleanor is telling her childhood friend, Nathan, that her mother has arranged a marriage proposal from their neighbor's nephew, Emery, down in Boston. Eleanor can still say no to the proposal, but she needs to tell her mother soon. The reader has gotten the impression that Eleanor would be making the wrong decision if she said yes. Nathan and Eleanor had been walking for a while through the woods after church, in the winter, and come upon a crosscut saw, glistening silver and newly left in the tree. Sawdust is scattered on the snow at the base of the tree. Later, they will walk to the nearby logging cabin and discover the dead bodies.

Standing at the crosscut saw, Eleanor tells Nathan she thinks she's going to accept the proposal, that she'd like to go to Boston, that she needs to see if there's any other life for her outside their town—that the farthest away she's been is Concord. There must be more to life, she says. A bigger life. Nathan reminds her that the man she's talking about marrying and maybe having children with is a stranger. She says that they've written a couple letters back and forth, and he seems like a nice enough fellow. The sun had set, the story read.

> Nathan looked up, seeing the last minutes of the sunlight held in the clouds high above them. Crows moved through the dead-gray canopy. The light was draining from the sky.
>
> "I suppose it's your decision," Nathan said.
>
> He had, he thought, long ago given up the expectation that he and Eleanor would marry. So, what was this feeling? Part jealousy, part confusion, but also just the simple line of fact that he knew she was making the wrong decision. She'd be unhappy if she went to Boston. Ever since they were children, she always got bored, unsatisfied, or disinterested eventually. She would be stranded in a city, want to return home.

"But," Eleanor said, "I want you to tell me I'm doing the right thing."

He felt anger now swelling up. "I don't think I can be part of this decision. You need to make it for yourself."

"That's somewhat harsh."

"I think you should live with your decisions."

"Lord," Eleanor said. "I just wanted support. For you to be a part of this."

She sounded nervous.

He reached out, touched the saw again. Whatever strange event had halted the loggers had also saved the tree. This huge, living thing had almost died, but didn't, just at the last moment. Maybe the cut would heal over, behind the saw, and the tree would live for a long time. He felt the cold metal teeth of the blade. There was a slim lip of grease still on the metal. The work-worn wooden handles were soft.

"You know that marriage is a bond until you die?" he said. "That you might be unhappy for a very long time. You might like the idea of it, but that's not real."

Eleanor breathed in, stared at him, and looked like she was about to say something. But she didn't. She held something back. She collected snow from the broad side of the saw and brought her hand to her mouth, licked it.

He knew by her silence that she'd marry this stranger, and that the two of them would drift apart. She licked the snow again. She smiled at him, in what he thought was a cruel way. So, they were already separating.

He felt it in the blood in his face, in his pulse. He wished her harm. Bad health. He wished that she'd think back to this moment by the tree, when she could have listened to him, could have changed her fate. Instead, her pride and curiosity were forcing her into a ridiculous life. Maybe it was good she was leaving. She was narrow. A narcissist. Someone he didn't want to be around anymore. He hated her, then. He felt the temptation to say all this to her, but was stopped when she turned away from him, breaking his chance.

She turned her hand over, and let the remaining snow fall to the ground, uneaten. She wiped her wet hand on her dress.

"Let's go," she said, walking toward the cabin, not looking around to see if he was following.

ELIZABETH WAS STILL AT WORK, and it was nearly seven. It had been dark for hours.

He had made dinner. Chicken, rice, and steamed asparagus that was becoming too soft, sitting in the pot. He had folded napkins a special way and put them on the table, with a bottle of wine between candles. He had put the plates in the oven to warm.

The magazine was upstairs, on his bedside table.

What would Elizabeth first say when he finished reading her the story? She wouldn't be wrong to be angry. To be used in that way, drawn into a story that he only wanted to publish for the sake of—what? Some small bit of entertainment for a few dozen readers? Maybe he had betrayed her. And then, he thought, what would that story look like? The story of him reading his fiancée a story about a century ago, in which the fiancée recognized herself from a decade earlier? And if he included the conversation they might have in bed that night, in the minutes after he finished reading, might that be a section of dialogue the editor would underline, bracket, and note in the margins: *Here is a question for the reader: Do you owe someone an explanation of a feeling that long ago left you? Does it feel like betrayal, distrust, anger? Or is there another word for that feeling? More here.*

The Journal of Thomas Thurber

December 11, 1907. We arrived to camp five days ago. The Fog River watershed. Another day walking & we'd be in Canada. We're here until March, as you know. As instructed, I'm keeping this journal for you, Isabelle, my dear wife, who has said many times that you're tired of me disappearing during the worst and coldest part of the year, that the least I could do is tell you what happens day to day. (The past week has been very busy. Sorry that I am just starting tonight!) Think of it as letters I wouldn't send, you said, but would arrive all at once on my return to Concord. You also said that I seem to have a better time in the woods with twenty men than I do with my own wife in the comforts of our own home, with downy pillows and dinner on good plates with good silverware, and you want to understand how that is possible. That I come back from the woods spirited and energetic, and am moody in our house. Isabelle, you are not wrong. The fresh morning air in the forest perfumed with the scent of pine, the daily work that is clear to me—it lifts me! Even today, splitting wood for Gabriel, the Cook, I was happy.

After some weeks here, my body catches up to my mind—my circulation clearer, my breathing better, my body limber and stronger. At home, I feel like pudding. Working at the Apothecary, a job which your Father has been so kind to give me—he will not let me forget that, won't he!—behind a counter all day, that is half a life. A maggot's life. (Well, it appears I've already drifted from material I would share with you. I am getting carried away, some!) I'll tear these pages from the journal before returning home. But, before I do, what I would tell you—never in these words—is: I love this respite every winter, away from our home (and so yes, away from our life together), away from Friday Suppers with your parents. I don't mean that I don't like being with you when I'm with you. But, what crime is it to take pause from home life, to be outdoors with satisfying work? To enjoy the company of men who have experiences not so dissimilar to mine? In addition, I hate the smell of the Apothecary. I know you won't understand all this, really. (Also, should I remind you what your father has paid me? We would never pay down our loan without my lumbering wages.) To be fair to you, I don't think I could well explain why it's so enjoyable here, in the woods. Why I like not speaking for a full day except for directions on cutting and chaining. Why I like the sound of the horses pounding through snow rather than the carts on Concord's streets. The tear of the crosscut saw and the thunking of axes, and the eventual crack! of a tree's side & its drop & hammering thud on the snowy ground. (After a dry snow, a felled tree sprays up snow—as if a hand slapping a dusty pillow—that flutters back down for minutes. I've heard it called Second Snow or Fairy Snow, because it glitters in the sun on its way back down.

What beauty is here, away from the city!) In my reasons for liking it here, I suppose I would reply to you: why is it that you like to sit for hours at tea with Alexandra, talking about who is marrying who or who is sick with what?

I can't spend all night on what I cannot let you read, and so I'll return to the task at hand: an account for Isabelle! From her husband, Thomas. The facts of his Wintry & Absent Life:

I am in my bunk, under lantern-light while the others play cribbage. The 5th day has passed. The first days were spent cleaning up camp—the cabin and the rest. Putting away supplies, chopping lots of wood for the cook's fire, digging a bean hole. There was one grim task I hesitate to write—and yet, you said you wanted to hear about Life in the Woods, Good & Bad. So, I offer this scene: Alvin (Crew Boss) had come here this past summer with a smaller crew to build the cabin in which I write, the stables and the outhouse and potato shed, to make ready for us lumbermen when we arrived come winter. He made the very bad mistake of leaving the carpenters' food supplies—casks of flour and potatoes—in the shed. I suppose he thought to save some money, we would use them this winter (or, with the potatoes, was simply lazy & didn't bury them). Guess what happened? First day we arrived, we were met in the cabin with many, many wood rats. They infested the roof & bunks and just about every place you could think of. The fireplace had turned into somewhat of a den. There must have been some breeding, too, just by the numbers. Anyway, vermin mean sickness, so our cook, Gabriel—old, short, and thin as a cornstalk, made it known he's angry he doesn't have a helper or a day off—said he had lots of experience with rats in cookhouses, and packs arsenic for it. He put powder in johnnycakes in the bunkhouse and cookhouse and around the edges of camp. He seemed to take odd joy in the activity. Rats were gone in a few days, expired in and around the cabin. To not attract other animals, we burned them. Perhaps I will leave that section out of your reading.

What else? A man named Stoddard is tuning up a fiddle, which is a Godsend for any crew—entertainment at night! You never know who is going to show up in your crew—some young men—boys nearly—coming for the first time, some lifelong lumbermen, who you'd think would topple over on the first day but can fell a tree in twenty strokes. This is the smallest team I've worked with—fourteen of us in all, including Gabriel. Alvin the Crew Boss keeps to himself. He's missing a finger. He has a good pocket watch. He is unlike other bosses I've worked for. He doesn't speak much to us. And he drinks. A cup of whisky at dinner—which I've never seen. Camps are usually dry as a bone. He doesn't linger with the crew after dinner, but retreats to his room. We sleep in bunks, two bunks stacked, on one side of the cabin. Except for Alvin who has his own room in the corner.

What else? There is a terrifically big, crackling fire. It is cold, cold, cold. I can feel the air through the wall by my bunk, cutting at my forearm. I will find some moss to patch the gaps. Night comes quickly and early. Day seems an afterthought of night.

As you requested, I've also rendered some compositions of "Life Around Camp." Here is my first drawing, above. James, Paul, and Winslow here. James is from a small town called Harrisville, in our Great State of New Hampshire. He is married. No children yet. He has done a few years a-lumbering, knows his way around. He has been making us all laugh with stories about growing up with his Father and no Mother (no explanation of why she died or left). He says his father didn't know what to do with the kids, and one day tied him, his brother, and sister in chairs and left bread on their laps while he was at work (Sawmill). I know you would think this is cruel, but the way he tells it, it is funny. One scene of his brother trying to escape, tipping over, and the dog eating his bread, made us all laugh hard. Then there's Paul, in the center, the tallest and strongest of the crew. He was born in Halifax, but lives alone in Concord now. If you think I'm moody, you should see Paul: he is a beast, barely talks, eats alone at dinner. I overheard Alvin saying to Gabriel that Paul is leaving a great sorrow behind. If I discovered that he had murdered a man I wouldn't be surprised. No, Isabelle, I'm not saying that I am living with a Murderer. I am only saying that he strikes some amount of fear into the world, which is a useful thing for a person, I think. He will be the most desired man to have on one's crew, due to his size. Finally, in this sketch, here is Winslow, who is just about the nicest boy/man you could imagine. He has a round & happy face with springy curls a-top his head, and isn't old enough to grow a beard more than a few whiskers on his chin and upper lip—which he is proud of. He's too eager, though. Talks too much. Also, this is his first time out and he is a Terrible worker. But, he'll offer the food off his plate to anyone who has finished before him. He says that he wants to be a Priest someday, which makes sense because of his temperament, but what he's doing here instead of at Seminary school is a question I haven't answered.

I feel bad how we parted. I should have said goodbye that morning. I regret that. I'm sorry. You felt hurt, and I shouldn't have disputed it. I feel only fondness for you, now that we are separated by a hundred miles of trees and a week's absence. It is easier to apologize on paper, isn't it? I don't want to fight with you. It all looks like such a waste of time, at this distance.

Everything else in camp is uneventful. Winslow sleeps on the bottom bunk, below mine. The air is warmer on the top bunk at night.

DECEMBER 15: Isabelle! My dear. Here is a drawing of Sally-Mae in her stable. One of the four horses in the skidding teams. She has the character of a Lap Cat and the power of a Bull. She touches my shoulder with her lip when I stand beside her. I don't know how you would train a horse to be so gentle—I suppose horses, like people, are born a certain way.

Yes: it's been four days since my last entry—I can't do the daily entries you wanted. I think I can write once a week, maybe less. I am too tired and my back too painful by the time I climb up in my bunk. (I am not so young, anymore! I surprise myself to think this is my 10th year logging!) I fall asleep within minutes, sometimes with my clothes on. I hear Stoddard's fiddle. No sleeplessness like at home—I think it must be my body working all the time, stomping through the snow, working my peavey, my exhausted limbs, and my empty mind. Nothing to think of here, to be upset by. All to say—I'm trying to write!

Food has been: beans, biscuits, pork, salt cod, johnnycake, and tea, tea, tea. Alvin has a rifle that he'll use to hunt, if there's a Deer or Moose we'll have fresh meat. No, beans and salt pork is not your Mother's Roasted Beef of our Friday Night Supper.

Sometimes, a man will bring biscuits with butter and jam and hot drinks from camp to the cutting site. We rotate turns doing this. There have been no significant injuries or accidents as of yet. Only, well, a man named Martin (Swede) broke his finger, but it's splinted up and he says it doesn't bother him so much.

Oh, there is one small drama that could add some color to this logging life: James said he returned to camp to get his sharpening file, and interrupted Alvin flipping over bedding. He said that Alvin told him that Gabriel said someone has been stealing rations, which, aside from sitting down on the job, is the Greatest Sin of a logging camp. There were biscuits missing.

Also: Winslow—the boy with the curls who wants to be a Priest—is more difficult to be around every day. My kind feelings about him are fading. He talks even when nobody is asking him questions—and lots about his Daddy, who is apparently a Big Deal Newspaper Man in Portsmouth. I heard him crying the other night under my bunk. If the others see him do that, he'll be the dog at the bottom of the pack, bullied to the very end. Years ago—did I tell you this?—there was a boy who complained about the food, left his things all around the cabin. Things got very bad for him—and he ended up running away. Winslow's already not well-liked. I see where it will end for him if he doesn't start to harden up. It is Man's Nature to find the weakest. I don't know why, but it does bring the group together to pick on the lowest one. James teases him openly and constantly. At breakfast this morning, he said Winslow sounded like a songbird that won't shut up.

Alright, I am getting tired, and the fire is still going and the fiddle is playing what you could call a lullaby.

December 21: Here: A drawing of The New Hampshire Woods. Despite your encouragement, I am not an artist. The trees tower higher than any building in Concord. Saw a Pine Marten the other day. Heavy snow was falling all yesterday. More snow means easier to skid the logs back to camp!

Today is the shortest day of the year, I was reminded. The Winter Solstice. I wonder what you're doing in our home on this long dark night? Perhaps your parents joined for dinner? Or—are you alone? Reading by the fire? Reading in our bed? What about right this moment? Maybe you are cupping your hand behind a candle, leaning forward to blow out the flame. Or, I barely imagine: maybe your thoughts are with me? Wondering how I'm faring under the cold sky? I wish we could talk to each other across this distance. That I might right now explain to you that I was not sincere in what I said to you that night. My words were sparks from a fiery temper—thoughtless debris. And now, my punishment is clear: tortured by the coming months, thinking how those words may still be like those sparks, singeing your feelings, burning out any fond thoughts you have of me. I can hear my father's reprimand. For this written record: Yes, I did see you standing alone at the Watsons' dinner. And, as you said—no, I didn't come to you. Yes, I did perhaps talk too much to Beth Holloway, and, yes, I did notice her touching my arm. I could have easily agreed with you. I could have parted on good terms with you, not been haunted by regret and unease. I am the one who misrepresented things, Isabelle, not you. Of course. You are, in fact, the least deranged person I know. (I cringe to think of what I said!) Perhaps I was ashamed that—an uncomfortable truth, easier written—I liked the attention from Mrs. Holloway. As you said, it was a betrayal, which I made larger by arguing. When I return, I'll prove to you a different side. Ah! The Fall of Man.

DECEMBER 22: Alvin shot a Deer yesterday. Praise! Gabriel roasted a leg over the fire, and it was one of the greatest dining experiences I've had. James asked if he could hunt on his free time, that he was good with a gun. Alvin said James must be slow in the head to think he'd let one of his workers go around shooting at whatever moved. Alvin is a good Crew Boss, I think, despite the drinking and his disinterest in the crew. He dresses in a necktie and vest for dinner, every night, even though we're a hundred miles from Society. I think he sets a good example, I mean. He eats with Gabriel and nobody else.

DECEMBER 25: Happy Christmas, darling! Alvin brought out one of his whisky bottles to share with the crew. He was toasted all night as the King of the Wood. Stoddard played some mighty cheerful tunes.

DECEMBER 26: Everybody calls me "The Author" now, due to this assignment you've given me. This morning, Lyman (from Keene, bachelor who I would never let you meet due to the stories he tells) said he thought he saw a light in the woods, late at night. Harvey (from Littleton, farmer) said Lyman was just drunk last night. Lyman said Harvey was drunk. Harvey said yes, he was drunk, but at least he wasn't seeing Christmas candles in the trees. Gabriel rang the breakfast bell to end discussion.

I feel bad for Winslow. These last few weeks/days have gotten only harder for him. James and Lyman (they have paired off as fast friends) now order Winslow around. It is embarrassing to watch. They'll tell Winslow to get them tea, and Winslow does it! If the tea is too hot or too cold, they dump it on the floor & sometimes on his boots. Alvin doesn't do anything because he's in his room. How can a man lower himself so much, Isabelle? Another thing: they'll make Winslow arrange their boots by the fire to dry, and turn them from side to side to dry each of the parts—as if roasting a chicken on a spit. Lyman just had Winslow blow on his tea for him.

DECEMBER 29: Northern Lights last night. Ribbons of green light over trees. I stood outside, watching until my toes were numb. Others came out to watch, and we had a moment of comradery, standing side-by-side, heads a-tilt. Jory (old & white-haired, the most knowledgeable on the crew and can still do hell to a tree) said that he worked at a mine in northwestern Canada one year with a fellow who said the Northern Lights were the souls of children arriving to earth. I thought of your worries. If I could lift the burden from you, I would. As your mother said, sometimes it takes years for children. We have time.

JANUARY 2: Happy 1908! A problem with the horses. When Clive—our Teamster—went to the stable this morning, he found the gate kicked down and splintered and broken. Two horses gone. He ran around like a madman, calling and calling. His bad luck: a flurry must have come and gone in the middle of the night, because a fresh blanket of snow covered up any tracks the two escaped horses would have left.

The other two wouldn't leave the stable. Clive pushed them from behind, yanked at their reins. Yelled many profanities. Hit them on flanks to get them out and hooked up to the sled. One kicked at him. Never, he said, had he seen anything like it. The horses pushed themselves together, in the back corner of the stable. Kept trying to back up more and more, as if they were hoping to disappear into the stable wall. Sally-Mae was one of the remaining ones. When I approached her, she turned her head down and away. When I put my hand out to her, she banged her head against the wall, like a lunatic. Clive is very worried about disease. Some brain-affecting or nerve disease. There's not a veterinary doctor within a hundred miles. He swore to high Heaven, then leaned against the broken stable gate, looking at the two remaining horses in total misery.

Alvin said he'd not let a day of work go by just because of some moody horses. He sent most of the crew out. A few of us went out with Clive to look for the lost horses. A useless activity—no tracks as I've said, and Clive didn't seem to have the faintest what to do. He just pointed off in one direction and then the next, ordering us to run ahead and see if we could see anything. Not like a work horse to leave the comforts of food and warmth. The only explanation I can think of is they were stolen and ridden out, but that doesn't explain the gate being smashed. Well, if they were stolen, they are very far away by now.

How Alvin expects to haul without a full team of horses is beyond me. I suppose that's his job—to find solutions beyond what I can see.

I do miss you, Isabelle. Now that the month has passed, I think back on those first days of excitement, of being in the woods again, with some disbelief. There is no washing, as you said, and I might have forgotten the stench of sleeping in one boarding house. The food is tasting worse. We've gone through the deer meat and Alvin said he doesn't have time to go hunting all day—but I suspect the real reason is laziness. And Winslow—despite wanting to pity him—is driving me mad. He uses a hair cream that smells worse than socks drying by the fire. Smells like tar and decaying roses. Every morning he puts a dab of it on his comb and combs it in. Who brings grooming supplies to a camp? This is what the son of a Wealthy Man does, I suppose. I don't think it's right to take a man's job when you don't need it. He seems to honestly hate the work. What is he doing out here?

If you thought I was grumpy at home, I have become a downright demon. I miss the sound of your footfall in the living room, the sound of your humming as you practice on the piano. I hope you'll forgive me leaving for so many months—and returning such a ghoul. My beard is already grown down to my neck (maybe I'll ask Winslow to use his comb before I return to you; I'll refuse the hair cream). The other day on site, I was suddenly struck with the memory of us on a summer's day, on the vacation with your parents on the Isles of Shoals. Do you remember when we had a moment alone, when we found a quiet side of the island—one of those many coves, with walls of granite that made private-like rooms for swimming? You had packed a picnic of cookies and lemonade. You are so kind! We were happy to be away from your parents. We fell asleep on the rocks to the sound of gulls overhead, & the sound of the wind in the rocks, beach pebbles washing across themselves with the waves. Oh!, that Memory is almost too sweet to me now, as I sit in this bunk, in the dark, feeling the icy draft cut through the siding (I haven't patched the gap in the siding, still), listening to Jory retell a story to Winslow, who has heard it before—like we all have—but is smiling like an imbecile and nodding because he's the only one who is polite enough or scared of Jory enough to listen.

I think this will be my last trip a-lumbering. I can find a more pleasing job in Concord. The Apothecary isn't the only job in all of Concord, is it? I think your Father would understand. This is the nice thing, I suppose, about getting away—it adds some perspective to life back home. I am tempted to say I am homesick, some—but I am Isabelle-sick! Isabelle-less!

Sending you many, many kisses. I await the March morning when I come back to town, when I am reading these (selected!) entries to you in our beloved home, when I can sleep beside you again—the smell of your neck!—every night. It seems too good a thought to be true. Here, a drawing of Stoddard fiddling.

JANUARY 5: Two horses still missing. The other two won't leave the stable. My guess is that there is some medical issue not too obvious. But something else I thought of, watching them in the stalls: My uncle Roger told me about something just like this—the way a horse couldn't be coaxed out—when he cared for the cavalry's horses during the war. Sometimes, he said, a horse just wouldn't take a saddle anymore, wouldn't let anyone ride it, stopped eating or kept hoofing at the floor, or would rub its neck raw against the gate. He guessed they were broken in a way, in the mind, it was from all that noise and cannon fire. Just like he'd seen in some of the soldiers. That doesn't seem so strange to me—you only have to have a dog to know that animals have all sorts of feelings, like shame and fear and all that. The question is, out here, without a war and under the peaceful skies & with lots of feed, what on Earth would have scared these horses so much? Roger said the worst part of his job was shooting a horse that had been broken.

But, now, worse than spooked horses, is that Clive has broken ribs. His temper got the better of him. Embarrassment, too, at being the Teamster who couldn't gather a team of horses together for what Alvin says are dollars stacking up on wasted days. Well, Clive just about beat to death Sally-Mae to get her out of the stable, and she responded with a kick to his torso, knocking him against the wall. I'm surprised his whole chest didn't cave in. He is in very bad shape. He is in bed now, and Alvin said he'll find a way to sled him out as soon as these G*d forsaken animals start cooperating. Otherwise, he'll have to let some of the crew go, three or four, to carry Clive out.

A snowstorm tonight, which is usually fine news, but there is a general discomfort among the crew; some saying that we should halt work for a week to trade out some animals.

JANUARY 9: Winslow this morning has his eyebrows gone, and bald spots on his head. I woke to the sound of him struggling, and heard James and Lyman's whispers and threats. They must have pinned him in his bunk, took a razor to him. I thought it better if I didn't interfere, as that might make things only worse, but now feel I should have. Winslow ate alone this morning, at the end of the bench, staring into his porridge, hiding his shaved eyebrows with his hat tilted low. He has some cuts on his forehead, too. I don't think it would do anything to tell Lyman and James to stop teasing. Human Nature is Human Nature. If it wasn't Winslow, it would be someone else. I just hope he can see it through for another month or so. Get his pay, and run back to his Daddy. I'll try to be nicer to him.

JANUARY 11: Darling Isabelle: I walked outside this evening, when the sky was golden and colored all the snow golden, to get away from this wicked crew for some time. The happiness I remember from other logging trips seems gone—it might just be that I'm stuck with a Bad Group! It is, I have decided, the worst crew I've ever worked with. "A few Bad Apples spoil the Bunch,"—thinking of James and Lyman.

Anyway, outside, some hundred yards away from the cabin, I was surrounded by moths. All white, & very small, like the size of fingernails. Thousands of them, as if hatching from the ground. Where did they come from? The snow? I looked up, and saw hundreds more in the trees. Nature is full of a thousand mysteries. It was very beautiful. Sending a kiss goodnight.

JANUARY 12: The moths have filled the cabin by now. What I thought was beautiful is a pest. They come in on our clothes, they flutter into the fire and into the lanterns. They line the bedding, and press themselves on the ceiling of the cabin. Lyman said it looks like a plague. Winslow said his Daddy said winter moths hatch from the tree bark. Then Lyman made Winslow eat one.

JANUARY 13: Some more issues: Gabriel now says there's flour missing. Alvin said that there's no flour missing, it's that Gabriel can't keep track of what he's used. They argued out in the open, which is not good for morale. Gabriel says he wasn't given enough money for rations, that he's worked to death, that if he wasn't in the middle of nowhere he would have walked off weeks ago. Clive said—from his corner where he's recovering from the broken ribs—that there's enough un-ground grain in the horse's barrel for four horses but only two are eating. Gabriel said that wasn't such a bad idea. He could boil the grain down, make a porridge or whatever else.

JANUARY 17: Blizzard last night. Terrible wind. Snow drifts up the side of the cabin. James Kelley (the other James), a quiet and generally invisible man—not even a very good worker, if you ask anyone here—has gone missing. Ned (father of ten, Portland) said he saw James Kelley walk through the door in the middle of the night, groaning, likely some bowel issue that makes its rounds on everyone at some time. This past morning his bunk was still empty. It was crystal clear this morning, icicles in the trees. Blue sky, fresh snow. Jory said someone should take a good long look in the outhouse, because he once worked with a man who died with his pants down, on the seat (sorry), from a spider bite. Lyman said Jory was welcome to stick his head in the toilet to look for spiders. Jory said doesn't matter, anyway, because it's winter and spiders weren't a problem, and James Kelley probably just got stupid and didn't have a coat and got confused in the Blizzard and froze to death. There is room to wander in a mystery, though, isn't there? Nothing to do but keep working, as Alvin reminds us.

I would die for news of Concord, even to hear of Alexandra's new "ailment."

JANUARY 18: One mystery solved. The horse mystery. Gabriel rolled a grain barrel from the stable to the cookhouse, opened it up, and saw that the grain was covered with black Satan-spur growths. Mushroom like. [*Ergot; toxic fungi.*] Clive is in a fury, says when he gets back to Concord he's going to kill Wendell—the man who sold him the bad grain. Gabriel says it doesn't matter when Wendell is dying—there's still not enough, and now the horses also need food that's not going to make them go mad. Gabriel also said Clive must be an idiot to not see that it was bad grain. Things are not looking good with supplies. I'm wondering if Clive doesn't have much experience—with the food and also seeing how poorly he handles the animals. You'd be surprised how many men can go through life without knowing what they're doing, telling people they know what they're doing. Which reminds me of Winslow.

Regarding Winslow: his bed was moved to the roof last night while he was in the outhouse. Not just the sheets, but his mattress, too. Alvin—who hasn't said anything about Lyman and James's treatment of Winslow—stood outside, watching Winslow trying to pull down his blanket with a stick. Then, in the middle of dinner, Alvin came from outside with a bucket of ice water and dumped it on James's head while James was seated at the table. Alvin said he had enough of James's bull, that this wasn't a schoolyard and to start acting like men and stop wasting time. And that if we were here to saw down trees, you better be thinking of sawing down trees instead of playing around with another boy's bed. James laughed, but he was faking the laugh, and you could see he was embarrassed. "Thank you for the bath!" he called to Alvin, who had already retreated to his room. I fear that Alvin might have done worse for Winslow's situation. Alvin should have kept to what he'd been doing, and kept out of the crew's affairs.

I dream about you almost every night now. It seems too lucky that I'll be able to sleep in the same bed.

James Kelley still missing. Considering no news of him, the crew seems unconcerned. I suppose he could have wandered off.

JANUARY 20: Was paired with Paul today. He works a saw faster than anyone. Rats, unfortunately, have returned. Another round of johnnycakes for them!

January 21: Sunday. Day off. I found myself alone with Winslow. I had gone to the outhouse, and heard him blubbering inside. He should pack up some supplies, and walk home. Guilt has settled in, though. I remember that I was teased in my youth. I went back in the cabin, waited, and then crossed paths as he exited the outhouse, as if by accident. I told him that I was going to the rock lookout, just for a walk, and asked if he wanted to come. Despite his bad fortune he remains polite. He said he would be "delighted" to join me for a walk. By his look, you might have thought I just asked him to be the King of England.

We arrived to the rock lookout. We sat. I asked about his upbringing, about why he came out here when it was obvious he didn't like it. Wasn't his father rich? I said nobody would be here if they didn't need the money. He said—quite plainly—he lied. His father wasn't a newspaper man. He said he didn't know why he lied, but he did, and he liked the sound of it. I asked him what his father did, then. He told me about his sad upbringing. Here is what I can remember: He was born in a house way outside of Concord, in the town of Tully. He said his father was a lumberman all his life. Away in the winter with that; and then away in the summer and fall working the slate quarries. His father would come back for short stays. He'd bring a wooden doll he'd carved for Winslow's sister (a few years younger). The comb Winslow used was the last gift his father gave him. He said his mother was better when his father was away—they were all better when he was away because he "knocked them all around."

Then, his father didn't come home. Winslow's mother died of a bad cough and not long after that they realized their father was gone for good, and so he took care of his sister, trying to keep the house going, working farm jobs around the hamlet. His little sister died in childbirth this past spring, in their house in Tully, (no mention of the father of the baby, suspect a scandal?), and he said he didn't know what to do with himself now that he didn't have to be at home putting food on the table for himself and his sister. So, he did what his father did—walked to Concord and signed up on the first lumbering job he saw advertised. I asked how old he was. He said seventeen. I asked if he had grandparents or anywhere to go after this. He said no. I told him not all jobs are this hard, or filled with bad luck. He thanked me for being nice, then about a hundred geese flew low overhead—way out of season, I think.

January 25: Assuming two horses are dead. Clive's ribs seem to be healing some—or at least in less pain that he moans about. Sally-Mae recovering, and hauling some logs, but seems weak. Spirits lifted, some.

January 29: Ned found James Kelley's boots and clothes, in the snow, a-ways from camp. Jory said he told us he was right all along, that James Kelley got lost in the blizzard and did that stripping some do before they die. He saw it happen before, in a camp in Maine in the 1880s, Jory said. James asked Jory how many men he's seen die on his crews and maybe he's Bad Luck or

Death Himself. Jory said something about how much longer he's been lumbering than James and then something rude about James's mother. Still, James Kelley himself is missing.

I find myself sleeping on my left side now, facing towards the door of the cabin, instead of my right side. I feel somewhat like a spooked animal, like one of uncle Roger's war horses, to be truthful. My back arches and my skin feels strange when I've had to go alone to the outhouse this past week. I do not sleep well, anymore. What were James Kelley's clothes doing out there? Alvin is openly drunk now.

I think of your rhubarb pie, of how you touch your earlobe when you read.

FEBRUARY 1: Winslow found his comb snapped in half. I'm somewhat glad that he can't put that cream in his hair, but I feel bad for him. He tried to repair it as you might splint a finger, with two thin lengths of wood and string. It didn't work, and I watched him throw the comb into the fire.

FEBRUARY 8: Over two months since arriving. I haven't felt the desire to write recently, I am sorry. This project of daily letters to you has waned, under the shadow of low spirits. We are stacking logs, under Alvin's commands, and will skid them—when?

FEBRUARY 9: James Kelley found, frozen and dead about two hundred yards from his clothes. After warmer days, the snow melted some. Winslow saw the bare arm held above the snow, as if waving for help. There aren't any marks on his body. The ground is frozen solid, so Alvin instructed a few men to wrap him in sheets, and pack him in snow, and we'll take him out in a few weeks when we're heading out anyway. What more can I write about this? The Devil is here, you might say.

FEBRUARY 11: Gabriel is convinced someone is stealing because he's running low on pork—and that this is the worst crew he's ever worked for. He says, blandly, we might starve if Alvin doesn't shoot something soon.

I have started thinking about my own Mother and Father. I should visit them, when I get back. You always tell me that we only get one set of parents, and that everyone makes mistakes. Maybe we can invite them—along with your parents?—to the Isles of Shoals? A vacation. August, when it's hottest. I can't forget to write my parents when I get home to Concord.

FEBRUARY 15: I woke to the sound of Winslow being hit. I think I'll burn this journal when the trip is over. I said hello to Winslow in the morning, and he avoided looking at me, but lifted his axe and headed for his lot, without waiting for anyone else.

FEBRUARY 16: Sunday. Mending clothes, washing. A tremendous Blizzard started late evening—heaviest snow and strongest wind so far. The snow is coming horizontal, and you can hear trees snapping in the forest. Cedar splits on roof are shaking and buzzing. Foul weather. Hurricane like.

February 17: Blizzard has not let up one bit. A very Big Storm. Can't work in this weather. Alvin has not left his room all day except to say that we're staying inside. How many bottles of whiskey did he bring, I wonder?!

February 18: Second Day of Blizzard, still not letting up. Snow is halfway up door, and we take turns shoveling out the path to the outhouse.

February 19: This will be known as The Great Blizzard of 1908, I believe.

February 20: I'm hesitant to write this evil. I wish I was home, Isabelle. A horrible scene tonight. After dinner, James chased Winslow around the room, pinching his arms, and knocking him down. *Stand up!* he would say to Winslow, and then push him down when he tried to stand. *Stand up!* And then push him down again. This is because we've been stuck in the cabin because of the Blizzard, and all the cribbage games have been played, and Stoddard isn't allowed to play fiddle anymore because Alvin said it gives him a headache hearing the same five tunes over and over. Everyone is a little loony. Winslow was starting to get angry the more James pushed him. I was sitting in my bunk, and called to James to stop, but he ignored me. Winslow kicked at James & then yelled like a wild animal for him to stop. He grabbed a fire-poker, brandished it around the room. Swung it at James. James stepped back, held up his hands. Said he was just fooling and to calm down. Don't be hysterical, James said. Winslow then gave what could be called a speech from the fireplace. He was about frothing at the mouth. He said he had tried to be kind and helpful. That in return everyone was a wicked bully to him. He said he was tired of being bullied. He said some of what he said to me, that he'd been bullied since he was a boy and he was tired of it. His face strained and he said a bunch of garble that didn't make much sense or sound like English. James laughed. Calm down, he said to Winslow. He was just fooling around, James said. He stepped toward Winslow with his hand out to grab the poker, and Winslow—I couldn't believe it—pulled it back and then swung it, like a baseball bat, landing with a crack on James's forearm. You could hear the snap of the bone. James swore and bent over, holding his arm, which made my stomach queasy because it looked like he had two elbows. James—must have been delirious—grabbed a hatchet from the fireplace, ran towards Winslow. Winslow leapt to the side, and James fumbled past him, and Winslow whacked James on the back of the head with the poker. James fell to the ground. Some men called out from their bunks. There was blood & the back of James's head was split open. Jory spoke from his place by the fire, said "G*d Almighty." Winslow was the look of Bewilderment itself, still holding the poker up. Lyman had snuck up behind Winslow, jumped at him with arms and legs and slammed him to the ground, punching his head.

Alvin opened his door—finally awoken. Alvin kicked Lyman in the back and told him to get off Winslow. Lyman held on. Alvin kicked Lyman hard in the side, and Lyman rolled over, groaning. Alvin told Winslow to get up. Then he told James to get up, maybe because he was drunk and couldn't see all the blood.

Jory told Alvin what happened. Alvin checked James's neck and said, that's right, he's dead.

Alvin said he was closing the camp down. This was a cursed expedition. After the storm ended, he said we'd cut until the end of the week, stack, and go. He said he'd return with new horses and new men in a few weeks to skid the logs. Jory said, 'Thank G*d.' Lyman said they needed to shackle Winslow. Alvin said don't be dumb, we don't have shackles and Winslow's not going anywhere. Where would he go? We're in the middle of a storm in the middle of nowhere. Alvin told Paul to help him wrap up James in a sheet and put him outside, beside James Kelley's body.

Winslow had gone to his bunk. He was touching his head where Lyman had punched and then looking at the blood. Lyman said to Winslow that he was going to jail for the rest of his life. That everyone here saw what happened. Jory said he'd been to prison and it wasn't that bad depending on where you ended up—free meals and such. "You're going to die in prison," Lyman said to Winslow.

More Blizzard.

February 21: Still snowing. 5th day. It's morning. I've taken up the journal because it is my only peace. I write with my back against the chimney for some warmth. Lyman is pacing around like a madman. He's asking what I've been writing, that I should put down every detail of what happened last night so that Winslow hangs. I keep the journal close to my chest—this is the only thing that is keeping me right in the head. Like I'm talking to you.

Wind has died.

Speaking of Lyman, Alvin should have put Winslow in a room by himself last night, instead of out with everyone else. Before dawn—I woke to the sounds of Winslow struggling, and to Lyman and Ned standing bedside. They pulled Winslow from the bunk, even though he was holding to the post. I swung my feet over and said stop, then Lyman held a knife up to me.

They pushed Winslow out the door. I don't know what happened, outside. I closed my eyes and thought about the sun coming up, about how we'd start cleaning up and moving out soon, and I'd toss this journal into the fire and forget about these months away from you, Isabelle. I didn't hear anything from the outside. I couldn't sleep. Sometime later, I saw Winslow walking across the cabin, to our bunk. Lord knows what they did to him.

I should have said something more to Alvin, or to Lyman & James, the first days he was bullied. I've never seen such a broken spirit as Winslow. I can't help thinking of his empty house in Tully, and of him being the only one left in his family. Some people are dealt a very hard hand in life. Maybe that's what had started the Trouble for him. Not his bad work or his chatter, but that Lyman & James and others saw the weakness he had—that he would have done anything to make friends, because he was alone in the world. What a horrible life this all is.

Later this morning: Winslow hasn't moved from his bed for hours. Snowing less heavily.

I brought Winslow a biscuit & water. He asked if I thought he was going to prison for his life. I said it might be true. He said James & Lyman were the ones who started the fight. I told him the honest truth, which is that the Law might not see things like that. He said it was an accident, didn't I see it? To protect himself. He didn't want to kill anyone. He wasn't that type of person. I told him I did see, and that things might be fine. But, I don't think I sounded very convincing to him. Plus, Winslow did hit James on the back of the head, which might not sit well with a Jury. He asked if I had written about it all in my book. I lied. I said I mostly just wrote about the weather and love letters to you. He looked thoughtful, then asked what I'd say about him, if this all came to a trial. I said he was polite and had lived a hard life, it seemed, and that I'd seen James and Lyman mistreat him. But murder, he said. "Would you say that I did it? If you were to be a witness?" I said that I wouldn't lie to a Judge, but I hoped the Judge understood the full story. "So you would say I murdered him." I didn't answer. "I don't want to go to prison," he said. He turned away from me, leaving the biscuit uneaten.

Evening: returning from my duty shoveling a path to the outhouse, I walked into the cabin to see Winslow standing at our bunk, then scramble down to his bunk. I found my journal not under my pillow as I usually leave it, but on the covers. I asked Winslow if he'd been reading it. He first pretended to sleep. I shook him. I said I'd just seen him standing up at the bunk, and my journal wasn't where I left it, and it was likely that he was reading it. He rolled over, looked at me, squinting, as if he'd just woken, saying they he'd been looking for his cap, which I could see was plainly on the bed-hook. He rolled back over, and didn't respond to anything else.

FEBRUARY 22: Idling by the fire after lunch, after a half-day of work! When I woke to a clear Blue Sky this morning, I nearly danced outside our cabin. I don't think there'll be another storm like this in our Century—I wonder what it was like for you in Concord? Are the streets filled with snow? Are you warm? I miss you! I miss you! I miss you!

The crews went to the logging sites all morning. Felt good to use my limbs again. A day closer to leaving. You'll be surprised to see me home a few weeks early. I've thought about the look on your face—hopefully a smile!—when I knock on our door.

It was soup and bread for lunch when we returned to the cabin. I sat across from Winslow, as I've been trying to lift his spirits. Alvin had told Winslow to stay in the cabin all morning—maybe Alvin didn't think Lyman was all that wrong, that a man who was facing a murder charge might take the chance to run away. I guess Gabriel put him to work because when we came back, Winslow was putting out the soups and bread on the dining table, and Gabriel was asleep by the fire. His first day off in months! What a sad sight to see—even in his situation, Winslow was carefully arranging the spoons and bowls like he was setting places for his own dinner guests.

At the table, Winslow said he was sorry. I asked what for. He said, everything. He said he was scared of prison. I told him that was reasonable. He said he felt like he never got a chance at a good life like other boys had. After much silence, I told him that I agreed he had gotten a rotten deal, but that he was a good man. I told him he might get a favorable Judge, and then he'd be off somewhere else, doing another job. He was still young. He had a lot of time left. He said that was nice to say, but he'd thought about it and understood he didn't have much of a chance. He'd probably spend decades in jail, he said. Probably die in jail, he said. I told him about the Isles of Shoals, about how nice it was in the summer, and that maybe he could get a job working in the hotel there, after this mess was over. To lighten the mood, I told him to never be a chef—that the soup I was eating tasted awful. The bread also was hard and tasteless as leather.

The potatoes for the soup must be rotting. I have a horrible stomachache now & a very bad headache, somewhat dizzy. Ned just threw up on the floor.

Paul and I are teamed up today, which makes me happy. Work will go fast. I'll end this entry now. I'll feel better moving around. I'll hide the journal, considering Winslow's curiosity. Love to you.

Radiolab: "Singularities"

SPEAKER 1: Hey, wait, you're . . .

SPEAKER 2: Okay.

SPEAKER 1: All right.

SPEAKER 2: Okay.

SPEAKER 1: All right.

SPEAKER 2: You are . . .

SPEAKER 1: . . . listening

SPEAKER 3: . . . to *Radiolab*.

SPEAKER 4: From . . .

SPEAKER 5: WNYC.

JAD: Ready? Jad.

ROBERT: Robert.

JAD: Radiolab.

ROBERT: Today we're talking about appearances . . .

JAD: . . . and disappearances.

ROBERT: Singularities. Moments in time.

JAD: Later we'll hear about the future of artificial intelligence. But first, a story from the past.

ROBERT: We're going north. Far north.

JAD: To a harbor town. Rocky coastline. Icebergs. A few hours of daylight in winter. Think lighthouses. Codfish. *Shipping News*. Newfoundland.

ANNA MOTT: The emphasis is on -land. Newfound-land.

ROBERT: To a story about a very rare animal . . .

JAD: . . . that was found . . .

ROBERT: . . . and, in a way, lost again . . .

JAD: . . . all in the very same moment.

ROBERT: The story comes to us from . . .

ANNA: Yes, I can hear you fine, Robert. Can you hear me?

ROBERT: . . . writer Anna Mott.

ANNA: *M. O. T. T.* No, not related to the apple juice people, unfortunately. I grew up in Halifax.

JAD: Who published an article that we really loved . . .

ROBERT: . . . which starts with a photograph. A mysterious photograph.

ANNA: Taken in 1991. By a man named Will Hunt. In the town of Mule Harbor, on the northwest coast. Will is sitting in his fishing dory, pointing his camera toward a small island.

ROBERT: What else is in the photograph?

ANNA: First, I should say it's perfectly clear—not blurry or anything. It's in color. The island is maybe ten meters away. You can see the bow of Will's boat at the bottom of the picture. It's a sunny, clear day. In the middle are all these rocks absolutely covered with seabirds, nesting there for the summer. Mostly murres—small black-and-white seabirds. But there's something strange standing with them. Way, way bigger than the others. Way bigger.

ROBERT: Which is?

ANNA: A great auk.

JAD: Giant seabird. Tiny wings. Flightless. Millions lived on the north Atlantic coastline.

ROBERT: And remind us why that's so strange, Anna?

ANNA: Well, the last time a great auk was seen was 1844, off Iceland. A pair of them.

ROBERT: So that's . . .

ANNA: Almost a hundred and fifty years before the picture was taken.

JAD: So, a long time.

ANNA: It was supposed to be extinct.

ROBERT: So . . . what was it doing there?

ANNA: That's the question, isn't it?

JAD: Wait, back up. What happened to all of them?

ANNA: Hunted to extinction. By the millions. Since, like, the 1500s. Sailors apparently thought they tasted really good, and they were super easy to catch. You didn't even need a gun. This is from an English sailor in the 1600s: "We filled two boats—collecting them was as easy as if we were picking up stones." They weren't afraid of people, and you could just go up to one, knock it over the head, toss it in the sack.

ROBERT: Oh no.

ANNA: Because their feathers were so oily, the hunters would skewer them, light them on fire, use them as torches instead of wasting kerosene.

JAD: That is—wow.

ANNA: Collectors and museums wiped out the rest in the mid-1800s. They wanted them for their collections. That pair off Iceland I mentioned? The last ones ever seen? They were strangled to death by a man sent for a collection. He also mistakenly stepped on the pair's egg, which was—well, maybe the last great auk egg on the planet.

ROBERT: OK. So, mass slaughter. Extinction.

JAD: Like the dodo.

ROBERT: Ah. The poor dodo.

JAD: People and flightless birds . . .

ROBERT: . . . deadly combination.

ANNA: That photograph is basically the same thing as a woolly mammoth in a herd of elephants.

JAD: Could it have been another seabird?

BOB BONTER: *Pinguinis impennis*. The great auk. Means something like "fat and lacking feathers."

ROBERT: This is Bob Bonter, professor of evolutionary biology and fellow at the Cornell Lab of Ornithology.

BOB: I specialize in the family of birds called Alcidae. Seabirds. Let me put it this way: there is not a single bird in the world that looked like a great auk. Totally singular. Like how an ostrich or peacock is singular.

JAD: Isn't there another type of auk, though?

BOB: The little auk. Which is eight inches tall. The great auk was two and half feet tall. That's as big as a toddler.

ROBERT: We asked Professor Bonter to talk to us about what he sees in the photo. From an ornithologist's perspective.

BOB: One hundred percent. Not ninety-nine. That's one hundred percent a great auk standing there. That photograph bothered me for years. Years! Haunted me, you might say.

ROBERT: So, you've seen the picture before?

BOB: Everyone's seen it! I don't think we'll ever get to the bottom of it. What was it doing there? How is it possible? It just—the whole thing is a riddle that really has no end. It's impossible. But, there it is.

ROBERT: But don't these things happen?

JAD: What things?

ROBERT: Everyone thinks an animal is extinct. Wiped from the planet. Then someone's out fishing or bird-watching or hiking and it just—appears.

JAD: Right. Like—the coelacanth. The ancient fish everyone thought went extinct millions of years ago. Then a fisherman in South Africa pulled it up in his net.

ROBERT: Ivory-billed woodpecker?

JAD: Giant woodpecker. Longtime extinct. Spotted again, only once, in Arkansas in 2004. Grainy footage. Okay. So, say it came back. But from where? How?

BOB: It would have had to come from a nesting colony. Because, let's remember, one bird cannot live for a hundred and forty years. Individuals probably lived twenty, twenty-five years tops. There must have been others to mate and continue the lineage. So, the question really is, was there a hidden colony? Sure. Chances are slim. But, sure—I suppose there could have been a limited population tucked away somewhere along the Labrador coastline, where people didn't go often. There are thousands of inlets and bays and coves that would make for good nesting habitat. This one could have gone off course during the winter migration, arrived at Mule Harbor accidentally, totally lost. But for a colony of great auks to elude people—for over a century?

ROBERT: So, it's possible?

BOB: Possible. Unlikely. But, even so, there's a big problem.

ROBERT: What's that?

BOB: It was never seen again.

ANNA: That's the issue. This one picture was all we had. Not really what you'd call a complete dataset.

JAD: But still people knew about it? How?

ANNA: The picture was printed in the local newspaper, then national papers. If you were living in Canada in the nineties, you probably heard of Mule Harbor and the reappearance of the great auk. *National Geographic* sent a photographer, did a long story on it. Dozens of bird-watchers showed up. They even got a visit from David Attenborough, which apparently sent the town into a panic.

BOB: People from across the world were searching the Labrador and Newfoundland coastlines. There was a reward. I mean, a huge reward. From a bird enthusiast in New York City. People who weren't even birders got binoculars and went searching. It was basically a yearslong treasure hunt. It got out of hand. That coastline is not a walk in the park. A few people in kayaks died looking for it. The whole thing was a mess.

JAD: Yikes. And still nobody saw it again?

ANNA: Not that summer. Or the summer after. Or the summer after. All the excitement died down pretty quickly. It's been thirty years now. And nothing.

ROBERT: Appeared and disappeared.

ANNA: But . . . there was something strange in all the articles I read about it. I noticed that Will Hunt, the one who took the photograph, never gave an interview. It was weird. Like, why wouldn't reporters talk to the guy who's responsible for the biggest news in zoology in decades? The only interviews are from folks around town, and from Will Hunt's neighbor, this guy named Fen Mack—who sounds like a character. He says that Will was out fishing and snapped the photo. Then Mack goes on to talk about how nice a place his town is, how it didn't surprise him the auk decided to settle there—with the beautiful views and such. Anyway. Not much more details about the auk itself, or Will.

JAD: That is odd.

ANNA: So, I flew to Newfoundland to find him.

JAD: And did you?

ANNA: Well, in a way.

ROBERT: We'll hear more about that trip soon. After the break.

[BOB BONTER: Hi, this is Bob calling from snowy Ithaca, New York. Radiolab is supported in part by the Alfred P. Sloan Foundation, enhancing public understanding of science and technology in the modern world. More information at sloan.org.]

JAD: Jad.

ROBERT: Robert.

JAD: Radiolab. Okay, so, Anna. Where did you leave us? You've gone to Newfoundland to find Will Hunt, the photographer, the only person who'd seen a living great auk in almost a hundred and fifty years?

ANNA: Right. It's a long way. A thirteen-hour ferry from Nova Scotia to the southern coast of Newfoundland. From there, I drove for like a day to get to Mule Harbor. It really is a beautiful town, especially in the summer. Green grasses piled on granite ledges. Sheep pastures. Clean air. Colorful fishing dories overturned on the lawns. All very picturesque. Bright blue ocean. You can see the island where Will took the picture. It's right outside the harbor. Not far. Lots of seabirds. Puffins.

ROBERT: Oh, I love puffins. Rainbow bills.

ANNA: Aren't they great? Anyway, for such a remote place, it was kind of bustling. There's one main street that goes along the coast. But there's a café, a couple stores. A tourist shop that sold auk keychains and postcards and hats and T-shirts. I ended up at the market, down on the waterfront. I told the woman working at the counter that I was doing a story about the great auk sighting.

NATALIE FAHEY: Oh, yes. I was a girl when it happened.

ANNA: This is Natalie Fahey. Owner of Fahey's Market.

NATALIE: It had the whole town in a scramble, didn't it? There was traffic for the first time. Folks driving up from St. John's. Our town was famous.

ANNA: Did you ever see it? The auk?

NATALIE: I didn't. Of course, when the reporters were here, we all were a bit coy. Saying things like, "I think I saw something, just down the coast a bit."

ANNA: But you think it was real?

NATALIE: Not a question whether it's real or not, is it? You saw the photograph that Will took?

ANNA: Well, that's sort of what I came here for. Do you know Will Hunt?

NATALIE: I don't think there's a person in this town I don't know. Of course I knew Will.

ANNA: Is he here?

NATALIE: Well, love, you're late. Will passed away years ago. He was quite private, anyway. I'm not sure what help he would be to you. I mean, he might not talk to you.

ANNA: I'm sorry to hear. Did he ever talk to you about the photo?

NATALIE: Some. He talked about Fen. He was quite angry at Fen for sending it in.

ANNA: Sending it in?

NATALIE: The photograph. Fen Mack was the one who sent it to the paper. I guess Will had lent it to him for some reason. There was some bad blood there for a time.

ANNA: What about Fen—is he here?

NATATLIE: Oh no. He was much older than Will. You know this all happened thirty years ago, love? Probably before you were born. How did you hear about this, anyway? I haven't had anyone ask me about the auk in years now.

ANNA: I told Natalie what I wrote in my article, what you read.

[MUSIC]

ANNA: That I'd been living in the States, in Brooklyn, with my boyfriend. I'd been pretty unhappy—for years. The week we finally broke up, the pandemic hit. I moved back to Canada to live with my parents, in Halifax. I couldn't write anything. I was getting pretty depressed. My parents and I had some trouble living together, but it's not like I could move anywhere else. There was a seabird sanctuary near a place where I would go walking every day. I started talking to one of the women doing work there. She said they needed more volunteers. So, that's what I did for summer the first year of the pandemic: counted seabirds. It kind of saved my life. One of the other volunteers I met there told me about the great auk. She'd grown up in Newfoundland, and said that she always kept an eye out for something big when she's doing her counting. She showed me the Wikipedia page of the Mule Harbor sighting, and then I found all the articles on it. Kind of got obsessed from there, and wrote some notes on it. It was the first writing I'd done in over a year. Anyway, I told Natalie a shorter version of that story.

NATALIE: The bird gave you something, didn't it? Lifted you up.

ANNA: Exactly.

NATALIE: You're not the first one.

ANNA: She put a sign at the register that said BACK IN 15.

NATALIE: Can I show you something? Out here.

ANNA: We walked down the street, and then up a grassy path. There was a hotel, up on a bluff, overlooking the bay. There were a few guests sitting on rocking chairs on the porch. A beautiful place. Sorry, the sound quality here is bad. Lots of wind.

NATALIE: Thirty years ago, you wouldn't recognize this. It was all run down. This was Will's family's inn. If you need to sleep somewhere tonight, you should stay here.

ANNA: Natalie led me around the back. To a little cottage. Shack, really.

NATALIE: This is where Will moved after Nora passed away.

ANNA: Nora?

NATALIE: His wife. I don't think he liked being around all the guests. He liked being left alone. It wasn't good, at the end there. He wasn't in a good place. My mother used to send me up to give him dinners every so often.

ANNA: She opened the door. It was one room, with a woodstove, bed, kitchenette.

NATALIE: Sometimes I come here when Gary is driving me crazy.

ANNA: Her husband.

NATALIE: To read. Or think. I don't think Will would have minded. I keep it clean, keep the mice out.

ANNA: She sat on the bed. Opened the bedside drawer. Pulled out the *National Geographic*, the one with the story of the great auk. She starting flipping through the magazine.

NATALIE: I must have looked through this a dozen times before I found this . . .

ANNA: She turned to the back. There was a photograph tucked in there. It looked almost like the one printed in the papers . . . but it was different.

NATALIE: That's Nora. Right there.

ANNA: It's a picture of a woman—of Nora Hunt, Will's wife—at the bow of the fishing dory, pointing to the rocks. She has this huge smile. She looks ecstatic, like she's on a roller coaster or something. Really happy. I see right off that the photograph was taken on a different day as the other one, the one printed in the papers. It's darker. It's cloudier in this picture.

NATALIE: Look where she's pointing. And look very closely.

ANNA: Oh my gosh.

JAD: Wait—what?

ANNA: An auk.

ROBERT: A second sighting!

ANNA: Yes. But what is really startling is what's beside the auk.

NATALIE: Look closer.

ROBERT: What is it?

NATALIE: You can see it clearly, can't you?

ANNA: Is that an egg?

NATALIE: It is.

ROBERT: No.

JAD: What?!

BOB: I almost fell off my seat when Anna emailed me that picture last year. A nesting great auk? That picture is what has renewed the search. It's just too exciting to not investigate. To not take seriously. It means that there are or were breeding pairs.

JAD: So, there's a nesting colony out there? Somewhere?

BOB: It's an enormous area to search. From Maine to Newfoundland and Labrador to Greenland, Faroe Islands, Iceland, Shetland Islands, Orkney Islands . . .

ROBERT: But that settles it, right? The great auk is struck from the extinction list?

ANNA: No, no. You'd have to document a live bird—with a video—and have many more sightings. We're a long way off. But, it's something. It's more than just the one in the paper.

But I started thinking, even if they don't find it, even if they find nothing, it already made an impact. It already affected people. Bird or no bird.

JAD: What do you mean?

[MUSIC]

ANNA: Like, it changed the town. Whether it comes back or not. I'm thinking of what Natalie told me, as we sat there leafing through the article.

NATALIE: Look at all the pictures here. What do you see?

ANNA: Houses. Marble Island. The ocean. The fishing dories. Fishing shacks. Sheep.

NATALIE: Do you see any big extinct birds?

ANNA: I don't.

NATALIE: But the town looks pretty, doesn't it? After the articles were printed, tourists came by the hundreds. We became a destination. A summer town. Everybody makes a living on the tourism now. We were on the edge of dying, and then Will's picture put us on the map. Maybe the bird will come back to us . . . but, it doesn't really matter if it doesn't. I've got to get back to the store now. I suppose you can stay here for a while if you want. Just shut the door when you leave.

[BELLS]

ANNA: The sighting resurrected the town. And it also changed my life.

ROBERT: How's that?

ANNA: I ended up staying in Mule Harbor. I never went back to New York. I'm working at the inn that Will's family owned. It's really nice here. I'm almost finished with my first book. And, the biggest change—I met my husband here. Natalie set us up. Luke is her nephew. I've been here two years now. Luke and I just bought a house.

JAD: That's a whole lot of change.

ANNA: But it came so easy. It made me think, why was I so interested in the great auk story to begin with? Why do certain stories grab your attention? If I believed in a higher power or whatever, I'd say the auk was leading me to this life, to Luke and my new home. It does feel, in a way, like fate.

ROBERT: Following something is worth it. Even if you can't see the end.

ANNA: Exactly.

JAD: I'd still like to think there's a hidden flock out there. Living happily away from people.

ANNA: Oh, I never leave the house in June without binoculars.

ROBERT: I guess you can always hope.

JAD: Even if the chances are small.

ROBERT: Right.

JAD: Okay?

ROBERT: Okay.

JAD: On to the future, after the break.

ROBERT: Thanks for listening.

[ANSWERING MACHINE: To play the message, press 2. Start of message]

The Auk

In 1991, I owned the only inn in Mule Harbor, Newfoundland, a town of fifty-five people who shared one of three surnames. The Grey Saint Inn had once been filled with seasonal workers—mostly those going north to gold washes in Labrador's rivers. My parents would serve you dinner, sell sugar and coffee, patch clothes. Before the miners, it was sealers. Before sealers it was bird hunters, and before them, whalers. Each animal hunted away, just as the gold had been and, now, the cod. Maybe the town was unlucky, forged in the name itself: about a century ago, a schooner carrying mules for the iron mines wrecked on the outer shoals. I guess some of the mules survived, swam to shore. My grandfather said he woke up to see one standing in the seaweed, braying. So, we were named after disaster.

The Grey Saint was about to fail. Nobody visited Mule Harbor anymore. Even my brother, Dan, hadn't come back up for Christmas. He wrote from Halifax saying that he and his wife couldn't take off work, even though they both were teachers, with holiday. The inn's reservations phone hadn't rung in a long time, and the last signature in the guest book was from three years earlier, when a nice English couple came for whale watching during the wrong season and left early. We weren't a ghost town yet, but if a dozen young couples with plans for procreating didn't soon decide that nine months of winter and a leaky schoolhouse was their greatest desire, we'd lose the town doctor, the government aid, all of it.

The town council floated the idea that we change our name, to make it more appealing. "To what?" my neighbor, Fen Mack, said at the town meeting. "A faithful animal," he continued, and spoke at length about his time working with mules in the mines back when he was a boy, which reminded him how good it used to be, and how it would never be that good again, and that we should have never joined Canada, that that was the start of all our troubles, along with church attendance. Once a year, Fen shot a moose and gave away the meat from his freezer, so he was well liked in town, though he had strong, some might say disagreeable, opinions.

Anyway, the name-change proposal failed because nobody could agree on a new name. The way I felt about it was, How the hell is changing the town name going to stop everyone from going on government support? After the meeting, a few folks came back to the Grey Saint's pub, which I'd kept open for tradition but long ago stopped serving food. Fen talked about living here like it was being on a losing team. He got fairly drunk, which wasn't common but not rare. I had to keep reminding him to quiet down, that Nora was sleeping in the next room. He ended the night singing a Beatles song to himself at the corner table.

By the fall of that year, I'd closed off the eight bedrooms, nailed plywood over the windows, and hoped the heating bills and taxes wouldn't bankrupt me. I fished, built a hothouse in the back lawn for winter vegetables, did some light carpentry for folks around town, and read the newspaper, which came once a week and which I read in parts through the week, always saving Politics for Friday so I'd have something fresh on my mind to discuss with Fen.

On one of my more desperate mornings, after staring at my last bank statement and seeing I wouldn't be able to cover tax and utility expenses by the end of the calendar year, I walked to the town library—a fairly new building gifted by national taxpayers—to look for books on business. I found only one, but it didn't make any sense to me, so I closed it after a chapter and sank into a couch in the sun, beside a tall window facing the sea that had once offered so much. On the coffee table in front of me was a book called *The Great Auk* and a notecard reading *Local History* in the handwriting of Gretchen McCall, the librarian and my mother's (since passed) best friend. On the cover was a painting of the auk—a teardrop body with a big bill, body divided in black-and-white.

I picked up the book, happy to stay away from troubles at home. In the first chapter, titled "Extinction," were drawings of men shooting birds on sea cliffs, others herding flocks onto boats by way of ramps. I read about a man in the Orkney Islands in the 1820s who caught an auk, kept it in a shed, and then, when a squall drowned a few fishermen, beat it to death with a stick because he thought it was a witch. Auks were unafraid of people, I read, always crowding together, killed easily. The last sighting, the most recent one, was not far from here—over on Fogo Island, in the 1800s.

I closed the book, held it in my lap. Turned it over. On the back was a picture of an egg—speckled and smeared with reddish-brown streaks. I've seen one of those, I thought. Up in the attic, when I was there just a few weeks before, looking for the deed that I had somehow lost but which I needed if I was, in fact, going to sell the Grey Saint. The egg was in a big wooden box, on blue fabric. I could see it perfectly in my mind.

I placed the book on the checkout desk, asked Gretchen about her holiday, and nearly ran home, thinking that I'd probably left Nora alone for too long.

THE WINTER BEFORE, Nora, my wife, started snapping her fingers in the air, having forgotten the name of her mother, for instance, or asking me, for the fifth time in a day, what I thought of the construction plans for the schoolhouse, where she worked. Then there were the times she'd spend an hour looking for a hairpin, or forget to put the bread in the oven after it had risen, or forget that the bread was already in the oven and so the kitchen would fill up with smoke. She would tell me that she was only overworked, that her students were tiring her out.

One spring morning, I woke and she wasn't in bed. I looked out the window, saw her standing in the snowy lawn, in her nightgown and without shoes. I opened the window and yelled down. She said she was looking for the bathroom. I ran outside, carried her back in, warmed her feet in my hands, made us tea, then walked with her to Sawyer's, the town doctor's, house. He listened to the stories about her forgetfulness, then listened to her heart, looked into her eyes, her ears, her mouth. He asked her to hold up her arms, then turn her hands side to side like she was screwing in light bulbs. "Well," he said, "not Parkinson's. You can be happy for that." He sat down, slumped over, draped his stethoscope over his neck, and said, "She is in perfect physical health." "But," I said, "she's not." He said there were a hundred things that could be happening: stress, sleep deprivation, early Alzheimer's, different forms of dementia. He said he'd take urine and blood samples to send away, and would call if anything came up.

Nothing came up. But when we drove to the hospital in St. John's one weekend to get brain scans, we saw she had had a few small strokes. Then, right there, in the hospital, a larger stroke came, which I suppose is lucky in terms of setting. There's not much to say about that day except that it was the worst of my life. We spent a month in St. John's, until the doctors sent us home with a wheelchair and more pills than I could keep track of. I set up our bedroom downstairs, in the old sitting room beside the pub, with all the furniture and paintings and decorations of our bedroom upstairs.

Spring passed to summer in Mule Harbor.

Nora would be lying in our bed, saying, in a whispering, closed-mouth way, that she wanted to go home. She asked one night if her mother, who had been dead ten years, was there. The memory scramble and the stroke could be connected, Sawyer said, but maybe not, maybe there were a couple things going on. "There's so much we don't understand about the brain," he said. "But, something like this? It affects everyone. Take care of yourself." I hated him for saying that, but thought of it more often than I'd like to admit. I'd lost my wife in a season, is how I felt.

When the harbor ice retreated and icebergs lingered on the

horizon, I'd wrap her in blankets and scarves, put her in the wheelchair, and walk along the shoreline. We watched boats come in and out of the harbor. Watched the lupines flop in the breeze. There were days when I wouldn't notice anything was wrong, and then, out of nowhere, she'd ask me when we'd met.

I subscribed to magazines like *Neurology Now* to try to understand what was happening, what I might do to help. I had a stack of them on my bedside table. Scientists were almost enthusiastically unsure about how the brain worked, I read. Just too complicated, they wrote. There was a case of a teenage boy who got knocked on the head and lost his identity, right down to not feeling anything for his mother; a story of an old woman who only remembered the facts of her life before she turned twenty-three; and many, many stories of people just like Nora, whose minds, in their early middle age, had dissolved.

I'd lay the magazine on my chest, close my eyes, feel the breeze coming through the bedroom window, and wonder where all my wife's memories had gone, and where my life was headed.

"Sailing in the fog," Fen Mack replied, when I explained to him what she was like now, what our life in the Grey Saint was like now.

AFTER RETURNING FROM the library that day, auk book in hand, I checked on Nora, then climbed the ladder to the attic. Broken furniture, cardboard boxes filled with light bulbs, old shoes, extra dishware, and costumes from the plays my mother used to put on for guests made an alleyway toward where I thought

I'd seen the egg. The wooden box—the size and shape of a small suitcase—was beneath a dusty window. On the lid was old, black script advertising soap. When I unhooked the latch and lifted the lid, I saw the egg resting on fabric, just as I remembered. It was larger than a chicken egg—more like a goose egg. Pale green, marked with the streaks, like the one I'd seen in the book. It was light in my hand. A little hole had been drilled in one end. I wondered if it was worth anything. Overhead, I heard seagulls scrambling on the roof, trying to keep their footing in the wind.

When I bent down to replace the egg, I noticed—my eyes adjusting to the darkness—a black feathery spike poking out from the edge of the cloth. I rested the egg on the floor and pulled back the cloth, knowing what I was going to find before I saw it.

The taxidermied bird was on its side—its small wing folded tightly to its breast, the head tilted upward. I lifted it out. The whole thing weighed almost nothing, as if a cushion. The feathers felt like horsehair, not feathers. On the leg was a square of yellowed paper small as a postage stamp, tied to a thread. I held the bird closer to the window. "Sam Watkins," it read. My great-great-grandfather. "1821, Marble Island."

I examined the taxidermy head to tail, then descended the ladder holding it in one hand, eager to show Nora.

She was asleep in the bed, sitting upright, her chin touching her chest and her hair falling over her face. Her breathing was heavy, and she moaned when she exhaled. Through the open windows, I heard Martin Sullivan's tractor and smelled the sweet smell of newly cut hay. A sheep bleated in a pasture.

I stood in the bedroom doorway, auk in my hands. I didn't

want to wake her. I'd show her some other time. I climbed back up the ladder, rested the bird back in the box, covered it with the cloth, put the egg over it. I made myself a cup of tea, sat in the kitchen, looked out to a spitting and gray summer day. Months of medical bills were fanned out on the kitchen table, like a hand of losing cards. "What happens if I just don't pay?" I asked Sawyer one time. "From a medical man's perspective?"

"Don't do that," he said.

I FOUND MYSELF THINKING about the auk when I'd take my daily afternoon walks, along the coastal road to the graveyard. I didn't understand why Sam had stuffed this one. Maybe he'd noticed they were declining and wanted to hold on to it—like when my mother used to press field thistle into her Bible just before the frost. I understand that you start missing something when it's about gone. Like, I thought of the times I was short with Nora when she was first losing her memory. I hate remembering that I raised my voice, sometimes, when she'd leave the downstairs door wide open, or not feed the chickens, or leave the faucet running. I wondered how it was possible that I hadn't been happy every minute she was herself, before all this. I missed cooking together, waking up and deciding which one of us would go downstairs to make tea, walking to the graveyard together, playing board games when the power was out and we couldn't watch television. Instead, on my walks alone, I wondered if my life would always be this narrow and difficult, and then, inevitably, would look out to Marble Island, and think of the auk in the attic that had lived there once, a century earlier.

Point being, the auk started to add some volume to my thoughts, a distraction. Sometimes, I'd go up into the attic and take it out of the box, just to feel its stubbly feathers.

A POSTCARD ARRIVED FROM my brother, who'd been sending me something in the mail every week since Nora's troubles. He's kind, my brother. It was his way of showing he kept us in his thoughts. Sometimes it was a picture of him and his wife, sometimes a postcard. This postcard showed a line of women in swimsuit bottoms only, standing side by side, facing away, arms linked, on a street in downtown Halifax. *Just Another Lousy Day in Canada!* the card read in bright pink cursive. I flipped it over. *Greetings from the warm south*, my brother wrote. *Anything interesting happening in town? How's the Saint? Send word or gossip when you get a chance.*

I smiled, then tossed the postcard into the woodstove.

I sipped tea at the kitchen table, wondering what I could send back to him. Through the window was Marble Island. The tall columns of rocks were topped with summery grasses—green lawns floating high above the waterline. Hundreds of nesting birds circled the island, flying into the cliffs where their nests were hidden. The sun cast long shadows down the rock faces and illuminated the water a nearly tropical blue. An idea came to mind as I looked at the island.

I got up from the kitchen table and went to our coat closet, looking for the Polaroid camera Dan had sent me for Christmas that year. I found it under a pile of scarves, then went up to the attic. I wrapped the auk in my raincoat, grabbed extra gas from the shed, and with the auk under my arm and camera over my shoulder, walked to my boat. I motored out to Marble Island.

It was a clear day, with high clouds and a rare light wind. When I approached the island, the murres scattered into the water. I found a cove out of the wind, nosed the boat up to the rocks, jumped out with the bowline. I lifted out the auk, unwrapped it from the raincoat and cloth, and placed it on a flat rock, out of the wind. I arranged some seaweed near its feet to hide the wooden taxidermy stand. When I was satisfied with the position, that it looked somewhat natural, I shoved my boat off the rocks, started the engine, and took my first picture. The photograph slid out of the camera, and I put it in my coat pocket. A murre shot out of the waves and onto the rocks, approached the auk, followed by a couple of his friends. I took another picture. The murre poked at the auk, and so I thought it was time to retrieve my taxidermy before it was pushed into the water.

As I steered back to the harbor, I composed what I'd write to Dan. *Life Returns to Mule Harbor,* I thought. *Have these in Halifax?* Something like that—I was never good at jokes like Dan, who said I was too serious as a kid and should spend more time smiling. "Lighten up," was the phrase I remember him repeating all through our childhood. I should draw a big circle around the auk, I thought, as I weaved my boat through the moorings scattered in the harbor.

I got home, put the auk in the attic. I left the photographs on the kitchen table, put on the kettle. The Polaroids came out well—you could easily see the old bird, and the murres surrounding it only added to the naturalness of the scene.

I looked at the clock. The mail boat would have already left. I'd have to wait to send Dan my response.

FIRST, I DIDN'T HAVE the postage, then forgot to give it to the mail boat, and then lost the momentum and wasn't even sure the joke was funny anyway. One day, I found Nora in bed with the photographs out in front of her.

"What are these?" she asked.

"Some nature photography," I said. "I went out on the boat the other day."

"This bird," she said.

"Hmm?" I said, looking over her shoulder. I was embarrassed that I'd spent this much time taking a fake photograph instead of scraping away the paint from the old shingles or trying to figure out why our water pressure had suddenly gotten so low.

"You took these?" she asked.

I did, I said.

"This is a great auk," she said. "I taught the kids about them in school."

"Is that right?"

She seemed a touch more lucid, in her speech and the fact that she, well, could recall a lesson she'd taught. She laughed, for maybe the first time in months. A short and mumbled laugh. I leaned in closer to her, looked at the photographs in her hand. I put my hand on her shoulder.

The photographs had developed in vivid, crisp color. The waves between the boat and island revealed, almost like a curtain parting, the great auk standing at the edge of the water. The waves, cresting, were skimmed by the wind. They were beautiful photographs, I would say.

"That's special," she said, tapping the pictures. "We should tell somebody."

I walked into the kitchen, took down two mugs from the shelf, put an herbal tea bag in Nora's, black in mine.

"Oh no," I called to her. "There's something I should say about those photographs."

I walked back into the room with the tea, and I was about to tell her the joke I was playing on Dan, but then she interrupted me.

"Can we go looking for it?" she said, taking a mug from my hand. "Will you show me where you took these?"

It's hard to describe why those sentences meant so much, at the time. Only, imagine that your spouse hasn't asked you to do anything with them for half a year, hasn't shown any interest in leaving the house for months, hasn't looked at you with a kind of soft smile that reminded you of how she looked at you years earlier.

I turned away, sat on the bed, and stared into my cup, watching the tea bag shed its color into the water.

"Sawyer said you shouldn't be out in the cold."

"Oh," she said, "I feel fine." She looked out the window. "It's a blue day. We have lots of sunlight. Take me on the boat."

"Now?"

Everything in her face and shoulders relaxed.

"Why not?" she said.

I agreed, kissed her on the ear.

I CARRIED HER OUT, set her up in the bow, in a couch of life jackets and blankets. She closed her eyes and faced the sun. We motored out of the harbor, toward Marble Island. She held her hand up to her brow to scan the rocks.

"See anything?" I asked.

I watched her looking at the rocks.

"No," she said, happily. She adjusted her wool cap. Squinted. Wiped her nose with her sleeve. Her cheeks were red. Living so close to illness often had me thinking about the body. "It's just blood and bones in there," Sawyer once said to me, when I asked what had happened, back in the early days. "It's like anything, like an engine—something can go wrong."

We circled the island three times. Halfway around the third time, the sun set, and the water went dark. Twilight would hold for a long time in this season. I told her that it was time to go, that maybe we could come back tomorrow to see if the auk returned.

"Tomorrow," she said, happily. She might not remember what we'd done today. But, right then, she was confident about tomorrow, that she would get another chance to look for the great auk.

THIS HAPPENED AGAIN, and again. I'd leave the photographs on the bedside table for her to discover in the mornings. She'd pick them up and say nearly the same thing she said that first time. I had read about this in my neurology magazines—people who suffer from memory loss or dementia will sometimes fall into repetition. Caught in a loop. We repeated this happy day on the boat a dozen more times that summer. Her looking to the rocks. Me pretending to look at the rocks but looking at her. Twice she called out that she thought she saw it with the other birds—always at the end of the day, when the shadows were long in the rocks and waves and anyone's eyes could be tricked. Even though I knew she hadn't seen it, I'd get excited with her, ask her where, and then we'd motor close, agreeing that maybe it had been scared away by the boat, gone underwater. It gave us a good moment, whispering to each other after I cut the engine, floating quietly with the sound of wavelets clacking on the hull, waiting for a bird that wasn't there to rise to the surface for a breath. It felt like the only times in those days that we connected, the only times I felt close to her. Which is why I might have taken it too far. Once, near the end of the summer, I snuck out early in the day, set up the taxidermy again on Marble Island, but this time put it higher up on a rock ledge, away from the surf. To make it look more real, I placed the hollow egg at its feet, pinned it tight with a little stone. Later that afternoon, I took us to all the usual areas around the island before steering us to my setup. I had my camera ready, so I could document the moment, show her what she'd seen, so she wouldn't forget about it. The setup worked perfectly. I'd never seen her so excited.

We were up for hours that night talking about the sighting, looking at the photograph of her pointing to the auk and its egg, a big grin on her face. As always, she woke up the next morning and had forgotten.

AUTUMN CAME, and all the birds left. Snow settled on Marble Island.

I went back to the library, borrowed the auk book. Nora and I read it together in bed, chapter by chapter. Because the great auk had gone extinct before scientists tracked their movements, nobody knew exactly where they'd migrated in the winter. The best guess was that they swam around the open ocean, each one alone, through the North Atlantic, maybe all the way to Europe—which unsettled me, thinking of a bird suspended in the fathomless and dark water, with no resting place, no direction of land.

Chopping and stacking wood, or shoveling a path from the front door to the shed, I wondered if some of the birds had escaped the hunters. That, come summer, on some remote spit of land in Baffin Bay and a thousand miles from any person, a small colony lived unaware that the rest of them had died.

Sometime after Christmas that year, Dan wrote saying that an apartment had just come up for sale in his building. Small, but cheap. I wrote back that I thought Nora was maybe doing better now, that we were just waiting for winter to pass, and that we liked it here.

The Children of New Eden

There they are, in 1696, newly married, happy, moving west, passing a lake near Worcester on an evening in summer, hearing a loon's two-note song. Philip and Caroline, nineteen and eighteen years old. A family of two, for now. Walking with them are eleven other couples, some with children, and five unmarried men and women. Ahead, leading the congregation, is Karl Dietzen, a soft-spoken Bavarian in a black coat, with long gray hair, a head taller than most, wearing a simple rope necklace, who arrived in Boston two years earlier. He carries with him the deed to land none of the others have seen, west of the Connecticut River, far north of Springfield, where they can worship openly and in peace. It is an enormous tract of land. A thousand acres and with—as Karl described at a service outside Dedham months earlier—a clear-water river edging a field with black soil a yard down. Philip had sold his inherited land to pay his share of the community land.

Everyone in their congregation, called the Children of New Eden, mostly keeps to themselves on the walk. Those with children are busy feeding and calming them, describing repeatedly how many days of the journey are left and when they will next eat. Up ahead, walking beside Karl, is Caroline's younger sister, Emma, who has fallen into easy conversation with him these past days. Emma is seventeen and unmarried. Only Emma had known about Caroline attending Karl's services, and, later, about the congregation's plans to settle in the western part of Massachusetts Bay Colony, in the Pioneer Valley.

It's been a stretch of warm and dry nights. Karl gathers the group together after dinners to describe what he sees in the constellations. He has encouraged every couple to increase their families as much and as soon as possible, and so, even in transit, after evening services, the couples spread apart for privacy, despite the open wilderness and occasional sounds of wolves. He tells them to not be afraid of the night, of the lies ministers and magistrates tell about dangers beyond the village in hopes of keeping people obedient and taxed. God is in the forest, Karl reminds them. He had lived on a remote hillside in Bavaria for years, alone, protected and nourished by his faith.

Lying in the grass in a meadow, off by themselves, looking at the moon, Caroline asks Philip what he thinks is beyond the stars.

"Light?" he says. "And beyond that?" she asks. "More light," he says.

She asks if he remembers the comet over Dedham, when they were very young. It was in the sky for a week. Her uncle left his family, she says—his wife and eight children—the morning after it appeared, so sure it was a sign from God. She hears the distant and singular laugh of her sister, who is by a big fire with the other unmarried congregants, including Karl.

"She is more spirited than I've ever seen her," Caroline says of Emma.

"Why would God send a sign to abandon your family?" Philip asks of her uncle.

Caroline says she doesn't know, but that's what her aunt told her.

On the third day of walking, near the ashes of their small cooking fire, Philip points out to Caroline a toad with a yellow-white stomach perched on the handle of their cooking pot. Its eyes are like mica flecks, and its throat small and beating as a pulse on a wrist. Philip brings the toad to the grass and nudges it off his hand with his finger. Caroline loves him for this gesture, feels the roots of herself inching farther into him. Philip says he wishes this part, the traveling part, would never end. He likes the feeling of going somewhere. There would be so much to do when they arrived. They would have to build the houses. Fence. Plant. Caroline says she's excited to start. She quotes Karl: "For the purity of wilderness to flush the soul as water cleans a festering wound." And, of course, she is eager for January 1, 1700, when they will all ascend.

Anyway, for now there is nothing to do but walk. Philip tells Caroline he feels very grateful, feels better than he ever has in his life. She agrees. They are starting afresh—away from the village ministers, from Dedham's elders, from her parents. He says maybe he'll keep bees, that he'll look for a swarm when they get there. Caroline asks if he thinks there are strawberries in the Pioneer Valley. He puts his hand on her neck. "Being with you is like putting down something heavy," he says.

The cart behind them rattles and knocks around with their

own belongings, which are few, and the community-owned items, which are many: nails, cooking pots, axe heads, pounds of lye, lengths of cloth, sewing needles, bags of seeds. Other families have pigs in their carts. Benjamin Lawson walks with two oxen. Some have chickens. The wheels of their carts knock against stones in their path.

Hail comes one day, when they are approaching hills. They stop at a rock overhang, nearly a cave, which shelters them some. The hail cuts loudly through the foliage. Rain follows. Waiting for the storm to pass, they kneel under the overhang. Karl leads a prayer. Water gushes above and below and behind them, sounding as if a hundred water jugs were emptying. When the storm passes, Philip notices the ground steaming in the sun. Water returning to the sky—proof of a soul's journey.

ON THE SIXTH DAY OF walking, Karl holds up his hand and tells the Children of New Eden to halt. They are in a swamp filled with maples, divided by a small stream. Just beyond, a forest of white pines slopes up a hill.

"Pray," he says. He motions for everyone to go on their knees. Philip and Caroline kneel, confused. "The woman fled into the wilderness," Karl preaches from Revelation, arms overhead and palms spread. "Where she has a place prepared by God, to care for her and to nourish her for one thousand two hundred and sixty days." With this, Philip understands: they've arrived. He looks at Caroline. There is no field soft enough for a light plow, as Karl described. No natural orchard. There is no river, only a sandy stream packed with fallen and rotting trees, and too shallow for fish. In his continuing prayer, Karl calls the stream New River Jordan and the hill Mount Saint Francis. The prayer ends, and Karl goes around to each couple, shaking hands and welcoming them home.

This looks like every other mile of forest they've walked through. Philip doesn't feel as he thought he would when they arrived—that the land would appear different, special. He feels nothing, really. How does Karl know this is the right place? He overhears Benjamin Lawson ask where they will be planting. There are no natural fields, Benjamin says. He has five children; it is months after seeding season. Karl sweeps his hand toward the pines, and says, "The field is right there, Benjamin, under the blessed trees that will make our homes, and given to us by the Lord."

Philip looks again at Caroline, who is looking at Benjamin's wife, Eleanor, who is sitting on a fallen log by the stream, nursing her baby and muttering to herself. Philip feels panicked. He walks to a nearby maple, cuts a thin branch, strips away its bark, sharpens one end, and then pushes it into the ground. He comes up with many feet of black soil staining the pale under-bark of the stick. He holds it up to Caroline. "Look," he says to her. It is good soil, just as Karl said. She nods. She walks away, toward Emma, who is playing with one of the children, seemingly very happy and oblivious of the amount of work that must be done to make this swampy and forested land home.

Philip is responsible for bringing the sisters here. He introduced first Caroline, then Emma, to Karl. The oldest daughter of the Thatcher textile family, Caroline had grown up in a comfortable house beside Philip's father's farm. Up until a few months ago, Caroline had been engaged to one of Mr. Thatcher's friends, the shipbuilder and widower Edward Owens.

She and Philip knew each other as children. Her older brother, Tom, and Philip were friendly. She and Philip exchanged pleasantries when they reached maturity, after service or while Philip was in the Thatcher field helping with hay. She had spoken to Philip at his father's, then his mother's, funerals—a week apart, due to a fever. Then, one evening, each alone, they coincidentally met on the road as they left their adjacent houses. Distressed by her upcoming marriage to Edward Owens, Caroline had been going for walks to avoid her mother's questions. Philip was on his way to a night service with Karl—whom Philip had met by chance while searching for an escaped hog in the fields outside town. Caroline was the one who stopped Philip after he nodded hello and nearly strode by. She then found that talking to her brother's quiet friend was one of the happiest moments of her week. He said he was late for a meeting. She looked disappointed. With his heart punching in his chest, he asked if she wanted to join. It was somewhat secret, he said. She turned from her house and told him to lead the way.

She loved the meeting. She loved Karl's expressions and calm and tranquility and certainty. The Bible, Karl explained, was composed of geometry of verse—numbers assigned to words—that could be translated into notes and then melodies that Karl had written down. Layered, the notes created harmonies. The harmonies were transmissions to Heaven. The language of the angels. They ended the service that night as they did all services: harmonizing notes that Karl had assigned each of them to hum.

When Caroline and Philip walked back to their homes, she felt something had turned in her, like a bird sensing winter and orienting itself to leave. For months, she snuck out of her home to meet Philip on the road, and together they walked out of town to see Karl and the Children of New Eden congregation.

When Karl said he was planning a settlement, she told Philip she wouldn't go. She would miss her family too much. Anyway, she was still engaged to Edward Owens. Philip said she would regret not seeing what Karl had promised: after forty-two months in the wilderness, as instructed in Revelation, a path of light that would drop like a drawbridge from the sky. At the other side of that bridge was an archway, beyond which was unimaginable beauty and light, illumination and joy. Warmth. No sickness or death. Songs and music sounding in the sky. Rest like one has never felt. How could you forgo that? Philip asked. Mostly, he was just in love with Caroline by then. He didn't want to leave without her. But he hated Dedham, his empty house, and he would follow Karl whether he could convince her to join or not.

Nobody in Caroline's family had known about Karl Dietzen. She decided to tell only Emma, to ask for advice. She described the services she'd been going to throughout the summer, about the harmonic ceremonies, about Karl's promise of heavenly entrance through angelic transmissions. Emma, who revered her older sister, who had taken every bit of advice Caroline had given her, said she was surprised by Caroline, didn't believe the nonsense, and wondered how Caroline could be fooled by such ridiculousness. So, Caroline invited Emma to join the services one night, to meet Karl, to hear what he said.

What happened to Emma happened to everyone who attended

his or her first service. Karl sat alone with the new members, asked them about their spiritual journey, their struggles, and what they hoped to improve in their relationship to the Lord, what he saw in them that felt special to him. On their walk home, Emma said to Caroline that she felt like she was being heard for the first time in her life, that she felt a holiness while talking to Karl. She'd never had a man of his age and confidence listen and respond to her so clearly, so enthusiastically, so lovingly. It was Emma who later convinced Caroline to go to the settlement in the Pioneer Valley. Also, Emma wanted to come. Philip and Caroline married in a private ceremony that Karl arranged. All of this was kept secret from Mr. and Mrs. Thatcher.

Caroline and Emma left a note for their parents because they knew they would never get permission to leave. The note said that they were resettling, and to please not look for them. Caroline added she was sorry for Edward Owens, and to send her best wishes to him in finding a more suitable spouse.

THEY CLEAR THE LAND. Benjamin's oxen pull out stumps. Fields are set out running perpendicular to the stream, plowed then planted. The men start construction on the Savior in the Wilderness House, where the congregants live until the family houses are built. Due to the zeal of their mission and Karl's direction, all the houses are done before the first snow. Karl's house, per his request, is built up the hill some, half a mile away from the others, so he can think clearly and be closer to the sky. Emma lives with Philip and Caroline.

Finally, they can worship in peace, readying themselves for

January 1, 1700. "A path solid as stone," Karl reminds the congregants in a service at the Savior in the Wilderness House. "Made of light." There would be seven paths in all, descending across the world. Each one created by an angel who has been called through harmonic transmission. The paths would only descend far from civilization, from cities and towns, away from nonbelievers. If any nonbeliever saw the path, it would disappear in an instant, like snow dissolving the moment it touches water. They needed to be as far out in the wilderness as possible for the prophecy to come true. They have morning, midday, evening, and night service to call their angel's attention, to say that they have arrived, and to give their location. "As if we are lighting a signal fire," Karl says.

He leads them on long walks. They stand under trees during a windy day—listening for anything that sounds like a word from the sloughing canopy, trying to put together a sentence. He leads them to a waterfall a morning's walk away, to sit at the edge of the pool and listen. This is how Heaven speaks back. The wind, breath; the trees, voice. Words in the sounds of water hitting stone and splashing into itself. At first, it sounds like nothing, but then, after a long period of silence, Philip does start to hear the rhythm of language, of loose vowels and snapping consonants in the thin waterfall. Karl instructs them to not tell anyone what they hear, but to hold the sentences in their minds and repeat them. He leads them up Mount Saint Francis to the large open crown of granite, to lie flat on the ground for a day of fasting.

They are mostly alone. In their first months, Philip sees men—Pocomtuc men, sometimes just one, more often a small group—standing at the edge of the forest, by the fields, watching. One day, Karl strides across a muddy field, kicking up clods of dirt, waving at the men, throwing open his arms in a way that he might have thought appeared welcoming but, Philip sees, is not. Perhaps Karl wants to talk to the men about the prophecy, or establish some trade. The men step back and hurry away. Later, two French trappers with long beards and dirty faces walk into the settlement. Karl allows them to stay for two nights, and somehow convinces them to leave three beaver pelts, which Emma volunteers to sew to a high-backed chair where Karl sits when he needs rest while speaking during his longer services—which can sometimes last hours. One of the fur trappers, Olivier, returns a week later, asking to stay. He is married to Benjamin Lawson's oldest daughter within weeks.

The following spring, when Philip finds an arrowpoint while plowing, he realizes that he hasn't seen any Pocomtuc men in many months. When he mentions this to Karl, Karl says that God has granted calm and isolation to their beloved community.

BY WINTER, EMMA is engaged to Karl, which surprises nobody and excites everyone. The ceremony, designed by Karl, is in the Savior in the Wilderness House. Emma stands alone at the altar, with a garland of evergreen. Karl crawls down the aisle toward her, worshipfully, praying loudly as he moves. With his gray hair sweeping the floor and his beard obscuring his downturned face, Karl nearly looks bestial, Philip thinks. When he finally reaches her, he puts his forehead on her feet. Emma touches Karl's head, inviting him to stand. With that, Karl announces that they are wedded. Emma smiles widely through the ceremony.

Caroline squeezes Philip's hand. Everything is going well. The next day, Emma moves into Karl's house up the hill. At first, Caroline is sad to not have Emma around the house. Philip comforts her, saying she will see Emma many times a day at the services.

A few days after Emma moves out, Caroline says, "I love my sister, but it is nice to have quiet in the house, isn't it?" Philip suddenly becomes more open in his affection, now that Emma's gone. In the kitchen, he touches Caroline's hip as he walks behind her. He kisses her before leaving to repair fences. One morning, he puts a sprig of forsythia on the kitchen table, which Caroline presses in her Bible. She finds herself on more than one occasion standing at the kitchen window, staring at Philip split wood, at his back flexing and turning as he swings his axe. She notices his forearms as he carries a stack of logs into the house and drops them in the woodbox. He slaps his hands together and brushes the splinters off the front of his shirt. She catches him watching her as she uses the hem of her apron to lift a pot onto a chimney crane. She wakes in the night to the feel of his hand on her head, and opens her eyes to see him, in the moonlight, staring. Since arriving they've been having sex most nights, because they are hoping for a child, but with Emma gone, it's sometimes more often. It might only take their knees touching under the breakfast table for them to reach out and hold hands, or for Caroline's hand to go up Philip's arm, and then they will fold their napkins and go back to the bedroom, close the wooden blinds, and undress each other. Without saying it, they are both sure that what they've been doing since the first days of marriage is unique—the way their bodies cross, press, lift, overturn, move into unlearned arrangements. They are certain they are remaking copulation, for divine and unknowable reasons, doing what's communicated from elsewhere. A hooked leg; a gripped hand; an unforeseen and easy urge of the mouth. During the day, they both feel shocking dissonance: they cannot talk about the most substantial occupation of their lives. Sitting at a spinning wheel, Caroline's foot keeps slowing on the treadle as she becomes distracted by the night before. Yoking up Benjamin Lawson's oxen one day, Philip is halted by a passing thought of earlier that morning. They know one thing for certain: that this daily ecstasy is because they are out here, at the edge of the frontier and away from their childhoods and parents, living in their own home, still young enough—Caroline turned nineteen just after Emma left, and Philip's twentieth birthday is later that summer—to feel grateful for the fullness of a free life. Lying in bed, Philip presses his face into Caroline's neck and kisses her collarbone. Caroline pushes Philip's arm above his head and puts her face to his armpit. She kisses his eyebrows. When Caroline's nose brushes his stomach, Philip calls out God's name, then asks forgiveness while touching her hair. When she wakes one morning to Philip's hand on her cheek, she turns her head and puts his thumb in her mouth without really thinking. He holds her hands and stretches her arms out. She lies on his back, aligning her legs with his, resting her ear between his shoulder blades and listening to his breathing. When Emma was here, they had to be quiet. Now, they aren't. What happens on their bed becomes the most anticipated part of Philip's day—or, more, the meaning of his day. Seeding the fields, watering the horses, sawing wood, and carrying buckets are all hours to be filled and passed as rapidly as possible, stopping points on the way to the stretch of night after dinner.

Even so, months after Emma moves out, Caroline is still not pregnant. They would like a child to join them on their ascent. There's time still, Philip says to Caroline.

Caroline does miss Emma sometimes. Especially during the day, when Philip is out in the fields. The chatter they shared while kneading bread and washing made the hours pass. When a period of days comes when Emma is not at service, Caroline asks Karl about her.

"Sadly, she is ill," he says kindly. "A fever. I am praying for her."

"Praying for her?" Caroline says, alarmed. "Is she very ill? I should go visit."

"Not to be concerned. She is fine. Tired. Exhausted, I think. I'm afraid she depended on you too much. She is not used to keeping a household, a husband. Let us pray she recovers her energy."

"I could bring her broth. Is the fever high?"

Karl takes Caroline's hand, tells her how kind she is, but that the best thing for Emma would be to rest, undisturbed.

MR. THATCHER ARRIVES. It's a warm July day, half a year after Emma's wedding. Philip is in the fields. John Heatherton sees Mr. Thatcher first and leads him to the Savior in the Wilderness House, asks him to wait there while he finds Karl.

After a long wait, Mr. Thatcher sees an emaciated man in a dirty gown and black bear–fur vest walking toward him. His head is slightly bowed, showing a small bald patch. His long hair has perhaps been greased purposefully, the way it presses flat to his face. His wispy beard is so long that it has a single wavelike look. He has concave cheeks and deep, nearly circular eye sockets.

Karl bows to Mr. Thatcher.

"Good morning," he says, and smiles. His teeth are rotted and discolored beyond a usual degree. "I am Karl Dietzen. And you are?"

"Emma and Caroline Thatcher are my daughters. Where are they?"

"The father!" Karl says. "I have been blessed to marry Emma." He compliments Mr. Thatcher on raising such a vibrant, beautiful young woman. He is sorry to say that Emma is occupied, though, with meditation prayer, and so will be unable to see him.

"In fact, I will be seeing her," Mr. Thatcher says. He is a tall, sturdy man with a strong voice. In his youth, he was trim and muscular from work, but has recently gotten heavier. He is accustomed to unquestioned authority, to requests being met.

"Where is she?" he asks.

"Prayer, as I said."

"You're forbidding me to see my daughter?"

"That's not what I said," Karl responds, still smiling. "She's unable to see you now."

"For how long?"

"Until evening."

Mr. Thatcher responds by asking to see Philip. Having been successful in his business, he has encountered enough obstinate men in positions of minor power to know that arguing will not help, for now.

Karl points to what Mr. Thatcher sees as a poorly built shack. "Likely in their house."

After startling Caroline when she opens the door to his pounding knocks, after the shock of his presence had come and gone, after his assurances that he only came to talk, Mr. Thatcher now sits at their table. It has been over a year since Philip and Caroline left Dedham. To Caroline's question of how her father found them, he says, "Allen." Allen Wellstone is Mr. Thatcher's lawyer but does many other things for him, including collecting debts, managing correspondence, finding new business ventures, shutting down competing businesses. Caroline was terrified of Allen when she was a girl—this silent man following her father around, coming and going from the house without knocking, suddenly appearing in rooms like a specter, his eyes always catching hers when she was staring.

Philip has never seen Caroline so reserved, so quiet and scared as she is now, sitting across from her father.

"Allen was here?" Caroline says.

"No," Mr. Thatcher says. "But he discovered you and Emma are here. Actually, he might have come once, to confirm you were here. At any rate, he would not have made his visit known. You wouldn't have seen him."

Mr. Thatcher says he is here to explain some things to Caroline. First, he says, she and her sister have disgraced the family. Second, Mrs. Thatcher has become ill from the grief Caroline has caused; she never leaves her bed, and he fears for her life. Third, there is a choice: Emma and Caroline can either come home, now, with him, or they can stay. If they stay, he will tell Mrs. Thatcher that he's confirmed Emma and Caroline are both dead. "Your marriages here are illegitimate," he says. "So, that will not be a problem. You can start again, back home. And Philip," Mr. Thatcher says without looking at him. "You are never to return to Dedham, on penalty of arrest."

"We are staying," Caroline says, without hesitation. "This is our home."

Mr. Thatcher changes his approach. He begins by outlining what he doesn't like about this community, starting with the filth he saw. "You cannot raise a child here," he says. "And what if you do have children? You would deprive your mother and I of knowing our grandchildren?" He leans forward, brings his hands around Caroline's. "Caro," he says. "Please. I can't help but see you as my child, my young daughter who is making a grave mistake. You are hurting me and your mother and brother. Do you remember how you used to be so scared of the night that you'd come to our bedroom, crawl over me to sleep between me and your mother? Do you remember how you used to make your mother set a plate at the dinner table for your doll, how we had to talk to your doll or else you would have a fit? You are still my sweet, sensitive daughter. And now, here you are, leaving me and your mother for—what? To be a part of some horrible experiment?"

Caroline thanks her father for his opinion. "But, we are staying here. This is my family now."

He lets go of her hand, leans back in his seat.

"You are living mindlessly," he says. "In sin."

Caroline takes a deep breath. "Please leave."

"Eating from the hand of a fraudulent heretic." Mr. Thatcher says their souls are bound for the fires of Hell, but he will pray for them.

"And we will pray for you," Philip says to him, speaking for the first time.

Mr. Thatcher looks down at his feet, rubs at a smear of dried mud from the top of one boot with the sole of the other boot. Finally, he says, "Where is Emma?"

"Praying, likely. Or at Karl Dietzen's house."

"Yes. That disgusting old man told me as much. But, still, I'd like to see her. Can you take me?"

"I cannot. I'm not allowed to see her now." Caroline regrets saying this the moment she sees her father's face.

"Not allowed to see her? Why?"

"It's forbidden. That's all."

"Forbidden? Caroline." Mr. Thatcher leans forward again, and with that, his head crosses into a path of sunlight that illuminates his eyes. Philip is struck by the brilliance of the blue in Mr. Thatcher's irises. Cornflower blue. "Caroline," he repeats, leaning back once more, out of the sunlight. "Your sister is young and easily influenced. She was a child just some years ago. I thought, at least, you would protect her. You haven't seen her?"

"Of course I have," Caroline says. She clasps her hands. "But." She pauses, looks out the window. "But not in some weeks."

"Some weeks?"

Philip watches her cheeks flush. He cuts in, sensing that Caroline is flustered. "I don't think you quite understand, Mr. Thatcher," he says. "There is a schedule here. Rules. Emma and Caroline are on different prayer schedules, and Emma has been sick."

"Enough." Mr. Thatcher holds up his hand to Philip's face. "Enough. Tell me now, Caroline. Will you and Emma return with me?"

Caroline shakes her head, then stares at the ground.

Mr. Thatcher stands. He grips the back of his chair, closes his eyes, and shakes his head slowly.

"Before I go." He pauses. "Before I go, I want to tell you another thing. Because I cannot force you to leave. Because I can see your concern for your reputation or your mother or brother won't convince you. There is another thing that Allen discovered. He has a skill, you know—a sort of love for accounting I never had. He requested from the General Court the filing for the land that Dietzen purchased. I assume that's why you sold your father's farm, Philip, and gave the money to Dietzen? Yes, well. Can you guess what Allen found?"

Philip and Caroline don't answer.

"No filing. No land grant. And because Allen is such a clever man, he imagined there must be a mistake, and looked for taxes to the Colony. There are—can you guess? No taxes were submitted to the General Court for anything west of the Connecticut River within the year. I don't know what Dietzen did with all the money you and the others gave him, Philip, but he never went to a seller or the Courts. So, as a matter of course, just so you are aware, you are settled illegally, and, for all intents and purposes, he has stolen your money."

"It matters little," Caroline says, before Philip can answer. "We won't be here long, anyway."

"I see," Mr. Thatcher says. Though, of course, he doesn't see, because in his anger, in his mission to convince Caroline to return with him, he hasn't yet asked about Karl's teachings, doesn't know what they are all waiting for, how they will all leave this world soon enough, together.

"Tell Emma I miss her," he says. "Tell her that she can come home whenever she'd like." Mr. Thatcher nods, turns to leave, but stops. "And one more point."

Philip wants Mr. Thatcher to stop. He feels a burning in his stomach. It would do no good to ask Karl about the money he gave him for the land.

"I passed an old man, a Praying Indian living with his wife near the Connecticut River. When I asked him for directions here, when I explained what I was looking for, his face looked like it lost its blood. He said he knew what I was talking about, but that the Devil is here, and I should stay away. Evil, he said. It seems that everyone knows you are in the fires of Hell, deceived, except yourselves."

Mr. Thatcher walks out without waiting for Philip or Caroline to respond. From the doorway, they watch him mount his horse.

"Is he right?" Caroline asks.

"About what?"

"Emma?"

"I think Emma is fine. She is in good hands." Philip says this to comfort her, even though he really has been concerned about Emma's long absence.

Mr. Thatcher and his horse disappear through a dark space of forest.

Philip suggests they do the couples' song—Karl's advice for practicing acceptance and calm. Caroline begins, facing Philip, closing her eyes, opens her mouth, hums a note. Philip joins, humming another note to harmonize. When she pauses to take a breath, he keeps going, and when he pauses, she keeps going. Their faces are almost touching, and they hear a third, fuller, buzzing sound that is not his voice or her voice, but a combination, which makes their faces and throats vibrate. The third sound is like a bolt going into a lock. It's further proof that what appears bodiless and without material is instead physical—including sunlight and their souls. Including, as Karl points out, love. Caroline, still humming, smiles when she feels the third voice in her neck.

That night they lie side by side, without touching. Caroline cries, and Philip puts his arm around her. Philip hates Mr. Thatcher for so quickly shattering their life, the space that they found away from Dedham. And then he wonders why or how it was so easy for their life to feel shattered. The next morning, Caroline is distant.

Days after Mr. Thatcher left, Emma finally returned to regular services at the Savior in the Wilderness House. She had been sick, she said to Caroline, who hugged her and said she missed her. Very sick, Emma said, but didn't offer any details when Caroline asked for them. Caroline told her that their father had been here. Emma appeared excited, asking where he was. When Caroline told her that he'd already left, days earlier, Emma looked shocked. She shook her head. "He's already gone? Why didn't you tell me he was here?"

"You were in solitary prayer. Karl instructed me to not disturb you. Didn't Karl tell you he was here? He met with Father."

"No," Emma said. "He didn't."

"I thought he would have," Caroline said. "I'm sorry."

"He didn't wait to see me?"

"We had a disagreement. He was disagreeable. It's probably better you didn't see him," Caroline said.

Their conversation was stopped by Karl, up at the altar, who called, "Welcome!"

MONTHS LATER, walking together by a stream in early autumn, Caroline notices that Emma looks weak. She's always been the smaller, slighter of the sisters, but she now appears ill. Her cheeks are sunken. Her eyes puffy and red. Her forearms and wrists are bony. Her hair is not neatly done as it usually is. She walks with languid, shuffling steps. After finding a way across the stream, they enter the reddish light of the sugar maple forest.

"What's wrong?" Caroline asks.

"Nothing." She flashes a quick smile at Caroline.

"Emma."

"I suppose I miss living with you and Philip. I find marriage difficult."

"I thought as much. Maybe I can help. I have more experience, if not much."

Emma pauses. Looks up at the vibrant foliage. "Karl is specific," she says. "About his meals. He doesn't wash, and I find it hard to be in the same room as him sometimes. There is a stench."

"Why don't you tell him to clean?"

"And if I leave anything out of place," Emma continues, "he becomes angry. Cruel. I was making dinner the other day and left for a moment to retrieve water, and when I came back, he had thrown everything I had on the counter out the door. All the bowls and kitchenware. As if he'd thrown them as far as he could."

"Emma," Caroline says.

"But if I try to order things, if I move his shoes or fold his shirt, he will be in a rage. And I won't tell you what he did the other day. I can barely think of it."

"What?"

"It seems improper to say."

"Tell me."

Emma picks up a maple leaf bright as blood, twists it in her fingers, tearing pieces off and letting them fall to the ground.

"He relieved himself in the bedroom, and told me to clean it up."

"Emma." Caroline touches her sister's elbow.

"At night, before coming into bed. I watched him do it. On the floor by the bed. I was too shocked to say anything. I pretended to be asleep."

They walk in silence for some time. Caroline doesn't know what to say because she knows there's nothing to do. Emma is Karl's wife, and she must stay in his house.

"Does he hurt you?" Caroline asks.

"He is cold. Sometimes he doesn't speak to me for days. I will ask him a question, and he will pretend he hasn't heard me. Maybe I am being too fragile. He is busy with transmissions; I am baking bread."

"Only for this life," Caroline says.

"Only for this life," Emma repeats.

Caroline thinks. "Let's go for walks. Daily walks. Tell Karl that the fresh air is good for your health."

Emma doesn't respond. She shuffles through a pile of fallen leaves.

"I shouldn't have told you this," Emma says. "Please, don't tell

Philip. I shouldn't have told you. Please don't worry about me. I'm fine. Karl and I are growing together. Forget what I said."

As fall passes to winter, then spring, summer, and finally fall again, more rigorous worship comes. Caroline is still not pregnant, but they are happy—if not as happy as when they first left Dedham, or during the months when Emma first moved out.

Karl has introduced fasting days and midnight prayers, in which they gather at the Savior in the Wilderness House to listen to him reiterate exactly how he's calculated the signs from the Bible, how he looks forward to seeing them all past the gates of eternity, lifted from the cold ground of Earth to the warmth above. During one service, Karl encourages the children to ask questions. When Eben Stoughton's young son, John, asks how his baby sister, who cannot yet walk, will climb up the sunlit ramp, Karl smiles and laughs and says what a dear boy. The congregants smile at Karl's tenderness. Karl says to John, kindly, that if a visitor to this earth, from another earth, were to arrive in the summer and see a pond, that visitor would have one thought about water. But if that same visitor arrived in winter and saw that same pond, he would see water as another way, and could walk right across it. The bridge of sunlight is the same. The air will thicken the way water thickens in winter—but, instead of cold binding water, it is prayer that binds light. John says too loudly to his father that Karl still didn't answer how Rose would climb the ramp. Eben says to John that he assumes mother will be holding Rose.

Not sleeping is a sacrifice for their futures. Karl also asked everyone to unload their earthly impulses and needs, which will only hold them to the ground like anchors keeping ships in place. Unburdening will make them lighter, he says, as cargo thrown off the ship. Karl will guide them in this process. Relationships between people weigh differently depending on the depth of bond. Spousal relationships are the heaviest. So, husbands and wives should practice celibacy. There are other mortal burdens to shed: jealousy, pride. Karl asks everyone to privately meet with him, so he can remind them of their shortcomings, strip them of pride and the cumbersome self that will keep them weighed down.

At one service, Caroline, standing beside Emma, notices that Emma appears flush, breathes in a shallow, irregular way. She keeps touching her right wrist with her left hand, and twisting her wrist as if it were in pain. Because Karl has already begun service, Caroline leans to Emma's shoulder, whispers quietly to ask if she's feeling ill. Emma shakes her head but doesn't look at Caroline, puts her finger on her lips to indicate Caroline be quiet. "Your hands," Caroline continues, nodding to the way Emma is trembling. Emma puts her hands at her sides, and pinches the cloth of her dress as if to keep her hands from shaking.

After service, Karl asks Caroline to please not stand beside Emma anymore. "It seems you distract her. And she you." He hopes Caroline will understand—we all must concentrate. "Perhaps," he says, "you are too much in your past lives, as sisters? You seem to have a complicated, burdensome bond."

She tells Philip what Karl said.

"It's nonsense," she says at dinner.

"Everyone heard you whispering to her. It was a disruption."

"Yes, but barring us from seeing each other is too formal a punishment. And that's the word. Isn't it? Punishment. We barely see her anyway, as it is."

"What would you like me to do?"

"Nothing. I'm not asking anything of you. All I want is for you to acknowledge that it's strange."

Philip nods. "I suppose it is harsh."

"I will talk with Karl," Caroline says. "Apologize for the interruption."

Because Emma leaves The Savior in the Wilderness House directly after service, straight for her and Karl's house up the hill, Caroline experiences a string of days in which she doesn't talk to her sister. She calls out to Emma one night, after midnight prayer. Emma is striding away, into the darkness. Caroline watches the light of Emma's lantern receding, without stopping, disappearing into the forest where the path to Karl's house begins.

In her house that late fall, Caroline builds, tends, and cooks over the fire. She pickles vegetables, spins yarn, washes clothes, repairs clothes, and helps stitch the special gowns they'll wear for ascending. She is tired from overworking and the new prayer schedule. There is food, but not quite enough to feel very full after dinner. More, Karl has forbidden slaughtering animals. People are the caretakers of animals, not murderers, he states one night. There will be no meat.

Sometimes, before evening service, she pretends to have forgotten something from her pantry. She'll raise a finger and say to

Philip, "I'll be right back." She'll go into the pantry, with her pots and kettles and barrels of flour and jars of honey around her, shut the door, and lean against it. She finds herself doing that more often—standing alone in the pantry, hoping to calm her mind.

It's during one of those times in the pantry, when Philip is out in the fields, that she notices a shoe by the flour cask. She steps forward, sees a pair of legs. She kneels, and then goes down on her hands and knees. It's Emma. She has wedged herself between the shelving and the casks.

"What are you doing here?" Caroline asks.

Emma looks up, slowly, as if it takes much energy to move her head.

"Please," Emma says. She draws in her legs, hugs her shins.

She rests her forehead on her knees. Caroline gathers her skirt and sits on the floor beside her. Emma says she wants to go home, back to Dedham. She misses their mother and father. Caroline says she misses their mother, too, but they can't go back. She notices that Emma's fingernails are split, and the skin around them red and scabbed. Her right wrist, the one she'd been rubbing weeks earlier at the service, is red and bruised. Emma says again that she wants to go home.

"Yes," Caroline says. "I know."

Caroline puts her arm around her little sister. Emma's head drops, onto Caroline's chest. When Emma leans against Caroline, Caroline feels almost no weight, feels her sister's bony shoulder digging into her rib. She kisses Emma's head, rests her nose in her hair, which smells like pond water and onions. Emma presses herself against Caroline. They fall asleep in the pantry.

Philip finds Caroline and Emma asleep against the flour casks, Emma's arm draped across Caroline's stomach.

"What's this?" he says, waking them.

Emma gets to her feet, apologizes, and says she'll leave.

"You don't have to leave," Philip says. "I wasn't expecting you. But, aren't you and Caroline supposed to be separated?"

Caroline reaches out and holds Emma's arm, and then stands beside her. "Stay with us for a while. You're ill."

"Does Karl know you're here?" Philip asks.

"No," Emma says.

"Oh," Philip says. "Well, maybe you should go back. He wouldn't like you being here, would he?"

"You'll stay with us for some time," Carline says. "Come. We'll tell Karl you're here."

"I shouldn't have fallen asleep," Emma says. "Is it late?" She shakes her head. "Oh no," she says. "No, no, no."

Caroline takes Emma's hand, and asks her to help cook dinner. "And then you can go, if you want," she says.

They walk past Philip, out of the pantry, and toward the kitchen table.

"Karl should know," Philip says, standing in the doorway. "But, why are you here?"

"Philip," Caroline says. "Let's just let Emma be."

Caroline is cutting a squash. She divides it with a long knife, scoops out the seeds, and slops them into a pile. Emma stands beside her, staring but not helping.

"He isn't a noble husband," Emma says. "He doesn't mean well."

"Doesn't mean well?" Philip says. "How?"

"Philip," Caroline says, "please build the fire for us."

"I'm allowed to ask why your sister is in our house, against Karl's wishes, without him knowing."

"Lots of things," Emma says. "He is not good for many reasons."

"As in?"

"Philip!" Caroline says. "Enough."

Emma sits, rubs her palms on her knees, and rocks back and forth.

"He says he can't think with me in the house," Emma says. "He doesn't let me sleep inside—that it would interrupt his dream transmissions, he says."

"Where do you sleep?" Caroline asks, holding another squash upright, her knife resting on its cut stem.

"The shed for cut wood," Emma says.

"The shed?"

"He said he had a dream that I ran away," Emma says. "He locks me in there at night."

"Locks you in?" Caroline says.

"No," Philip says. "It is too cold. You are exaggerating."

Caroline slams down her knife and lets the squash roll to its side.

She says to Philip, "It seems Emma is unwell. Please tell Karl that she'll be staying with us until she's better. Indefinitely."

"I can't do that," Philip says.

"Tell him," Caroline says. "Or I will go and tell him myself."

"Emma," Philip says. "Come with me to your house. Let's talk to Karl together."

Emma keeps rubbing her hands together, in her lap, rocking.

Philip finds himself alone, lantern in hand, walking up the hill and between the pines. He's never been to Karl and Emma's house. He can only see as far as the edge of his lantern's light. Off to his side is an orange smudge of sunset low in the trees.

The house is dark. He knocks on the door. He doesn't hear anything. He calls Karl's name. He walks around the house. Perhaps Karl is in the back, splitting wood. He sees the shed. There, oddly, is a door. And then he sees a padlock, open and hanging from the door's latch. He walks up to the latch, touches the cold metal. He extends his arm through the doorway, holding the lantern into the shed. There is a white blanket on the dirt floor, twisted and pushed up against the far wall, by stacks of split wood. He dips his head and walks into the shed. Under the blanket, he sees a chain and open manacle.

"Yes?" he hears Karl call from around front.

Philip hurries out of the shed, and walks around the side of the house.

Karl stands at the doorway. He moves the hair from his face and rubs his eye, as if he's just woken.

"Philip," Karl says. "A surprise."

"I'm sorry to bother."

Karl yawns and asks Philip what he's come for.

"Emma. She's at our house. She wanted you to know that she'd like to stay with us for a night, or perhaps more."

"Oh no," he says. "That won't do, Philip. You know. She must come back here. Now. But thank you for telling me. Should I go down to retrieve her, or you?"

"Yes, well," Philip says. "But she's insistent on staying. And my wife, too. She didn't want you to worry where she was."

"She needs to come back," Karl says. "This is her home. And this is not the first rule Emma has broken. I'm not sure you're aware, but your sister-in-law is not the ideal disciple. She's somewhat immature—not her fault. She seems to think we're playing a game at this. I'm worried for her."

"Yes, I understand. I'm only telling you what I've been sent for."

"Did your wife invite her in?"

"She just arrived, I suppose. Caroline found her in the house."

"But why?"

"Emma seems to think there were—discomforts. Here. I'm only relaying messages. Something of a sleeping arrangement."

Karl smooths his long beard. He shakes his head.

"Come in, Philip," he says. He opens the door wider, and then steps into the dark.

It is very cold in the house. A putrid smell surprises him. A small ember in the fireplace, no bigger than a coin, shows a fire that went out long ago. Karl asks Philip to sit with him, and arranges two chairs in the center of the room. Philip places his lantern on the floor.

"Shall I build a fire?" Philip asks.

"Of all human flaws," Karl begins, ignoring Philip's offer, "lying is perhaps the most repugnant. Perhaps because the fabric of a community is woven in trust. I cannot eat unless I trust that you will not steal the crops from my field. Trust is what we have.

It is all we have. You trusted me to bring you here, to this new Eden. Trust brings meaning to our lives. What is disturbing about Emma is that she has no regard for trust, for truth. She lies, often and without remorse. Whatever she has said, I assure you it is false. Now, this new mess of her and Caroline. One of the principles of this prayer cycle is to reduce the weight of human relations. Dramas. Pathos. To lighten our loads, as it were. Emma and your wife have a complicated relationship that binds them to a nearly animal instinct. Emma is exactly like a young animal, in fact, distrusting of the higher calling in rational thought. She wants comfort like a wolf pup to a mother. She requires too much. She is still a girl in many ways. She needs lessons. As we have laws and consequences, Philip. Lessons."

Karl's chair creaks under his weight as he leans back.

"So," Karl says. "Go to Emma. Tell her to come back to her husband. The family, husband and wife, is the most important structure. If there is discord within our community here on Earth, it risks the clarity of our calling to those above. For the sake of everyone's destinies, Emma should return, to live in harmony with her husband. Go, and tell them. You are the head of your house. Not Caroline."

Philip nods, but he is thinking of the dirty blanket in the shed. The chain and open manacle. The padlock. Emma was not lying.

Karl holds out his hands, palms up.

"Now," he says. "Before you go to her, pray with me."

Philip obeys, resting his hands in Karl's. Karl pulls him forward, so Philip is sitting uncomfortably on the edge of his chair. He nearly kicks over the lantern as he adjusts his footing.

Karl hums. Philip closes his eyes. He concentrates on the voice as practiced; and with that, he begins to feel calmer. All this difficulty with Emma and Karl and Caroline is material difficulty. Earthly problems that will be reduced to nothing in the light of eternity, just as clouds transcend water and are carried distantly. Karl once described what awaited them on the other side of the bridge of light not "as a place, but as a feeling." He asked his congregants to think of their most euphoric moments, and then to imagine those moments expanded by millions upon millions of degrees. "The beauty that you'll feel, the purity, it is too immense to describe," Karl said. Philip wants to experience what Karl has foreseen. The discord he anticipates with Caroline when he returns to the house to tell her that Emma won't stay—and the discomfort he feels in thinking of the blanket on the ground of the shed—are only pebbles on the mountain one climbs for a view of the divine. Even if Emma were cold or in a little pain, she will forget it all after she ascends. The frigid mortal nights will be blanketed in the warmth of eternal love.

And so, Philip knows that he will, after this prayer and with as much certainty and duty as he just placed his hands upon Karl's, thank Karl, walk back down the hill, between the pines, to his house, tell Emma to return to her home, and that if she refuses or Caroline tries to bar him, he will carry Emma out, if needed, all the way back up the hill. Even the thorn of this decision that has now pricked his conscience, this droplet of blood it produces in his mind, dissolves into the much larger living body of their mission, into imagining the moment when they will all stand atop Mount Saint Francis on that winter night, holding hands, and see a bridge of light cut through the night sky and descend to offer them entrance. This life—with its comforts, its cooling wind, birdsong, its purplish frost on fallen maple leaves, its fire-warmed clothes, the sound of Caroline humming to herself in another room, her hand on his back, Caroline's neck, moments lying in bed after hours of plowing, Caroline's foot moving up his calf—will be faint lights compared to what awaits them.

Philip joins the prayer, harmonizing with Karl, together transmitting from the cold, dark room.

Introduction to *The Dietzens: Searching for Eternity in the North American Wilderness*

Many texts on the Colonial New England frontier describe the daily physical and mental struggles of European settlers that would later define American attitudes of independence and enterprise, but few illustrate how, at times, anti-American, experimental, and plainly bizarre the fringes of the frontier could be. One of the leading examples is the Dietzen Community. At the very center of that thinking is the Dietzen Bible. The horror that eventually befell the Dietzens is, additionally, an indication of how limited frontier settlements were in escaping Europe—its wars, politics, human rights abuses, and capitalist aims—despite their best attempts.

I still remember the first time I saw the Dietzen Bible. It was in the spring of 1989, when I was eleven. My parents and I had driven from New Haven to Deerfield Academy to pick up my sister, Mary, who was a senior—of the first class that included girls—at the boarding school in that historic town. Thirty-one years later, with Mary's permission, I can describe the circumstances of our visit: Mary was pregnant, though I didn't know it at the time. The night before we left to retrieve her, my mother told to me to pack an overnight bag, and that Mary was sick. I was excited to skip school for a few days. I packed my toothbrush, pajamas, and my drawing book.

The highway to Deerfield followed the Connecticut River, partly the same route that Pioneer Valley settlers walked in 1670 to claim the eight-thousand-acre land grant given by the Massachusetts General Court, a section of which became the town of Deerfield. Our car followed the muddy river up the valley. It was dusk when we arrived on Deerfield's Main Street, which is still lined with much of the original architecture—boxy clapboard sections street-side, shanty kitchens garden-side, slack rooflines, handblown windows, neat stone foundations. Limbs of hemlock, oak, and buttonball arced over the street. My father parked under a tree with leaves the size of printer paper.

"Wait here," he said. He and my mother disappeared into a colonnaded brick building. I left the back seat of the car only once, to snatch one of the buttonball leaves, which I put in my notebook and still have, pressed and framed above my writing desk. Looking at it now, it hasn't lost much of its green of that day.

From a distance, Mary, walking out of the building with our parents behind her, looked herself—shoulders back in her constant pose of athleticism. Her copper-blond hair, cropped short and tucked behind her ears, was darker than I remembered it when

I'd last seen her at Christmas. I leapt out of the car to meet her, and she leaned down to hug me. Because of our seven-year age gap, we had a wonderful relationship. We never fought because we had nothing to share. She became a second mother to me when our mother withstood personal difficulties for some years while I was in elementary school. I cried every night for a week when Mary went away to boarding school, and I blamed my parents for sending her. I later discovered it was Mary's idea to go, and that our grandmother paid for it. In retrospect, it wasn't surprising Mary wanted to leave home. I know her relationship with our parents had once been sweet, as a child, but for reasons that plague many families, her transition into adolescence soured their bond, especially with our father. From an early age, I remember my father's voice booming from downstairs, scolding Mary for any number of small transgressions.

We drove to a nearby restaurant for an early dinner, during which there was little conversation. We'd leave for New Haven early the next morning, my father said. He'd gotten us rooms at a motel down the road. Mary and I would be in one room, and my parents in another. I was thrilled.

Later that night I woke to Mary standing over her bed, clothed, her suitcase open, packing.

"What are you doing?" I asked.

"Go to sleep," she said.

"Are you leaving?"

She said if I told my parents that I'd seen her, she'd never forgive me—at least that's how I remember her saying it. She said she loved me, and then walked out the door.

I dressed, snuck out of the motel room, and found her waiting in the parking lot. She was not happy to see me.

"I want to come with you," I said. The thought of her disappearing again, like she had for boarding school, was too painful. I was bored back at home in Connecticut, having dinner alone with my parents as they drilled me with questions about my school day.

"You're not coming," she said. She kept looking at her watch.

Headlights flashed on us. A pickup truck drove through the parking lot and stopped where we were standing. The driver's door opened, and a young man came toward her. He was about her age, I thought. He looked at me, then at Mary, then at me.

"My brother," she said. "He's going back inside."

The young man smiled, put out his hand for me to shake, like an adult.

"Pleasure to meet you," he said. "I'm Jim." This was Mary's boyfriend and future husband. I'd later find out that Jim lived one town over, in Conway, and was a docent at the nearby Memorial Hall Museum, where they'd met when Mary's class had gone there on a field trip.

"Ready?" Jim said. He lifted her suitcase into the pickup. I felt, then, the gravity of what was happening. They were running away.

"Where are you going?" I asked.

"I'll write you."

She shut the door of the truck, and through the window I saw her put her hands on her face. I stood there, by her window, watching, waiting for them to leave. Mary was shaking her head. Jim was talking. Then she rolled down her window.

"Do you want to come with us for a little while?" she said. "Just an hour, and then we have to bring you back." She opened the door, moved to the middle, and I climbed in. The truck smelled of cigarettes and leather, and the seat was covered in white dog fur. My heart pounded as we drove away from the motel. Jim asked what she wanted to do.

"He likes history," she said. She was right. My room was covered in posters of the Greeks and the pyramids, and whenever somebody asked me what I wanted to be when I grew up, I said an archaeologist.

"You could give him a tour of the museum?" Mary said.

The Memorial Hall Museum was about a half an hour away from the motel. I guess they were in no rush to leave, but I don't really know if they had a clear plan that night. It turned out they didn't need to worry about making a fast escape: the following morning, when I watched my father talking to the police in the motel lobby, an officer told him they couldn't force an eighteen-year-old to return home. My parents responded to Mary's departure the following months by talking about her in the past tense, as if she had died. My father eventually told me I wasn't allowed to talk about her at all, even mention her name in the house, because it upset my mother too much.

The grass in front of the museum was wet and soaked my shoes. Jim opened the back door, and the three of us slipped in. He said he couldn't turn on the lights, because someone might notice. He found a flashlight in the office, and we walked upstairs to the exhibits. His beam swept across glass cases filled with antique farming equipment, blankets, guns, kitchenware, and tinware. He showed me Deerfield's famous Sheldon House door—in the middle of the room, held up by overhead wires so visitors could walk around it. The door was splintered and studded with time-worn nails. The wood, like all old wood left to swell and shrink with the seasons' moisture, looked oily, and there were cavities where wood beetles had been. In the center of the door was the gash where an axe had struck on a cold night in 1704.

We moved on to a room filled with lanterns, rushlight holders, candleholders, and stoves until we reached a small desk topped with a glass display case.

"This," Jim said, "is my favorite artifact. It's from a house just south of the Vermont border." He unlatched the top of the display case, opened it, and lifted out a book. "Most people who visit the museum don't even stop to look. It's over three hundred years old." He opened the book. He motioned me to come closer. "The Bible of Karl Dietzen."

And so, this was my introduction to the Dietzens, which would become the seed for this book. Jim held his flashlight over the opened Bible, to the marginalia written by the eponymous leader and German émigré Karl Dietzen. Those notes, I'd later read, promoted fasting, vegetarianism, periods of celibacy, and a range of occult rituals both euphoric and, to a modern reader, wildly anachronistic. One of the more fascinating elements of Dietzen's teachings was his musical theory proposition, which I describe further in Chapter Two. What primarily defined and drove this community was a bedrock belief in a Second Coming of sorts in the North American wilderness, which Dietzen had figured would arrive on January 1, 1700. Sadly, none of them saw the day they'd all been waiting for. What happened to this peaceful, music-loving fringe group on the edge of the frontier illustrates, as I've mentioned, how entangled Colonial North America was with Europe. As Jim told me that night, "They were all killed. A massacre. Women, children, everyone."

I remember Mary telling Jim that he should maybe stop there, that I was just a kid. He agreed. A more complete picture of the Dietzen Massacre came to me later, which I'll give here in brief, before exploring it fully in Chapter One. On an early winter night in 1699, on the orders of the distant French commander Jean-Baptiste Hertel de Rouville, thirty-eight Frenchmen (some soldiers, some fur trappers acting as guides from Montreal) followed the Connecticut River south and encircled what they thought was an English settlement, misunderstanding that it was, rather, the Dietzens—a very anti-Puritan, antiestablishment, anti-English venture filled with a mix of Germans, Dutch, French, and English. The raid was part of a long-term campaign in which one Colonial power was attempting to dislodge another. As the French and English fought to control what is, today, New England and southern Canada, the French terrorized frontier villages that were creating footholds for the English. In essence, the Dietzen Massacre was a case of mistaken identity: they had the very unlucky fate of being in the wrong place at the wrong time. That wintry night, forty-eight men, women, and children were killed. Some were executed in the fields; some were later found trapped in their burned homes. The massacre was the beginning of a decade of frontier terrorism, befalling Holbrook, West Valley, and, most infamously, Deerfield. In fact, the most vivid firsthand accounts of the aftermath of the Dietzen Massacre can be found in the letters and journals of the few Deerfield men who first arrived at the scene. They'd witnessed in the night sky the glow of a burning village, and trekked north the next morning to see what had happened. It's within those Deerfield citizens' accounts that we know the fate of Karl Dietzen himself: he was found in his house, in his bed, his throat cut. Fortunately—if perplexingly—unlike all other houses, his house was spared from burning. Thus, his Bible was saved.

In the museum, Mary continued down the hall and disappeared into a dark room. Jim told me he would be right back, and left me at the desk. I'd later find out that he had gone to make photocopies of the Bible.

I walked down the hall, following where Mary had gone. I stood in the doorway. The room was a replica of an eighteenth-century bedroom. There was a simple wooden bed with a table on which was a chamber pot. I saw Mary's shoes on the rug. I heard her say my name from the bed. I stepped over a rope cordoning off the bedroom display, approached the bed, and saw her lying under the covers. She threw back the heavy blankets and quilts to invite me in. I took off my shoes, put them beside hers, then crawled in bed, just like we used to do before she left for boarding school. She drew the heavy blanket over me, and hugged me. I felt awash in joy.

It was only then that I learned the real reason my parents had come to take Mary home. She whispered it in my ear, as we were lying there. She said that I'd be an uncle, and that she couldn't wait to introduce her baby to me. She told me she loved me, that she couldn't live with our parents and they wouldn't understand why, and not to worry, we would see each other again. She said, "We're going west. To the mountains. Idaho. To Sun Valley. Doesn't that sound nice? Sun Valley." She told me to keep it a secret. "You can never tell Mom and Dad," she said. "But I want you to know where I'll be." Then we both fell asleep, because it was the middle of the night.

I'd like to pause here. A note of explanation. In a way, this moment in the Memorial Hall Museum is at the heart of my long-winded and rather personal introduction to an otherwise research-driven, impersonal text. The question you might be asking yourself right now is: How does this story bear any relevance on the chapters ahead? (No, I'm not simply a frustrated novelist, despite my wife's insistence.) The answer emerges, I think, by interrogating what it means to be writing history today—how we write about our subjects from the past, what authority we have in writing about them, and why we choose to write about them in the first place. For some historians, it could be an interest in a cultural history that shapes their present experiences in the world. For others, a charismatic professor or discovering a rare primary source may have inspired a line of research. For this book, it was this: sharing my sister's secret in a dark, fake bedroom when I was eleven years old. The Dietzen story and Mary's admission were like two epoxies in a polymer of feeling I've carried for my whole life. Only when I sat down to write this introduction did I see how bonded the two were, beyond Jim first showing me the Bible. I feel close to the Dietzen story because I felt so close to my sister. She trusted me, treated me as a confidant, as a friend; even though I was so young, she chose me over our parents. I think I'm compelled to research and tell the Dietzen story because, in many ways, of Mary. I'm reminded of what my thesis adviser, Professor Adams, once told me: history is personal, even when it isn't.

Jim woke us eventually, said it was time to go.

Mary squeezed me, then asked me to help her make the bed. We swept it with our hands, puffed the pillows, ensuring that the display appeared as if nobody had been there. They drove me back to the motel. Mary again made me promise that I'd never tell my parents that I'd seen her go. "Just pretend that you woke up and I was gone." Mary and Jim drove west the next day, to Sun Valley, where they have lived for the past thirty years.

My parents came into the motel room just after dawn. My dad was clean-shaven, shirt tucked in, ready to leave. He sat on Mary's bed, asking me again to remember if I heard her leave that night. I said no. They called the police, who came and asked me if I saw her leave. I said no. I never told my parents the story of the night in the museum, not even after they eventually accepted Mary's invitation to visit her and Jim in Idaho. They had a few good years with Mary and their grandchildren.

The rest of my childhood and adolescence was untouched by the Dietzen story, until I arrived at the University of Massachusetts Amherst to complete the graduate program in history. An invitation to the Memorial Hall Museum in my first year of the program brought me face-to-face with the Dietzen Bible for the second time. Seeing it again was like striking a match—the memory of that night with Mary and the accompanying bond I've described, the thrill and terror of what Jim told me about the fateful night, it all lit a fire in my mind. I needed to know more, to get inside the story and community. I knew exactly what my thesis would be.

AND SO, A FULL DECADE after seeing the Dietzen Bible again, I have finally arrived at this book, *The Dietzens: Searching for Eternity in the North American Wilderness.*

The text turns on three primary sources (in addition to the minimal descriptions French commanders documented of the ambush, tactics, goods taken, and casualties). The first source is Karl Dietzen's Bible, packed with lengthy notes illuminating the strange mind of its owner, of his belief in the path of light that would descend from the sky in answer to their prayers. The second source is the written accounts of those Deerfield men who first found the horrible aftermath of the massacre and spread word to Springfield, Boston, and beyond. For a long time, those were the only two primary sources I had. Then, a couple years ago, an unexpected document came to light. Newly digitized archives of libraries and cross-reference databases allowed me to uncover a firsthand account from an actual Dietzen community member: a deposition from a woman named Emma Thatcher to a magistrate on behalf of the Albany General Courts, a document that had been kept in the Albany Historical Association archives and only recently been transcribed and put online. From the deposition to the court magistrate, we can see that Thatcher had been arrested as a "vagrant," being tried for "petty theft." Thatcher states that she came from the "House of Karl Dietzen," and relays the horrors that befell the community. After weeks of sifting through more court documents, I found that Thatcher spent only a few months in the Albany penitentiary before a man named Allen Wellstone presented evidence to prove Thatcher's innocence. There was no mention of that evidence of proof, which, oftentimes, can mean that some amount of bribery or political manipulation was involved. Perhaps Thatcher had a benefactor. Regardless, she was released, and doesn't appear in any Albany records again—or anywhere, for that matter. (I have been unable to establish Allen Wellstone's role or relationship to Thatcher with much certainty.) Emma Thatcher's account is included in Chapter Three, and the full transcript of her deposition can be found in the appendix.

There is one—*nearly*—final note I would like to address to contextualize this book. The other day, I visited the Dietzen site, not far from the town of Leyden, Massachusetts, with my colleague, the brilliant archaeologist Dr. Abigail Eatherly. Her help—and ground-penetrating radar technology—has allowed me to paint a much more vivid picture of daily life in the community than I ever dreamed I could have. Standing on-site with Abigail, I heard cars speeding on Route 5, that constant *hush* of the automobile that makes one feel as if there is nowhere untouched by development. Overhead, I saw streaks of airplane contrails painting the sky. Disheartened, I said to Abigail that I wished we could go back in time, to the years of the Dietzens, when we'd be standing in an old-growth forest in absolute silence, in untouched wilderness. "That's not true," she said immediately. "Far from it. There were people here for ten thousand years before Karl Dietzen showed up."

I am deeply indebted to Abigail for correcting me, and for

setting a more conscious course for this book. She is right, of course. Though the Dietzens might have felt as if they were alone in the Pioneer Valley, they certainly were far from it. Modest estimates show that well over a hundred thousand Indigenous people were living in New England at the time (a population much reduced by a century of European diseases). In the Pioneer Valley alone were thousands of Pocomtuc men, women, and children. Whatever untouched wilderness the Dietzens imagined for their social and religious experiment was just that—an illusion, a few dozen Europeans playing out an isolation fantasy. But for believers like the Dietzens, that fantasy was essential: seventeenth-century forests of western New England presented a proxy Eden, the type of virgin landscape European newcomers claimed had disappeared from their homeland. They were looking to settle in a place that felt like it was back in biblical time, new, untouched. See the landscape paintings of Albert Bierstadt and the voluminous scholarship on nineteenth-century westward expansion and Manifest Destiny to understand how this same Edenic framework played out in America for centuries thereafter, the line moving farther and farther west as the spear of settlement pierced deeper across North America with each passing decade.

And finally, as a coda to how one might best process the following chapters, I'd like to make one last point. It's easy to think of the average seventeenth-century person as limited in their understanding of the world—in scientific and theoretical terms. It's easy, for instance, to pity the Dietzens for their beliefs. Let's just remember why they were there: to pray for an angel to make a ramp of sunlight that would lead them through the night sky. It sounds absurd! Easy to dismiss. And, in a way, it is. We all know that sunlight will never come at night, that you certainly can't walk on sunlight, and that, most important, the afterlife itself—the supposed end of the sunlit ramp—is likely a space imagined by people hoping to ease their grief for the ones they've lost. These poor people, you might think, following a blathering cult leader into the woods and chanting at the stars. But, as I remind my students, you must remember that before the mid-nineteenth century it would be hard to find a single European settler who did not believe in the divine, who did not believe that his or her very distant ancestors had actually once lived in the Garden of Eden, and that one was guaranteed a very horrible or very sublime eternity depending on how one acted in this brief and mortal body. In other words, the afterlife was real—as real to New England settlers in 1699 as the state of Connecticut is real to you and me. It was a place where you could go, that you would very much see if only you took the right path. Or, for that matter, it was as real a place as the snow-dusted mountains of Idaho, the elevated, euphoric escape far from home.

So, I ask you, reader, to suspend your disbelief as you fall into this strange, luminous world of Karl Dietzen and his devoted followers. We open on a frigid winter night in 1699. The French are approaching the sleeping village, slipping through the winter-stripped trees with guns in hand.

Cal Owens
Amherst, 2020

Origin Stories

Annie was on the couch, watching evening TV, eating a bowl of cereal, alone. Henry didn't like TV. That's what was good about their relationship, she told her friends. They liked doing their own things. This was back in 1983, when they were still married.

She landed on Channel 2. It was *Live from the Common*—a talk show with host Ted Rosen. Ted was too chatty and interrupted his guests, but he interviewed interesting people. He traveled around Boston, to secret gardens in Beacon Hill, bakeries and pie shops in Cambridge, to artists' studios in Somerville, talking to folks about their passions or jobs they loved. Annie did not have a job she loved. She worked part-time at a nonprofit. Henry had a job he loved. He was a scientist. A behavioral biologist. People liked talking to him about what he did, how he conducted his research, how his year was divided into fieldwork, what he'd discovered. People had few questions about Annie's job.

In this episode, Ted was sitting with a much older man at a table in a pretty library—wood paneled and shelved with leather-bound books. Maybe a part of the Boston Public Library she hadn't seen? Somewhere hidden? That was just like Ted—always finding cool little nooks in the most everyday places. A book was placed upright on the coffee table between Ted and the old man. *Roots and Branches of American Ballads*, the title read, over a photograph of fog-covered, green hills.

The man wore a blue oxford button-down rolled to his elbows. His exposed forearms looked—not inappropriate, but something like that. He had glasses—perfectly circular little frames—which he touched and adjusted as he spoke.

"No," the man said, shifting in his chair, leaning on his elbow.

"Are you sure?" Ted asked, cocking his head, smiling.

"I'm sure." The man shook his head. "I don't sing anymore. Only in the shower. And very much alone."

Ted laughed. "We'll see about that. So. This wonderful book. It was your father who introduced you to folk music?"

"And my mother," the man said. "I suppose it started with them. But, when I went to the Conservatory, that fell away. It wasn't very popular to like the fiddle or, God forbid, a banjo."

"And why did you return to folk music?"

"I suppose. I suppose . . ."

Here, the man paused. He looked uncomfortable. He shifted in his seat. He adjusted his collar. He looked around, as if someone had just said something to him off camera.

Something weird was happening. Annie turned around to see if Henry was there, to show him, but he was upstairs, working on a paper.

"Are you OK?" Ted asked. "Water!" he called to someone.

The man looked down in his lap, rubbed his hands together. Maybe he was having a health issue. A producer or assistant brought over a glass of water, put it on the table. The man strained a smile. He lifted the water glass from the table, sipped.

"Are you OK, Dr. Worthing?" Ted asked again.

"Sorry," he said. "Yes. I'm fine." He touched his forehead and adjusted his glasses. "One moment."

Annie noticed then that his hand was shaking. He took a deep breath, like he was having trouble catching his breath.

A panic attack. She had them, too. This man looked just like she did before she rushed to the bathroom and sat on the toilet and held her hands together because they were shaking so much. It used to happen only a few times a year, but now at least once a month. Her skin would tingle, and then, *bam*, her stomach would twist into a knot and she'd feel dizzy and her chest would tighten. Like an asthma attack plus food poisoning. Sometimes an episode lasted hours. Sometimes her throat would close so much that she couldn't even respond when Henry would gently knock on the bathroom door asking if she was OK. After the attack was over, after she would leave the bathroom, they wouldn't talk about it, really. Henry would hug her, ask if she needed anything. She would say no, and then he would say "good." That was another reason they worked so well together: he never got very upset or sad, and if she didn't get upset or sad, then no drama. Not like Beth, her best friend, who said she and her husband were in arguments that lasted years, and that they sometimes argued so late into the night they forgot what it was that had upset one of them in the first place. That sounded like hell to Annie. Annie could remember two, maybe three arguments, early in their marriage, when they were discussing having children before deciding against it. But not arguments like Beth's, or like Annie's parents, who had yelled at each other for her whole childhood and then separated to live significantly happier lives.

"Can we continue?" Ted asked, after a few moments of silence on the TV.

The man nodded.

"You were saying that you returned to folk music, because—?"

"My father, in a way. You know, the book is dedicated to him."

"What do you mean by that? 'In a way'?"

"I suppose it was—a friend, really, to be honest."

"A musician?"

"He and I were students together," the man said. "At the Conservatory. Before the First World War. It was his passion to find and record old songs. I was learning from him. I went along for the fun. We went on a song-collecting trip one summer. Walked through Maine, recording with wax cylinders."

People live such interesting lives, Annie thought. Free, interesting lives.

"America was a different place then," the man continued. "A different time, you understand. People would sit together in the evenings, on their porches, singing songs. Seemed like everyone could carry a tune. I mean, where I grew up, in Kentucky, you could go to one side of a mountain and people would be picking banjo this way, and then go to the other side and they'd be doing it another way. And then, well, TV came along in the fifties and sixties and everybody just started sitting on the couch and stopped being together, in community. TV ruined a lot."

"No offense taken!" Ted said.

"Well, offense should be taken," the man said. "We live in a more boring time. I'm sure it will get worse."

"Is that so?"

"Yes."

God, Annie thought, what would it be like to be that confident? To be able to talk to a famous person—to someone like Ted Rosen—like that? To just say what you wanted, to just be sort of truthful-cruel and not care?

"Anyway," the man went on, "I left folk music behind, after that summer collecting. Career, and other things, changed my life. I sang in Europe—London, Geneva, and Rome. I had this apartment on the Tiber River that looked out to umbrella pines rising out of ruins. It was so beautiful back then, in Rome. Nothing was shut off to visitors as it is today—you could have a picnic in the Forum. My friends and I celebrated Christmas of 1929 in the Colosseum—had a dress-up party and brought champagne into the ring. But that's another story."

Champagne in the Colosseum? How the hell did people make lives like his? How did you live in a foreign country and get friends and have the idea to picnic in ancient ruins and even know where to buy your groceries in Rome? If only she'd been alive before TV, she thought. Maybe things would be more interesting. Maybe she would have more interesting stories of her own, by the end of her life. Hard to see that happening now.

"To your question," the man said. "Yes, I left American music behind. But there is something special about these ballads, I think."

"And why now?" Ted asked. "Why write this book now?"

"Oh. I don't know. I'm getting older. Reaching the end of something."

"The end of what?"

The man breathed in, heavily. Annie looked at his hands. When her attacks hit, it was always her hands that started. Then blinking, too. For some reason her eyelids fluttered.

His hands were steady.

"Well," he said, "isn't it obvious, Ted?" The man leaned forward at the waist, held up his arms, as if to show himself off. "The end of me! I'm eighty-four. I'll be dead in a couple years."

Annie loved this man. He had some vital energy that she could feel through the TV.

"I see," Ted said, smiling but looking to the ground. "Well, let's just hope you'll stay with us a little longer. Thank you, Dr. Worthing, for your time. It's been a real pleasure."

Ted turned to face the camera. "My guest is singer and author Dr. Lionel Worthing. His new book is *Roots and Branches of American Ballads*. This has been *Live from the Common*. Next week: one Quincy woman who's gone to the Westminster Dog Show . . . three times!"

A commercial cut in. Annie turned off the TV. She stood, and looked at all the boxes that were still piled up behind the couch. That was the rest of her Sunday evening. Clean and organize and unpack her and Henry's things. Pack and move out the previous owners' things.

This was her day.

LAST MONTH, SHE and Henry had moved from their countryside house to one closer to Bowdoin College campus. Ten minutes from Henry's office. It was also a nice move for her. She could walk downtown to work—instead of driving forty-five minutes three days a week.

They had been the first ones to look at the house when it went up for sale. The former owner—a woman in her eighties—had offered a below-market-value price with the nonnegotiable condition that the house be bought as is, with all the furniture and junk left behind. They'd have to move everything out, do all the cleaning. Their real estate agent, Liz, said that the woman had a summerhouse on an island Down East, and she was in a rush to move out. She didn't have any relatives to take care of the mess here, and didn't want to deal with it.

"I've been in this business awhile," Liz had said to Annie and Henry. "Something like this doesn't come around often. Almost never, actually. This neighborhood? Minutes from campus? You'd be crazy not to take it. Nothing like this will come up for another decade."

Annie liked Liz. She was smiley, had what people would call a breezy confidence, and dressed in practical, heavy wool sweaters. Annie trusted Liz. So, she and Henry bought the house right in the middle of fall semester, and it had—without a discussion, just an understanding because of Henry's teaching schedule—fallen to Annie to move them in, and to move all this woman's stuff out. There were clothes in boxes. Old furniture. Broken lamps. Rugs that needed replacing. In the basement, there were about a hundred jars of pickles and unmarked tin cans. Everything was left, even the old photographs on the wall. "What kind of person doesn't even take their family photographs?" Annie had asked Henry. "A pragmatist," Henry said.

Only after they bought the house and moved in did the

immensity of the cleaning and moving project become clear to Annie.

"Maybe we should hire a moving company?" she suggested to Henry.

"Why? We have time to do it ourselves. It'd just be a waste of money, right?"

She knew what he meant. She had time. She had four free days a week. What else was she going to do?

Some mornings, when Henry was off teaching, she'd walk around the house for almost an hour, from room to room, just looking at all the things, not knowing where or how to start. Somehow, the house felt both too big and too small.

"DO YOU EVER THINK of what it would be like to be born before TV?" she asked Henry at dinner, the night she had watched Ted's interview.

"What do you mean?"

They were eating beef stew, which she'd made that afternoon instead of cleaning out the downstairs pantry.

"Like," she said, "do you think our parents' generation lived more interesting lives?"

"I think every generation thinks the one before them had more interesting lives. It's a function of escapism—nostalgia. That your own life would be better if only you lived in the year . . . fill in the blank."

Henry blew little puffs of air over his soup spoon, then parted his lips too wide and bit down on the metal. His teeth clanged on the spoon, and then dragged off a cube of beef. She clenched her jaw at the sound of his teeth on the metal.

"I just think," she said, ignoring the impulse to ask him to stop biting his utensils as she had before, only to have him treat her with silence through the rest of their dinner, "that we live in a more boring time. Like, a long time ago, people played all these instruments in different styles depending on which side of a mountain you lived on."

"Instruments?" he said. "What instruments? And what mountain?"

"Or, everybody used to sing."

"Everybody used to sing? Sorry, honey, what are you talking about? I feel like you started a conversation without me."

"No, I didn't," she said. "But I had this idea."

"Sounds dangerous."

He blew over the spoon, and as he brought it to his mouth, she had the urge to plug her ears.

Instead, she said, "What if we went to Rome? For a holiday."

"Rome? Why? When?"

"Christmas?"

"We can't miss my parents' Christmas dinner. You know that."

"Summer?"

"My fieldwork," he said.

"OK," she said. "Next year. Fall. Let's just go! Rome is prettiest in the fall, I heard."

"I'll have teaching again. You know. What's this about?"

Annie looked beyond Henry, over his shoulder to the kitchen

sink, where the faucet was dripping. She hadn't turned the knob all the way.

"Just an adventure. The ruins. The Colosseum. And there's always the food, I guess."

"What about," Henry said, "we make a nice Italian dinner every once in a while? My mom used to do that. Eggplant parmesan and baked ziti and stuff?"

Annie folded her napkin and put it beside her plate. She pressed her hand to it, and stroked it.

"Having spaghetti and meatballs is not the same as going to Rome."

"I know," he said. He bit down on his spoon, and dragged it out of his mouth.

"Oh God," Annie said. "Doesn't that hurt?"

"What?"

"How you're eating? Your teeth?"

He raised his eyebrows and stared into his stew.

SHE AND HENRY had an origin story. One of the best. People loved hearing about it. "It's actually fate that you two met," Beth said, when Annie told her that Henry had proposed.

The first part of the story began fifteen years ago, in 1968, when Annie was nineteen, a freshman at Cornell University. She was taking the Intro to Evolutionary Biology class, and the professor noticed that she kept acing her exams. One day, he asked her to stay after class, and then he said something very kind: "You have the mind of a scientist. You're good at asking the right questions." He asked her what her major was. "Communications," she said. "You should switch to biology," he said. She said she couldn't. But after some back-and-forth about why she could or could not change her major (her uncle, who was paying for her college, had helped her choose her major and had a job lined up for her at his firm), the professor offered her an internship: "How about you try a summer at a research station. Couldn't hurt, right? I have a graduate student studying spiders in California. If you don't like it, then you come back and study communications. Your uncle can't tell you what to do with your summer, right?"

Six months later she arrived at JFK airport one warm June morning, flew to San Francisco, took a bus to Monterey, met her professor's graduate student, Carl, and together they drove east, to the Carmel Valley—a very, very beautiful place filled with live oak forests and rolling grassy hills.

Henry was also at the research station. He was from Berkeley, studying acorn woodpeckers. As far as Annie could tell, he was just following around birds, catching them in nets, and spending hours trying to find where each one went. It seemed like a difficult, slightly absurd task. She didn't know what he was trying to do—but, then again, when she first got there, she didn't really understand how field research worked. She walked around the hills with Carl, taking notes as he looked in and called out what he saw in the spider burrows.

She and Henry had nine weeks together that summer in 1968. They were assigned to rooms on the second floor of an old ranch house where all the other interns and graduate students lived. One studied wild pigs. Another, western bluebirds. They'd lasted in their separate bedrooms for a week, until Carl gave the house a bottle of vodka, and Annie ended up in Henry's room. Every day was the same after that: he woke before her, because birds woke early, and made breakfast downstairs with the bluebird interns. She'd stay awake, in his bed, until she heard the front door open and close, and then watch him through the bedroom window, walking with his spotting scope over his shoulder, cutting through the tall grass that would, by the end of the summer, turn dry and pale. He'd disappear into a grove of live oaks, toward the trees where his woodpeckers were. Then she'd get up, walk across the hall to her room, shower, dress, drink coffee with the other research assistants, then go to check the spider burrows. Henry always ate lunch out in the field, so they wouldn't see each other again until the evening, for the shared meals their house cooked together. Dinner would end; Henry would go to bed early so he could wake up early. Annie might stay up later, playing a board game or cards with her housemates. She'd go upstairs, into her room. Wait for five, ten minutes. Then she'd get out of bed, cross the hall, and get into Henry's bed. "You know we all know that you two are together," Carl said, a couple weeks after their first night. Annie couldn't help smiling, but didn't acknowledge anything.

When summer ended, when the station was boarded up for the school year, they all returned to their colleges. Henry and Annie wrote each other for a few months. But then Henry moved apartments, he missed a letter from her, and they fell out of touch.

The second part of the origin story came three years later, in 1971. She was a senior. By then, she had switched to majoring in biology, after her uncle agreed to keep paying tuition. She had a big exam that she was studying for. Beth—who'd transferred to NYU—called, saying she was going to a party at her friend's apartment, and that Annie should drive down to come. Annie told her about the exam, about needing to study through the weekend. Beth said they hadn't seen each other in months, and that she'd been through a bad week, and that she wanted to see Annie. "Just stay for a night. It's good to take studying breaks. Just be a good friend and come," Beth said. She gave Annie the address.

There had been traffic on the way and all through the city, and so Annie had to take a roundabout way, stopping every ten blocks to ask someone for directions. She got lost. Tired, she parked at the first empty spot she saw, in the neighborhood but not very close to where she was going. It would be easier to walk. The parking space was in front of a small liquor store. It would be nice to bring a bottle of wine to the party, she thought, after she locked the car.

She walked through the door of the liquor store, and there was Henry, in the aisle, kneeling in front of the wine section. As she would later say at this point in the story, she almost didn't go to New York that weekend. There were a hundred reasons not to go, but she did.

As she walked down the aisle, toward Henry, her heart beat and her arms tingled. She said, "What are the chances?" when she got to him. He looked up, still kneeling. His mouth moved but he didn't say anything. She'd never made someone go speechless. He looked as if he was going to cry. "Annie," he said. She laughed. "Are you OK?" she said. He stood. "How?" "I should ask you the same," she said.

He was living in the city, doing graduate work at NYU. She said she was just passing through.

She didn't go to the party. She stayed with Henry that night, then the next night, then the next. She missed her exam. Every time she tried to leave, Henry asked for just one more day. They went to the Met, to the Museum of Natural History. They stayed in bed until lunch. It was, perhaps, the best week of her life.

Winter break came, and when she went back to school the following semester, she felt like she couldn't concentrate. She missed Henry, felt unhappy and lonely in gray, dull Ithaca. She wanted to be back in the city, back with Henry in his little apartment. Back to walking in Central Park. He couldn't visit her; he was applying for teaching positions and had to prepare lectures. So, she spent a lot of time in the car, from Ithaca to Manhattan, every weekend, sometimes during the week.

After she had missed her exam that fall, she got a C in the course. Her lowest grade yet. And now that she spent so much time in the car, she couldn't always finish her homework. She failed an exam in February of her senior year. She lost energy. She couldn't catch up. She gave up on organic chemistry first, then behavioral biology. It felt surprisingly good, exciting, to stop trying to do something that was so hard. Her evenings were free. She asked Henry one day on the phone what he thought about her coming to the city. For a longer time. She was thinking of taking some time away from school. "So close to graduation?" he asked. "Yes," she said. "Do you not want me to come?" He told her to please, please come. So, she did. She got a job as a receptionist at an accounting firm in their neighborhood. She was very happy, is how she still remembered it.

They married two summers later in a small ceremony at her parents' house. Beth gave a speech about fate and chance and how certain people were meant to be together. She told a joke about Annie disappearing into Henry's apartment for weeks, how she'd thought to call the police about a kidnapping. Guests laughed. Annie's uncle was there. He didn't laugh. After the ceremony, her uncle and father got in an argument that ended with her father kicking her uncle out. Her uncle had apparently asked Annie's father to reimburse him for the forty thousand dollars he'd spent on her education, which was, as he said, "Useless, now that Annie's going to be a housewife."

When Henry got the teaching position at Bowdoin, they moved to Maine, where they'd lived for the past ten years.

WEEKS AFTER WATCHING Ted's show, Annie was upstairs one morning, standing in what must have been some sort of home office at one time. It was a corner room with two tall windows. Lots of light. It would make a nice space for her to start on her own projects.

A wooden desk was pushed up against a window, beside a floor lamp with a broken bulb. There were stacks of browning papers and old, leather-bound books in a bookshelf. There was a closet behind the desk, on the wall adjacent to the entrance. She went into the closet, which was filled with old bedsheets, curtains, curtain rods, and what looked like collections of vacuum cleaner parts. She left the closet, sat down at the desk. She drew her finger over a film of dust on the windowsill. There was dust everywhere. On the windows, on the floor, on these curtains—which she'd probably have to throw away—on the rug under her chair. She looked closer at the rug and saw piles of mouse droppings on it. Great, she thought. Now she was going to get hantavirus. This house was actually going to kill her.

She moved the chair off the rug and went down on her knees. She inhaled over her shoulder and held her breath while she rolled the carpet, careful not to disturb the aerosols around the droppings.

When the rug was halfway rolled, she saw that something was weird with the floorboards. There were parallel cut marks, running through and perpendicular to the boards. She kept rolling. The cut bisected two other cuts, to make a square. There was a little metal ring at the top of the square. A hatchway.

She dragged the rug out the door, and went on her knees again. She pulled the little ring. The hatch opened easily.

Just under the hatch was what looked like a brown suitcase, fit neatly into the cavity in the floor. She touched it. It was hard, maybe hollow. She felt around the sides, found a handle, and lifted it. It was heavy. She dragged it out, set it beside the opening. There was a strip of paper peeling off the box, faded and illegible.

She opened the box. Inside were papery containers the size of soup cans. She pulled one out. She unwrapped the paper to see a hard and hollow cylinder, which, when she put her nose to it, smelled like beeswax. It looked like it was a part of an old sewing machine, maybe? Something people didn't use anymore. Weird, she thought.

She took out a few more cylinders and lined them up on the desk. There was a little paper tag on one of them. It read: *Cormac Shaw; Glasgow, Maine. Pretty Saro.* And below that, *Lionel Worthing & David White, 13 August 1919.* Her recognition of the name and the coincidence of knowing it came together. "What?"

she said into the empty room. With the cylinder in hand, full of excitement, she walked out of the office and stood at the top of the stairs.

"Henry!" she called downstairs. He didn't answer. She called his name again, and then looked out the window to see that his car wasn't there. He'd left for the day without saying goodbye.

She sat in the office awhile, looking at the cylinders. He should have these back, she thought. She still didn't understand what they were, but he should have them. Maybe she could contact Ted Rosen, somehow, tell him she made a discovery.

She wrapped the cylinders back in their paper, fit them back in the box, and put the box back in the cavity, where she'd found it.

She spent the rest of the day cleaning the office space. She didn't tell Henry about the secret compartment because he'd come home after she'd gone to bed. Then he'd left early to teach the next morning, and by the time he came back that day, he was in such a terrible mood that she didn't feel like telling him anything at all, really.

Days later, on her way to see Liz at the real estate office in downtown Brunswick, Annie stopped at the bookstore. She asked the cashier if he had a new book by the musician Lionel Worthing. The cashier said, "The one about folk music? I think we do."

"I saw him on Channel Two," Annie said.

"Over here," the cashier said.

Together, they walked to the nonfiction section, scanned the shelf. He pulled out what Annie had seen on the show: a book with foggy, green mountains on the cover. She paid for the book, then went to the little café connected to the bookstore and ordered a cherry Danish. The café tables were filled with college students, so she took her Danish and new book to the park across the street and found a bench. It was a warm, late-fall day, anyway. Puddles scattered across the park. The season's last songbirds sifted through the bushes.

She looked at the author photograph first. She then read the introduction, where Lionel Worthing wrote about having perfect pitch and something called aural synesthesia, which made him see colors and taste flavors associated with musical notes. He wrote about growing up in Kentucky, humming along with the trees, listening to insects at night. About his difficult mother and overworked but musically genius father, a farmer who had learned to play the fiddle when he was only five years old, in 1878, because he had broken his legs in five different places when a horse carriage ran over him. His father had been in bed for almost a year, first healing, then learning how to walk again, and because nobody in his family could read, he spent all his time learning tunes on a fiddle his grandfather had given him. His father, Worthing wrote, was what today would be called a prodigy.

She closed the book and put it in her purse. "We live boring lives," she said to herself. Or, no, that wasn't it. What did he say on Ted's show? "We live in boring times"?

She pulled her coat around herself. It was getting colder. Winter would come, and she and Henry would go to her mother-in-law's Christmas dinner like every year. Henry would spend long hours in the office, mentoring his new group of advisees. Winter semester was always the worst for her. Spring would come. She knew right where the daffodils in the park would come up—she had watched them come up in the same place for the past decade. Maybe she should buy some flower bulbs. Plant them around the new house. It would give her something to look forward to.

Across the street, she could see through the bookstore café window a girl and a boy, college students, sitting at a table together. The girl was at the edge of her seat, leaning in, her elbows on the table and a mug of coffee or tea between her two cupped hands. The boy was leaning back, arms crossed. The girl moved her foot to the boy's legs and touched his shoe with her shoe. He drew his feet in, away from hers.

Annie looked at her watch, stood, and made her way to Liz's office, just a few blocks from the bookstore.

YEARS AGO, IN THE beginning, she felt that Henry was special. He saw patterns in the world other people couldn't see. He'd even become somewhat famous in ornithological circles for what, as such a young man, he discovered about the woodpeckers in the Carmel Valley—and she felt lucky to have his attention, his rare power of observation, fall on her. She had a friend from the early days in New York, from the accounting firm, who said nearly the same thing about a new boyfriend who was a concert violinist—about his hands, how she loved looking at his hands, knowing how many years had gone into making those hands do something so rare and exact. Her younger self imagined Henry seeing her more clearly, with the observation he brought to his studies. He wasn't like other men.

Henry had proved what nobody believed at first: that the oak trees were heirlooms. These old trees into which the acorn woodpeckers had drilled hundreds or thousands of holes—storage shelves for their acorns—were passed down through specific lineages of birds. The oaks were the birds' estates, tended and guarded from one generation to the next. After that first discovery, there was a problem that kept Henry going back to the valley every summer, looking for answers: sometimes the woodpecker families left, suddenly and without apparent reason. Families that Henry had witnessed at one oak for a decade suddenly vanished—leaving all their acorns, and sometimes even their chicks, behind. "It just doesn't make any sense," Henry said to her when he first saw it happen. But he'd seen it enough that he knew it did make sense, somehow, just not yet to him. This was his skill—knowing that there was an explanation for everything that appeared confusing, that it only needed an application of patience and observation.

Recently, she'd thought of a conversation they'd had a few weeks into that first summer together. She and Henry had left their bed in the middle of an August night, had gone outside to lie on the hillside. They were both in their underwear. The ground was cement-hard from the heat in the valley and still, even at night, warm to the touch. The grass had been baked dry. The sky out there, so far from a city, was crowded with stars spread around a thickened Milky Way. Midway up was the Teapot asterism, which her dad had first shown her on a vacation to the Arizona desert when she was in middle school: a cloud of stars that looked like steam billowing from a constellation shaped like a kettle.

"Do you think people are meant to be together?" Annie asked. "Like fate or something?"

"Maybe," he said. "But, no. I think statistics could probably explain everything."

She asked him what he meant, annoyed that he didn't see that she was just trying to say how she felt then, about them, on the hillside, nearly naked and under a view of the universe.

"Like you and me," he said, to her momentary relief. "We are objectively the most good-looking people here, in a similar field of study, in a remote location. It's a reduction of variables."

She lay back on the hot ground. The dried grass pricked her skin, but she kept down. *A reduction of variables*, she thought. The nearby oak trees shifted in the wind; in the distance, an owl murmured to nothing.

"Yeah. Maybe that's what fate is," she said. "A reduced equation."

"I think so," he said.

He put his hand on her knee. He brought his head down to kiss her stomach, which ended the conversation. He crawled over her, kissed her shoulder, her neck, then her lips, and so blocked her view of the asterism.

LIZ GREETED ANNIE at the door of the real estate agency, and then brought her into her office in the back. Annie felt underdressed, in her puffy jacket and sneakers.

"So," Liz said. "What's up?"

"I know this isn't normal to ask," Annie said. "And you'll probably want to run me out of the office."

"Just don't tell me there's something wrong with the house?"

"No. It's lovely. But. Now, I know we took on the responsibility of cleaning, but there's so much in there that I just can't bring myself to throw away. Old photographs. Antique clocks. Dolls. Family photos. Other things that seem really important. I mean, I can't think of what type of woman would just leave this all behind."

"Is it too much for you?" Liz asked. She looked impatient. "It was part of the deal."

"No. Not at all. I mean, yes, it is too much—but that's not why I came here. I'm wondering if there's any way I could contact the owner? The last owner. Just—I just want to make sure she really wants me to throw all this stuff away. It feels like a sacrifice or something."

Liz put her hands on the desk.

"You know I can't give out sellers' information."

"Well, yes, of course. But. Maybe you can just see? Ask if she's willing to meet? I could drive the most important things to her. I worry that she didn't realize what she was leaving. Is she, you know, all there? Mentally?"

Liz leaned back in her chair.

"Please?" Annie said.

"Let me see what I can do. I'll make a call to her real estate agent. See if it's something we can arrange. Maybe she wants to come back to take a look."

"Thank you. Or, I'd be happy to go to her. I feel like I need a little break from this town anyway."

"Tell me about it," Liz said. "I'm already exhausted from a winter that hasn't started."

Annie left Liz's office, walked past the bookstore, and noticed that the girl was now sitting alone at the table by the window.

Henry was standing at the front door, like he'd been waiting for her.

"I have something for you," he called to her, when she was still on the sidewalk, walking toward their house.

He was smiling, giddy. "A present."

"Oh," she said. "Aren't you nice."

She climbed the stairs.

"If you don't like it," he said, "we can return it. It comes with an activity."

"An activity? Is it a massage? Please say it's a massage."

He disappeared into the house. She followed him.

"Here!" he called from the kitchen.

She took off her coat, hung it on the rack, and then walked into the kitchen. Henry was standing at the sink. On the old butcher's block in front of him was a little tableau. A still life, it looked like. There was a straw basket—a nice basket, handmade—filled with spaghetti, tomatoes, canned tomato sauce, and a big wedge of parmesan. A glass jar beside the basket held a bouquet of basil. There was a bottle of red wine. And, leaning against the basket, was a book titled *The Tuscan Plate.*

"What's this?" she said. She smiled.

"If we can't go to Italy, we'll eat our way through!"

"Oh."

She touched the pasta, the basil, the handle of the basket, the cover of the book. The loose pasta shifted in the jar as it separated under her touch. The tomatoes, she noticed, still had the grocery store stickers on them.

"It's just," he said. "You looked so sad the other night. I thought this might be fun."

He looked very pleased.

"Henry," she said softly, looking at the basket. "This is spaghetti and sauce. This doesn't need a recipe book."

She picked up the book and leafed through the pages.

"That's just for the presentation. I mean, it's not just spaghetti and sauce in that book. I flipped through, there are some pretty wild dishes. I don't know where you'd get zucchini flowers. Do you know that's a thing? Eating flowers on pasta? You'll love it."

She stared down at a page in the book that read, *Don't forget about bowties!* with a silly cartoon of a man wearing a bowtie pasta.

She started crying. She shut the book. Her skin began to tingle. She felt a wave of nausea.

"What?" he said. "Wait. Are you OK? What's happening?"

"It's a nice thought. It really is."

"Then what's wrong?"

Her throat tightened. She felt her face flush.

"You want me to cook us pasta?" she said. "Is that what you want?"

"Honey," Henry said. "It was just a fun idea. I'm sorry."

She forced herself to look up. He was staring out the window, away from her. He looked like he was in pain. He was biting his lip. He put his hands in his pockets. He was fidgeting. He looked weak, defeated, like he wanted to leave the room as quickly as he could.

She needed to sit down. She walked over to the kitchen table.

Sank into a chair with plastic upholstery patterned in big blue flowers, which was on her list to replace. She let her hands shake.

"I don't do anything now," she said.

Henry didn't respond for some time, but she sensed him, somewhere by the sliding glass door.

"What do you mean?" he said, annoyed but trying to sound tender. "You have a job. And interests."

"I'm not doing anything with my life."

"I'm sorry about the cookbook," he said sourly. "I thought it was nice. I'll give you some space."

He left the kitchen. She heard his feet clunk up the stairs, toward his office, and then back down the stairs, out the door, to campus, likely.

She stayed at the table. Long enough for the sun to have set. She should turn on the lights, she thought, but didn't. She only stood when the phone rang.

"Annie?" she heard. "It's Liz. Listen, it sounds like the woman, the former owner—her name is Belle LaSalle—she's fine with having you drop off some things. She called right back and said it was fine."

"Really?" Annie said. "Great."

"Yes. Well. I'm not sure you'll want to. She lives way the hell out there. On Isle au Haut. You take a ferry from Stonington. It's not an easy place to get to. You don't have to do this if you don't want to. It sounds like Belle doesn't really care either way."

"I want to."

"OK. Do you have a pencil? Take down her phone number?"

After she hung up, Annie put on the teakettle. She listened to the heat crackle up the metal sides. The house was quiet otherwise.

Henry came home late, again, after she'd gone to bed.

"I'M GOING TO go to Isle au Haut," she said the next morning.

They were at the table, each with a cup of coffee. They hadn't talked about what had happened the night before. She wouldn't even know how to say what had happened.

"Where?" Henry said. "What's that?"

"An island a couple hours north. I want to give Belle some things."

"Who?"

"The woman who owned this house before us."

Henry scrunched up his face and shook his head. "How do you know her?"

"Liz called her. Or, I mean, she called her agent. Anyway, she gave me her address. There are some old photos and things that I think she'd want back."

"Really?"

"Yes, really."

"OK," he said, holding up his hands like he was surrendering. "OK."

After Henry left, she found a cardboard box and put in a selection of what she thought looked important: old photographs, children's drawings, cards. Before leaving, she went up to the office to look at the box under the floorboards. She still hadn't told Henry about it. She wondered if she should take that, too. But it was heavy, too heavy to drag downstairs and into the car and then lug onto the ferry.

THE ROAD TO STONINGTON was desolate and beautiful. The blue morning sky in Brunswick was filled with thunderheads, lit by the sun, and by the time she made it two hours north, midafternoon, a snow flurry had come and gone.

She parked on the street and learned that she'd arrived with only ten minutes before the mail boat was leaving for Isle au Haut. She grabbed the box of Belle's things from her car and walked onto the ferry.

Placing the box under one of the passenger seats, she stood on the deck, leaning against the boat railing as they left the dock. The clouds were gone, and again it was a stretch of blue overhead—the kind of day where the sky seems frightened up, far away. Her eyes watered from the cold wind, but she felt invigorated by the heaving boat, the spray splitting at the bow, the leathery smell of diesel fumes. Lines of ducks drew over the waves. The island was ahead. A hummock overpacked with evergreens. The boat arced around a peninsula, and into view came boxy houses. The boat rocked to a stutter once past the breakwater. The harbor water was tropically clear, and Annie saw a seal hovering over seaweed below.

She and Henry had spent a week on an island like this the first month they moved to Maine. Their rental house had a potbelly woodstove, and copper pots hanging from the rafters in the kitchen. There was a sunroom with wicker chairs that looked out to sea. The floor of their bedroom was painted light blue, like a dollhouse. One late afternoon, after a swim in the frigid water, she stood in the outdoor shower, looking to the islands scattered in front of her. That night, in bed, he told her that he'd dreamt about her after he'd left the Carmel Valley. "Almost every night, for weeks," he said. "The one I remember the most was that you and I were on this little bed that was only big enough for one of us, and I fit my body into yours—like, my fingers to your fingers, my feet into yours, my legs into your legs." "That sounds like a sex dream," she said. "Except it wasn't," he said. "In some way it wasn't."

The boat eased to the dock, and the captain poked his head out the cabin door.

"Welcome to Isle au Haut," he said. "There'll be another boat in three hours."

"Can you point me to the house of Belle LaSalle?" Annie asked.

"It's right there," he said. "The big white one. At the edge of the field. Just go up the road. You can't miss it."

ANNIE FOUND HERSELF in a very cold living room, with Belle, sipping tea. Annie was nervous. And cold. And wondering why this woman would want to live out here, so far away from a hospital or anyone to talk to.

"It's very beautiful here," Annie said. "I'm sure the sunsets are lovely."

"Winter is horrible," Belle said. "It'll be hell here for the next three months. But then spring comes and all the lupines come up around the house and the birds return and, you'll be right then, it is beautiful. Heaven, I think."

They talked about the house in Brunswick. About how Belle had lived there since she was twenty, how she'd raised her family there, how she'd had one son, who now lived in Utah and wanted nothing to do with the house so they put it on the market. How her husband had died last year. "I just didn't want to mow the lawn anymore, you know? Albert did that. And I never liked that place, anyway."

Annie nodded, and then put her teacup on the table and reached into the box.

"So, there are these."

She held a bundle of old photographs.

"I thought . . ." Annie smiled, looked down in her lap. "I thought you might want them. I think—is that you there?"

She held up a black-and-white photograph of a young woman, in a wide hat, standing against a black car with two men, one on each side of her.

Belle took the photograph. Held it close to her face.

"Yes, from my family home in Newport. That one on my right is my brother, and the other is my first husband. But, what am I going to do with all these?" She pointed to the pile of photographs in Annie's lap.

"You don't want them?"

"Why?" Belle said. "I'll be gone soon, anyway."

Annie sipped her tea.

"Don't get uncomfortable," Belle said. "It's embarrassing."

"You don't want them?"

"I don't think so."

"So why did you agree to meet me?" Annie asked.

"I never turn down a visitor. It livens up my days."

"I see."

"But," Belle said. "There was one other thing. I wondered if, in your searching, if you did find something that I wanted to talk with you about."

"What's that?"

"Music. Sheet music. It would have been old. Over sixty years ago. Handwritten."

"I don't think so," Annie said. "I mean, no. I didn't find any sheet music. Was it yours?"

"Not mine," Belle said. She held her hands together. "My first husband's. David. He was a composer. A somewhat brilliant composer, I think. I don't know much about music—I do play piano, but not like him. He was, yes, he was very good."

"And—are you still in touch with him? Is he asking for the music?"

"Oh no," Belle said. "He's long gone. Died a year into our marriage. It was horrible. Don't ask me about it. The worst experience of my life. But, now, well that was a long, long time ago. Before the moon landing, you know? Lifetimes ago. We were very young when we fell in love and married."

Belle smiled, which felt like an invitation for Annie.

"I fell in love with my husband very young, too," Annie said. "He was my first love."

"And you're still together?"

"Yes. Well, we had a period in college when we weren't. But we came back. It was like fate. So. I guess I'm lucky."

"I see." Belle sipped her tea, then said, "I suppose."

"You suppose what?"

"It's not for me to say."

"Say what?"

"Well. I guess I am too old to keep anything inside, anymore. Sorry if I offend you. First loves never really seem to work out, do they? Don't you change too much? I was practically a child when I married David. And I think it's good to have a bit of heartbreak in your life. A story to tell. I went through something terrible with David's death when I was younger, and then I had these years and years of grief. But, when it was all over, I felt like I had arrived."

"Arrived?"

"To my real self, or something. Like I had been floating along." At this, Belle held up her hand, extended her finger, and moved it slowly as if her finger were drifting. "And then I moved up." She lifted her finger up, above them. "It was the best thing that ever happened to me, in a way. Which might sound selfish, or cold. But you should have a little pain in your life—humans are meant to have a little pain. Endings, I suppose, like seasons, like winters. That's where all the good stuff is. Ripped apart, so you can feel the mending. There's nothing like it. I wouldn't wish an uneventful life on my worst enemy."

Annie listened. Belle didn't seem to care that Annie hadn't responded.

"Albert was my second husband, but . . ." She paused. "He was the bigger love. He was expansive. Like the ocean. With David, even in that first year of marriage, I felt imprisoned by my obsession with him. I was obsessed. Like I didn't want to break it. Until he broke it. No, no—one must leave first love to Shakespeare's advice."

"Shakespeare?" Annie said.

"With Romeo and Juliet."

"What advice is that?"

"Well, he killed them both, didn't he? Don't you know the play?"

"Oh," Annie said. "Yes."

"End first love while in bloom, before it dies petal by petal."

"Right."

"You look disturbed," Belle said. "I've scared you. Albert always said I should edit."

"No," Annie said. "You didn't. I was just thinking." She felt comfortable around this stranger, compelled to say more. Maybe it was being way out on the island. Cut loose from everything back in Brunswick. Like she was standing at the water's edge, leaning forward to jump. Nothing she said here would really matter, anyway.

"What?"

"Maybe I'm sharing too much. But maybe you're right. With Henry, my husband—something has felt different lately. Like I'm watching my life from the outside instead of just living?"

"Oh dear," Belle said.

"And I see these people in the world—just people shopping or ordering a coffee or walking down the street talking to someone, and I think, *How do you do that?* Like, how do you just live without thinking about it?"

"I don't have advice," Belle said, "if that's what you're looking for."

"No," Annie said. "Of course not."

"But I can say, it doesn't sound like you've found yourself in a good situation."

A gray cat meandered in and pressed itself against Belle's calf. Tapped its tail on her knee. Belle lifted the cat into her lap, talked quietly to it.

"Why do you want the sheet music?"

"Sentimental. David still was my husband. Also, I don't have a television and winter is long and I'm looking for more music to play. I thought, wouldn't it be wonderful to hear David's melodies again? I used to hear them all the time, over and over. He didn't record anything, so the only way to hear them again would be to find the music. Oh well. Keep your eyes out, if you can. He wrote on everything. Newspapers. Notebooks. Whenever and wherever inspiration struck. Kept a stack of papers beside the bed. He dreamt in music, sometimes. I'd wake to hear him scratching away in the dark. I even found a few bars written on the wall by the toilet, one day."

"I'll look around," Annie said.

"Thank you," Belle said.

They sat quietly. Annie listened to the wind roar over the island. This poor woman, she thought, who only wanted to be left alone, who Annie had assaulted with artifacts she wanted to leave behind.

"Well," Annie said, looking at her watch. "Ferry leaves in half an hour. I'll take all these back with me." She held up the photographs.

"You can leave them here if you'd like, darling," Belle said. "You don't need to lug them back and forth for me. I don't mind."

Belle stood and so Annie stood.

"Thank you for the tea," Annie said.

Together they walked to the front hallway. Annie found her

coat, scarf, and hat on the rack. As she put her coat on, she looked across the front stairs to the living room, where there was an upright piano beside a bay window. On the bay window was an old-fashioned steamer trunk with a blooming geranium on it.

"Oh!" Annie said at the door. "There is something. I almost forgot. In the upstairs room, at the top of the stairs, I found a suitcase of what looked like toilet paper rolls. And, strangely, they had the name of a famous musician I'd seen on TV. What are they doing there?"

Belle smiled. "My Lord." She stepped back, leaning into the coats. She turned away from Annie, straightened a coat on the rack. She touched her forehead.

"What?" Annie said. "Are you alright?"

"You found them."

"Found what?"

"I was looking for them. For forty years."

"What are they?"

"Music."

"Music?" Annie said. "No. I don't think so. Maybe you're thinking of something else. They're like little, well, like toilet paper rolls, almost."

"Phonograph cylinders. Recordings. Lionel Worthing and my David made them one summer."

"That's right!" Annie said. "Lionel Worthing. I saw him on TV. Your husband knew him?"

Belle nodded. "Where were they?"

"Under the floorboards. Beneath the desk, under a rug. Very hidden."

Belle touched the coats on the wall. "All David's secrets," she said. "He went through so much trouble hiding everything. For what?"

"What should I do with them? Do you want me to bring them back here? Do you want them? I don't mind."

"Not at all," Belle said. "They don't belong to me, really. Wait here."

She climbed the stairs, and then came back down holding a piece of torn paper.

"I have Lionel's address. He wrote me a letter a few years ago. I think he still lives here. Harvard Square. He would be very grateful to receive them, I'm sure. They would mean a great deal more to him than to me."

Annie took the paper, put it in her pocket.

"Just do me a favor?" Belle said. "When you send them?"

"Yes?"

"Don't mention me. Or that you met me."

ON THE LONG DRIVE home from Stonington, Annie thought of the research station, of that summer. Of watching Henry walk from the house every early morning, leaving a darkened trail through the dewy grass. There was a detail that, in telling their origin story, she never included: Henry had left the station over a week before her, to get back to Berkeley early, and Annie had some time alone on the top floor. The first nights Henry was away, she slept in his bed. She could still smell him on the pillow. But after a few days, she moved back to her own room, which she liked very much because it had a window facing east, so she could watch the sun rise over the ridgeline and cast orange light onto her wall. It was quiet on the second floor, without Henry. A lot of time to think. She decided then, definitively, that she'd switch her major. She'd be a biologist. It was the first decision in her life that really felt like her own. She spent the evenings walking in the hills above the research station, taking notes in her journal, wondering at the size of her future, at how big all the decades in front of her felt. She'd sit in the grasses on the ridgeline, the sunbaked earth warm on her legs, after sunset. In the valley, she heard the screeching *coo* of Henry's woodpeckers. There might be wild pigs roaming on a far hillside. At the time, she thought that it wasn't the loneliness and quietness in itself that felt so good, but that her loneliness was enriched by knowing that Henry was out there, thinking of her.

But driving back from Stonington, thinking of Belle, she wondered if, during that time at the station by herself, it was simply her solitude in and of itself that felt so good. Maybe her longing for Henry had nothing to do with her happiness—he wasn't, perhaps, part of it. It had been a very long time since she'd felt the kind of frictionless joy she experienced on the ridgeline above the oak trees. That feeling of not just being by herself but being by herself and with purpose.

And then, well, came the thought that had arrived more often this past year, the thought she tried to ignore but which only grew bigger. If there hadn't been traffic coming into Manhattan that night, if she hadn't gotten lost trying to find a quicker way to Beth's friend's apartment, she wouldn't have stopped at the liquor store, and she wouldn't have seen Henry, and then she wouldn't have stayed in New York. She would have made it back in time for her exam. She wouldn't have taken all those trips from Ithaca. She would have graduated, gone on to grad school, and become a biologist—like her professor said. She would have her own study species. There was a life of hers, right now, in which she was walking somewhere distant, in some cloud forest, maybe, taking notes on the sounds of frogs or the color patterns of birds of paradise. A life she had cut away when she got in the car to drive from Ithaca fifteen years ago. And now, she wasn't in a cloud forest. She was driving along a road skirted in dirty snow, back to a dark and messy house in a town she didn't like, in the winter, without a job she cared about, without any shape or purpose in her days besides unpacking boxes.

She hadn't passed a town or a gas station for a while, and needed to pee. She took an exit off the highway, onto a country road. There were no lights, no houses. She walked from her car, without her coat, into the forest. She found a big tree to hide behind. High above her, branches clanged in the heavy wind. There, she let the story of her second life fill her mind. Of the research she never did; of the life's work she never had. She didn't push it away this time. She saw that hers and Henry's meeting in the Carmel Valley was not only an origin story. Standing in the forest, looking at the headlights of her idling car illuminate nothing in the road ahead, she considered this for the first time: that what she thought was the beginning of her life might have been the end.

IT WAS DARK BY the time she got home. Henry had left a note on the kitchen table. *In office grading exams.* He had made some of the pasta from his presentation but had been messy about it. There were a few uncooked noodles on the kitchen floor, scattered in disordered lines.

She folded his note and put it in the trash.

Then she went to the downstairs bathroom, sat on the toilet, turned on the light, and scanned the wall to her left, looking for the music. At first, she didn't see anything in the faded and stained wallpaper—only the brown lines of water damage. It was beautiful wallpaper, oak-and-acorn patterned, made in royal blue. She ran her finger along an air pocket by the door's trim. Then she saw it: notes within a staff, written in pencil, thin as a finger and only a few inches long, by a pattern of an oak leaf curling out from the door's trim. She'd been looking for a rigid scribble across the wall, not this, as if the notes had been written to blend into the pattern, to be hidden.

She wished that she could read music. She might have hummed the melody, or at least understood why this phrase of music was important or original or innovative enough—or elusive enough, at risk of being forgotten—to require being written out so urgently. But she couldn't read music, and so the artifact remained just that: something from a long time ago that she would never really understand.

Acknowledgments

Thank you, John Knight, Stephanie Jenkins, and Pat Walters, for your guidance and notes. Many thanks to Caitlin Wylde, Alex Kanevsky, and Hollis Heichemer for offering me space to write—and thank you, Jen White, for giving me time. Thank you, Claudia Ballard, for all you've done for me and for this collection over many years. Thank you, Allison Lorentzen, for bringing these stories into the world, for your guidance and encouragement, for brilliantly navigating us along this journey. Thank you, Camille LeBlanc, for all your support. Thanks to David Winkler, David Bonter, the Cornell Lab of Ornithology, and Shoals Marine Laboratory for igniting and sustaining my love of birds. A special thanks to the Nantucket Historical Association and the E. Geoffrey & Elizabeth Thayer Verney Fellowship program; thank you, Betsy Tyler and Libby Oldham, for all your help in the archives. I'm so thankful that the Cuttyhunk Historical Society and The Museum of the Elizabeth Islands kept old journal transcriptions. Thanks to Chloe Garcia Roberts and Christina Thompson at the *Harvard Review* for publishing earlier versions of a couple of these stories. Michael Fauver read my first short story and gave me a bit of hope—and thanks to Benjamin Percy for your invaluable encouragement. Within that lineage, thank you to my English teachers, Karinne Heise and Peter Rowley, for your kindness and care. Jennifer Acker, editor of *The Common*, published the short story *The History of Sound* years ago; I'll be forever grateful to you, Jen—for that, and for your continued guidance.

Many books helped build this one, especially these: *The Great Auk* by Errol Fuller; Scott E. Fulton's *Glass Flowers: Marvels of Art and Science at Harvard*; Nathaniel Philbrick's *Away Off Shore: Nantucket Island and its People, 1602–1890*; and Donald A. Wilson's *Logging and Lumbering in Maine.*

My lifelong thanks goes to the families that made our corner of Massachusetts a very special place to grow up: to the Burnes family, the Sullivans, Covers, McMahons, Powels, Sommaripas, McGowans, Garfields, and Kinnanes. Thank you to the Slate family for all your kindness, for being so warm and welcoming. Thank you to my parents and brother, who endured my childhood poems and stories. A special thanks to Dedee, who read through this collection in record speed and made key corrections. Jenny: thank you. I can't believe my luck, that I get to spend my days beside you, that you are, right now, in your writing studio a short walk away, and that I can just stop in to see you. Your brilliance and attention to all things is so rare, so precious. You are the brightest thing in my life. And that naturally brings me to you, Ida. Where did you come from? Your timeless and tender spirit is almost too much for me sometimes. You have expanded everything with your sweetness. This book is for you and *Mama*.